A FLAWED PROMISE

———

A Novel

A FLAWED PROMISE

Ellen Schmalholz

Layout and design by Sharon E. Rawlins
Author photo by John H. Mayer

GOLDNWORKS PRESS
goldnworks@gmail.com

www.ellenschmalholz.com

ISBN 978-0-692-09791-5 Paperback
ISBN 978-0-692-09792-2 eBook

Printed in the United States of America

Dear Carolyn,

TO DREAMERS AND BELIEVERS

To Love and Forgiveness,

Ellen

ix

Prologue

I'm at a cocktail party in the garden of a large estate. My red hair is done, my make-up perfect, my emerald green cocktail dress shimmers, showing just the right amount of cleavage. The flowers in the garden are in full bloom. A breeze, scented with roses and honeysuckle, caresses my bare neck and shoulders. I look around at all the couples at the party — on the verandah, in the gazebo, lounging around the pool. I wonder where I belong. Each statuesque woman dressed in a black, form-fitting evening gown stands next to her tall, muscular mate. A necklace with a two inch gold key suspended above her large breasts adorns each woman. My hand touches my bare neck. I shiver. Then, as if some bell signals me, I run to the side of the house and drop to my knees. With my hands, I dig through the dark moist earth of the flowerbeds, searching desperately for my gold key.

1979

PART ONE

1

NEW YORK CITY

July 1979

*T*he red-eye from Los Angeles arrives early. With only light traffic, the cab cruises along Grand Central Parkway to the upper Eastside. Just past The Metropolitan Museum the driver pulls up in front of the well-kept Manhattan co-op.

"Welcome home, Maddy. It's been a while." The doorman retrieves my luggage and walks me to the elevator. "How long are you staying?"

"Just long enough, Bill."

He pushes the button for the fourteenth-floor and waves as the door closes between us. I watch the numbers light up. Twelve, skip thirteen, fourteen. Who are those superstitious architects kidding? I smooth down my hair and wonder how I'll style it tonight. Two weeks ago when my mother asked me over the phone what I planned to wear, I snapped, "Don't worry, I won't embarrass you."

My mother waits outside the doorway of the apartment. Short, round and pretty, she looks sleepy in her green cotton robe pulled carelessly around her. I roll my two suitcases down the hall.

"How are you?" She reaches up to hug me. "Tired?"

"I'm fine," I say, my hands full. I don't hug her back. "I'll take a nap before tonight's three-ring circus."

My mother doesn't deserve my aloof behavior or sarcasm. I need to tone it down to try to make this visit pleasant, but my body remains

3

tense, my jaw clenched. I follow her into the apartment. The metal door, with the dangling chain lock, clangs shut.

I glance at the tall glass vase filled with red gladiolas on the table. My father sits in his imposing black leather chair that dominates the living room. It looks out of place with the other bold turquoise and green fabrics and teak furniture. The Saturday *New York Times* is perched neatly on his crossed legs. He skims all the sections, goes back to the ones that interest him, then folds them in that way New York subway riders do.

"Hi, Daddy." I cross the length of the room knowing he won't get up to greet me. Holding on to the arm of his chair, I lean down to kiss his cheek. "Did the Mets win last night?"

"No, they're still bums, but your mother won't give up on them." He uncrosses his long legs. "Are you hungry? Mother went to Zabar's for you yesterday."

Zabar's is a specialty store on the other side of Manhattan, a fair distance from where they live. As a special treat for me, my mother shops there. I smell the coffee percolating in the kitchen and she offers me a fresh cup.

"Thanks, but I'll wait. I want to unpack, take a shower. What time do we have to leave for the Bar Mitzvah?"

"Between six and six-thirty."

"Perfect. That'll give me time to sleep, eat something, and call Beth and Linda to make some plans." I start to walk away, then turn. My mother stands with her arms crossed. My father resumes reading his paper. This is not the homecoming I want. "Sorry you had to get up so early," I say. "We'll visit later."

She nods.

I retrieve my suitcases and walk down the hall. My heels click on the cool white tile floor, as I pass the bathroom to my old room, now my mother's craft room. In one corner I see a life-size naked mannequin, and in another corner, a profusion of gold and red yarn piled high. I stuff my smaller suitcase in the closet and put the larger one on a chair to unpack later. I plunk down on the daybed my mother has made ready for me. After six hours on the plane, I feel crunched up like an accordion.

The early morning sun bounces off the tall buildings and comes in through the blinds casting shadows across the family photographs on the wall. There are portraits of both sides of my family — my grandparents, parents, aunts, uncles, cousins, and babies.

I get up and move closer to focus on my father's sister, Renee, when she was young, tall and slender. Contrary to the image on the wall, the one in my head is of a bald, skeletal woman lying in a hospital bed much too big for her. No one told her the truth about the cancer and her impending death, and true to Gold family dynamics, she'd never asked. She died unmarried and childless.

I don't want to end up like her. I'm supposed to be married and have babies by now. My babies' pictures should be on that wall along with the others. I unpack my black silk cocktail dress and try to shake out the wrinkles. I hang it in the closet, find my bathrobe and escape into the bathroom.

In the early evening, I drive my parents and their friend Mildred out to Long Island. My father relinquishes his car keys to me because I like to drive and he doesn't. We're behind schedule and it's my fault. I slept later than I planned and talked to my friend Beth way longer than I should have. I'm also ambivalent about going to a synagogue and supporting organized religion. Rather than bringing people together, it separates them. But I remind myself, I'm here for family. We drive across mid-town Manhattan to pick up Mildred on the Westside and then battle several traffic jams on the Long Island Expressway. Except for an occasional direction from my father, "turn left" or "turn right", I hear only the sound of his teeth grinding.

I've been to many of these events before and hate the way they bring up the reality of my single life in the way only family affairs, celebrations and rites of passage can do. Mildred breaks the silence and starts in on me in the car. "Aren't there any men in California?" Like my father, I grit my teeth.

Stopping in front of the synagogue, I let my parents and Mildred out of the car. Before I can say, "meet you inside", three doors slam shut leaving me alone to watch them hurry away. I find a place to park, dash across the lawn and run up the stairs of the temple. Clumps of earth and grass clinging to my spiked heels fly off. The dark wood sanctuary doors, carved with the tree of life, are closed. I was hoping the service would start on Jewish time, but the sound of organ music spills out into the lobby. I walk inside and look for my parents. I can't find them so I sit among strangers in the last row and stare ahead.

The Bar Mitzvah boy will conduct the evening Havdalah service that signals not only the end of the Sabbath and the start of a new week, but that the thirteen-year-old is ready to take on the responsibilities of becoming a man. Sitting up on the bimah in front of the congregation, little Robbie Levine, the Bar Mitzvah boy, almost disappears into a large, hand-carved oak chair. I watch my very pregnant cousin Arlene climb the four stairs to bless her son and present him with his tallit, a beautiful, blue and white silk prayer shawl. I take in the pride of the mother, the discomfort of the son, the solemnity of the service and all the things I want that might never be mine. As I look up at the bimah, I force myself to concentrate on the service. Prayers and speeches mix with a parade of parents and grandparents blessing the Bar Mitzvah boy, until finally the service ends.

I stay seated waiting for my parents, as the organ music plays softly in the background. Watching congregants and guests walk up the middle aisle to exit the sanctuary, I wave to a few people I know. I'm unusually peaceful, happy and proud for Arlene and her family.

As the crowd thins to a few stragglers, my father strides across the front of the sanctuary towards a white haired guest. He begins gesticulating and poking the air with his index finger as the man slumps in the corner of a pew in the third row. I'm too far away to hear what he's saying, so I stand up. My mother, petite even in her high-heeled shoes, tugs on my father's sleeve, trying to pull him back. I start down the aisle when a heavyset woman in a yellow and white striped dress runs toward me. When I step out of the way, I recognize her.

"Anna? What's going on?" I hadn't thought about Anna attending the Bar Mitzvah, but she'd been part of the family for years and still cleans house for Arlene's mother.

She doesn't even glance at me as she hurries up the aisle and out the rear doors. I turn back. My father's deep voice echoes throughout the now empty sanctuary as he points his finger at the guest's face. "You're a dead man to me," he yells. His olive skin tone face turns red. He looks like an overgrown man in a boy's suit as the sleeve of his white dinner jacket inches toward his elbow. I had experienced his anger many times before — a long-lasting, quiet rage that made me beg to know what I'd done wrong.

"I warned you years ago never to show up around my family," my father shouts. "I want you out of here. Now!"

"Simon, stop. Maddy's here," my mother says as I approach. Her expertly applied make-up doesn't hide her pale, distraught look.

"What's going on?" I step closer. "Who is that?"

"Get out of here, Maddy." My father waves me off. "Go join the others."

My eyes are riveted on the old man. His dark blue suit jacket droops from his shoulders and his white shirt collar could easily house another person. His milky brown eyes radiate fear, while his lower lip trembles. My stomach clenches.

"Sherry, take her out of here. Now. He'll leave soon and I'll meet you in the lobby."

Without another word, my mother takes my elbow and pushes me toward the back of the room. Confused, I look over my shoulder toward my father.

"Is that Anna's husband, Anthony? I've never seen Daddy like that."

"It's nothing."

"Nothing? Are you crazy? What's going on?"

"Not here, Maddy. Not now. We'll talk about it tomorrow," my mother says in a low, controlled voice, her jaw almost stationary.

I know that look and that voice. It brings back my lonely childhood when I was taught to obey and keep everything inside. Then, as though some imaginary internal engineer throws a switch, my mother smiles broadly, takes my hand, and pulls me through the doors. "Come on," she says. "Let's have a good time."

Across the lobby, two ushers swing open the doors to the social hall in grand fashion. I peer inside. Great planning has gone into every detail of this gala celebration for Robbie. Baseball, football, and tennis memorabilia line the walls. Sky-blue dyed floral arrangements adorn the tables with matching helium-filled balloons floating high above. At the rear of the hall, a grinning photographer snaps photos of guests with one of three life-size cardboard cutouts of Robbie in his various uniforms. Across the way, near the children's table, a magician performs card tricks to entertain the kids.

I walk toward my table still trying to make sense of my parents' behavior. My father rarely loses his temper like that — he broods instead. I make my way around some empty chairs and stop. Out of place, out of context, and hidden behind a full black beard with a gray streak, I recognize a man I knew in college. He pokes a piece of lime in a tall glass with a swizzle stick.

"Howard?"

He looks up from his gin and tonic and rises to his lanky, six-foot-three height, still the perfect gentleman. "Maddy Gold. It's been a long time." He reaches for my hand and kisses me on the cheek. His smile reveals two crooked front teeth, the only imperfection in his chiseled Grecian face. His hazel eyes sparkle. I back away and smooth down the bodice of my black dress.

"Who do you know?"

"The Bar Mitzvah boy," he says. "Actually, his father David was my divorce attorney a few years ago." A flash of sorrow crosses his face. "We got to be friends. You?"

"Arlene's my cousin."

"Nice." A grin replaces his sadness. "I never got over you, Maddy Gold." He points to a chair. "Why don't you sit down?"

I thought about our blind date my senior year at college. We'd had a five-month relationship, but I wasn't willing to abandon the Peace Corps and my two-year commitment to save the world. How naive I'd been.

"I'm sorry your marriage didn't work out," I say.

He nods, a look of grief in his eyes.

"You've been home what, eight, ten years?"

I laugh. "I've been back in the States for ten years. I live in Southern California now, Marina del Rey to be exact. I teach learning disabled high school kids."

"And you're not married?"

"No. Maybe I never got over you."

"That's good to hear." He takes my hand and pulls me to my feet. "Let's dance. We used to be good at that."

I'm happy for the distraction — an old love, someone to dance with, and who knows what else? The dance floor is empty in the partially filled room. I move against Howard's body as his arm slides around my waist and his hand presses against my bare back. I wonder if my parents are watching. My mother would remember Howard as the one who got away. But I don't want to dwell on her disappointment. Concentrating on the music, we glide to the rhythm of "Fly Me to the Moon". I like his cheek against my hair, the scent of his English Leather cologne. I like everything.

———

The smell of fresh coffee floats under the closed door of the guest room. I open my eyes and slip my left leg over the edge of the single bed.

If I were at home I'd have a larger bed and more hours of sleep. I badger myself to get up and have breakfast with my parents. I want to talk to them and find out about last night. As I stretch, I think of Howard. We spent the whole evening at the Bar Mitzvah dancing and laughing. We even stole a kiss behind the coat rack like we were still in college.

I exit the bedroom and walk along the cool white tiles toward the dining area. My parents sit at the oval table, covered with the green and white, hand embroidered cloth I'd given them from my trip to Guatemala. They're eating the remains of the Zabar's shopping spree in my honor.

"We didn't expect to see you until mid-morning," my father says as he peers over his rimless glasses.

I glance at the grandfather clock — just after nine. I sit down across from him and next to my mother.

"We have to talk about last night," I say.

"Not really."

My father slides the bridge of his glasses higher on his nose and looks at my mother. "But we can talk about you and your life in California. We don't want you to end up like Aunt Renee."

"I am not Aunt Renee. My life is nothing like hers. I'm independent. I have friends. I travel. I have a life."

"You're alone. She was alone."

"You mean I'm not married. Don't you think I want to be married?"

"You could have been," my mother says.

"You mean if I hadn't gone into the Peace Corps?"

The phone rings. My mother answers, then quickly hangs up.

"It was Mildred, thanking us for the ride." She brings back the coffee pot and puts it on the table.

"And that's what I need to talk about," I say. "What was going on last night?"

"What are you getting at?" my mother asks.

"Don't be condescending, I'm not a child anymore." I turn to my father. "Last night with Anna. Was that her husband, Anthony?"

My father looks toward my mother again. Neither one says anything.

"You told me he was dead."

"We thought it was better."

"Why? I didn't even know him. Maybe I saw him once. I went home with Anna one Christmas, right? And you never let me go again. I thought it was because she took me to church and I had somehow betrayed Judaism."

I fold my arms and lean back in my chair. The electrical charges prickle my skin.

"It doesn't matter." My father glares at me. "It's in the past. If he hadn't been there last night we wouldn't be discussing this."

"But he was there and you had an extreme reaction." I hesitate. "Did he do something to you?"

My father shoves aside his half-filled coffee cup spilling its contents onto the tablecloth. "I told you it doesn't matter. We will not talk about him again."

My head jerks backwards as if I've been slapped. My eyes open wide as I watch the swishing waves of café au lait in his cup. I look at my father and then my mother. With one swift movement I stand up, scraping the metal chair against the white tile floor, and run out of the kitchen. I retreat to the guest room and into the silence of my childhood.

I'm determined to crawl into bed, pull up the covers and hide for as long as I can, but the family pictures on the wall catch my attention again. Happy people of all ages on different occasions. I study each face. One particular 5" x 7" black-and-white photo of my father catches my eye. His salt-and-pepper hair frames a face lined with deep creases and furrows around his eyes and lips. A small white cloud of cigarette smoke envelops him, blurring the image. My mother once told me about his year long depression when I was a little girl, too young to remember.

I sit on the bed thinking of another picture of my father in an album I have at home. A black and white photo of the two of us taken with an old Kodak Brownie camera. No more than two months old, I'm lying on my belly on a changing table, lifting my head as I push up with my hands. My father, wearing a white shirt and a tie, is standing in front of me looking down, watching over me. Maybe he'd just come home from work? Young, handsome with dark hair, he looks proud. Proud of me? Proud of being my father? His face beams. I am his baby, his daughter, his joy. Whatever happened to change all that? I look closely at the blurred picture on the wall again.

————

When I emerge from the guest room in the afternoon, it's as if nothing has happened. My father sits in his black leather chair with sections of the Sunday *New York Times* scattered around his feet. I stand in the doorway watching him work on his crossword puzzle in ink. An organ plays, "Take Me Out to the Ballgame," on the television in the den where my mother watches her beloved New York Mets.

I go into the kitchen and pile a bagel high with smoked fish and cheese left over from the morning. I put the plate on the table and walk across the living room to get the Opinion section of the *Times*. Since my father is doing the puzzle, he has finished reading the paper. We nod to each other and then I sit by myself in the dining room eating and reading. Growing up I struggled to understand the secrets and silence of the Gold family dynamics, but now I'm mostly resigned. It's the way we are.

While I eat my bagel, Howard calls and rescues me. Someone gave him two tickets for the evening's special benefit performance of *The Fantasticks* and he asks if I want to go. "Yes!" I say, jubilant to get out of the house.

After the performance at the Sullivan Street Theater, I wait for Howard to come back from the bathroom as the crowd thins out. Seeing this popular, long-playing musical for the second time brings back memories of the sixties, of high school and college, when I hung out in the Village during vacations in black pants, black sweaters, black jackets and thick black eye make-up. I hum "Try to Remember" from the show and study the framed old playbills featuring various cast members.

"Maddy Gold. I don't believe it!"

I turn and come face to face with Jake Miller. Passionate, rumpled Jake was my friend Linda's ex-lover and my secret crush. What are the odds of bumping into two men from my past in New York City?

He leans over and kisses my cheek.

"Jake, what are you doing here?"

"I live here, remember? This is my city. The one you abandoned."

I laugh. I grab a strand of hair and hook it behind my ear.

"You and Linda will never forgive me for that."

To Jake's left, I notice a young, slight, sad-looking woman. Could this be Claudia, Jake's new ex, the one that Linda told me about?

I had met Linda and Jake and their group of friends on Fire Island when I returned home from the Peace Corps. An old friend invited me to share a house for what turned out to be a revolutionary summer experience for a very conventional and innocent me. Thirty people living together in different quarters in what I came to name The City Commune. Everyone slept with everyone. Nothing was sacred. Even people in committed relationships turned out to be unfaithful. I spent the summer wondering how I had become a part of that.

"Maddy," Jake says, "this is Claudia."

I smile. I understand the dark haunting eyes that face me. Jake and Claudia may have split up, but she is still connected.

"So what are you doing here?" Jake asks. "Did you come to your senses?"

"I'm not getting into that East/West battle with you. We have culture. And great weather."

"Just visiting then?"

"For about two weeks."

Howard comes back and slides his arm around my waist. His arrival creates an awkward silence so I rush to fill the void by introducing everyone. I shake hands with Jake and Claudia.

"It was good to see you both."

"Give me a call this week." Jake flashes his bad-boy grin. "We'll have lunch and catch up."

"I promise."

Howard takes my hand and pulls me away.

"Who's that? He looks familiar."

"Jake Miller. We met the summer I came home from Kenya — he and his latest, Linda. We became friends. I haven't seen him since they broke up."

"Is that the Madison Avenue Jake Miller? I didn't realize he was so short."

I laugh to myself.

"How do you know him?"

"Trust me," he said, putting his arm through mine as we walk toward Washington Square Park, "anyone who reads *The Wall Street Journal* knows Jake Miller. He's been around a long time and runs one of the most successful, cutthroat, advertising agencies in the country."

I shrug.

"When you see someone on weekends with their kids, flipping hamburgers on a barbecue, you forget that professional aspect."

"Maybe." He checks his watch. "It's still early, Madd. Why don't we have a drink at my place? I'd like you to see it."

We walk down the street arm in arm. I think about our kiss last night and lean my head against his shoulder.

Howard is right about his place. He's always had good taste and I remember that as soon as I cross the threshold. His apartment is one large room partitioned by Japanese silkscreen panels that can be pushed aside into a kitchen, a living room and a bedroom. As I pass his neatly made bed, I wonder if this evening will be more than a nightcap.

Howard hands me a glass of red wine as we walk into the garden outside the glass doors of his sleeping area. Trees are carefully arranged for privacy and accented with an array of brightly colored flowers. Accustomed to gardens in Los Angeles, it surprises me to see something so lush and green in the middle of Manhattan.

"You're lucky to have found this place." I lean against a small, white birch tree, sipping my wine. "It's heaven."

"I'm out here a lot, whenever I have free time." He complained earlier about how hard he worked teaching biochemistry at Columbia and doing his research projects. "I grew up in the country and always had a garden. I still have green thumbs." He smiles and wiggles them in front of me. I giggle at the silly gesture.

He pulls me to him and kisses me lightly. "I've been waiting to do that all evening." He takes my drink out of my hand and sets it down. "Time feels very precious." He embraces me, nibbles my ear lobe and kisses my neck. As his hands slide under my blouse, he caresses my breasts. His mouth gently sucks my lower lip. I want this to feel good, but instead I hold back. Crickets chirp, a saxophone wails. I stop and push away from him.

"I'm sorry," I say, "maybe we're rushing this a bit."

"Rushing? I've been thinking about you for years. I never understood why you left. I felt like you ran away."

"Howard, you knew when I met you what I wanted. I never hid the Peace Corps from you. That had been my dream since Kennedy talked about it."

"Dreams change." He strokes my cheek. "You told me last night you tried to find me when you came home. Why?"

"I never wanted to hurt you and didn't want you to be angry with me."

He puts an arm around me.

"Anything else?" He sounds playful.

I look up at him. "I was curious." I pause to find the right words. "Things were unsettled between us. Sometimes I felt it had to be your way or no way, and I spent too many years watching my parents do that dance. I didn't want it for myself."

"I wanted us to be together. If that made me too pushy…"

The sparkle in his eyes disappears, separating us again. The night is warm and I don't want to feel cold.

"We don't have to do this right now."

"Good," he says. His shoulders relax, his head tips sideways. "You wouldn't sleep with me back then," he teases.

I close my eyes and remember our fights. I remember the late-night talks with my girlfriends wondering about sex and what "doing it" would be like. I remember the girls who did and how they were called sluts.

"Virginity was prized." I laugh, embarrassed at how silly that sounds now.

Howard puts his arms back around me. "More like a booby prize." He takes my hand. "I don't want to rush you, but I want you." He leads me into his bedroom. "Come on, Madd. Relax." He kisses me again as he strips off his shirt. He lays on his bed and pats it. When I don't respond, he reaches up and takes my hand. He pulls me down and undresses me. I make him use a condom. With little foreplay and little tenderness, he enters me.

———

The dimly lit hallway to my parents' apartment is empty. I turn the lock of the steel door and close it quietly behind me. My mother has left the floor lamp on so I don't go bump in the night and hurt myself or wake them. I walk by the ebony upright piano and touch the lid that covers the keys. I can't recall the last time it was open. Maybe when I was a teenager and my father yelled from the bedroom, "Why does she always start to practice when I come home from work?" Or it might have been when Mr. Sutton suggested I stop taking lessons. I must have been really awful.

I turn off the lamp and walk over to the window. The light from other apartments slips through the blinds creating geometric patterns on the floor and walls of the living room. One beam bounces through the Steuben glass elephant on the green credenza creating a prism that sparkles on the ceiling. The elephant's trunk, high in the air, symbolizes good luck. I gave it to my parents on their thirtieth wedding anniversary.

I pull up the blinds and sit on the windowsill hugging my knees. In my mind's eye, Howard's face stares at me, questioning. I left him without saying a word. I can't explain what I don't understand. Give me a man who is interested in me, wants me, and I will speed away faster than the IRT express train. Give me a man who toys with me, is distant, and I will pursue him like an addict looking to score.

Tired, but not ready for bed. I close my eyes and take some deep yoga breaths in through my nose, out through my mouth. The next thing I know I'm hyperventilating from the recurring dream I've had since I came home from the Peace Corps. Tears stream down my face.

> *The flowers in the garden are in full bloom. A breeze, scented with roses and honeysuckle, caresses my bare neck and shoulders. I look around at all the couples at the party — on the verandah, in the gazebo, lounging around the pool. I wonder where I belong. Each statuesque woman dressed in a black, form-fitting evening gown stands next to her tall, muscular mate. A necklace with a two inch gold key suspended above her large breasts adorns each woman. My hand touches my bare neck. I shiver. Then, as if some bell signals me, I run to the side of the house and drop to my knees. Using my hands, I dig through the dark moist earth of the flowerbeds, searching desperately for my gold key.*

I've had that vivid dream before. I shudder, tired of feeling alone. I think about my cousin Arlene. Growing up together in the fifties, we wanted to be as cute and perky as Doris Day, whose blonde, blue-eyed, virginal cheeriness attracted the likes of Cary Grant and Rock Hudson. Arlene and I wrote letters and talked on the phone. When our parents allowed us, we spent weekends together on Long Island sharing our dreams of boyfriends, husbands, and having babies. Now Arlene is living our dream. What if I never share all the love I have to give? What if I never have a baby? Never feel life growing inside of me? I put my feet on the carpet and step out of the windowsill. I search for the gold key I want close to my heart. Barren and bare, I retreat to my room.

The next morning, still in my pajamas, I go into the kitchen while my mother fills the dishwasher. I kiss her and open the well-ordered refrigerator. I reach in to get some orange juice from the left side of the top shelf. Everything has its place in her spotless kitchen. Even the pale yellow counters are devoid of any appliances except those being used.

"What time did you get home last night?" my mother asks.

"After midnight."

I need an aspirin from the cabinet near the sink, but that will raise more questions I don't want to deal with.

"Did you have a nice time? Was the show good?"

"Yes to both." I pour some juice in a glass and take a sip. "When are you and Daddy leaving?"

"We were waiting for you to get up." She turns off the faucet and starts the dishwasher. The machine clicks and sputters. "Are you coming out to the country before you go home?" Her voice sounds hopeful, pleading over the water whirring around the dirty dishes.

"I doubt it. Too many things I want to do here." There is no contest in my mind between spending time with my friends Beth and Linda, and maybe seeing Jake, or taking a train ride to upstate New York.

"Are you going to see Howard again?" My mother's voice sounds hesitant.

For years, an emotional barricade has prevented us from having a close relationship. I would never, could never, tell my mother what happened last night. I didn't understand it myself. How could my passion and desire to be warm and loving, turn me into an unresponsive, cold receptacle? What's wrong with me? And why with Howard, his breath, his touch, all I wanted was it to be over?

"I don't think so," I answer.

"Oh." My mother's energy deflates. She turns away and puts groceries into paper bags to take to their country home. "Daddy wants to talk to you, Maddy. He's in the den. Tell him I'll be ready to leave in ten minutes. And be nice. He only wants the best for you. We both do."

I close my eyes and stand still. My head pounds. I can't imagine what we have to discuss. I shuffle toward the den. My father sits at his antique oak desk writing out some checks. The sunlight from the window behind him lights up the room. I walk around his desk to kiss his cheek and sit down on the opposite side to face him.

"Mom says she'll be ready to leave in ten minutes," I say, my voice light. "Are you looking forward to getting away?"

He puts down his fountain pen, clasps his hands and looks me in the eyes. "Since you took that leave of absence from school for the year, you'll have no income. How are you planning to live?"

This is the presiding judge of many years. I'm in the witness seat. His questions are straight, to the point. Taking a leave is a major concern to my parents who are frugal and spend wisely.

"I've been saving. If I need extra money, I can get a part-time job. Maybe tutoring. I'll be all right."

He leans back in his chair and puts his hands behind his head. To my right hangs the Picasso-like portrait his friend painted of him sitting in that exact position wearing his black robe, with a scale of justice and a chessboard against the skyline of New York.

"Plan A is to write full time," I continue. "If it doesn't work out, I'll go back to teaching."

The wrinkles in his brow deepen. He sits up and tears a check from its binder. Reaching across his desk, he hands it to me. "I want you to have this. Mother and I want you to have this." I look at the eight hundred dollar amount.

"We'll send you one every month for a year so you don't have to worry about money and you can concentrate on your writing."

"You don't have to do this."

"I know. We hope you'll find what you're looking for. Maybe this will help."

My emotions spin — guilt, gratitude, fear, excitement, relief.

"Thank you."

"We want what's best for you."

Tears form at the edges of his eyes. He closes the large black ledger and pushes back his chair. He walks over to me and cups my face in his hands. "I love you," he whispers and kisses my forehead.

———

I take the elevator in Beth's building to the eighteenth floor. The morning with my parents came with its highs and lows, but two aspirins, a hot shower and the prospect of a week in New York with my friends, revived my spirit. Like Mary Richards from *The Mary Tyler Moore Show*, I'm ready to toss my hat in the air. I know I'm going to make it after all.

As I drag my bags out, I almost collide with my best friend. Dressed in a flowing, royal blue silk caftan, wine glass in hand, Beth is as excited to see me as I am to see her. We embrace, then stand back and assess each other. I start to ruffle her newly shorn hairdo.

"Damn. Almost forgot. You hate anyone playing with your hair."

She blushes.

"You look great, blonde highlights and everything. So New York sophisticate."

"Yeah, right. Come on, I have a glass waiting for you."

She grabs one of my bags and leads the way. We enter her spacious one bedroom corner apartment, with its southern and western exposure, and no towering buildings to block the sun. Light pours in through every window allowing her plants to thrive. They add warmth to her white, modern, made-in-Manhattan co-op. To the left of the door, photographs in Plexiglas frames decorate the wall, along with her five book jackets and excerpts from her various newspaper and magazine articles. With Beth's writing skills, she has turned her single woman exploits into a lucrative career. I wonder if I can support myself as a writer too. She hands me a glass of red wine and makes a toast.

"To the summer of '79, your trip and our visit."

"Just what I've been thinking."

"And why not? Good things might as well happen to us." She points to the couch and we choose our spots. "Fill me in on your family and the Bar Mitzvah."

I sip my wine. I can tell her all that later. There are other things I want to talk about. I smile at the woman who knows all my secrets, supports and challenges my decisions, and most of all makes me laugh. I take another sip of wine and set it down on the coffee table.

"What?" Beth asks. "What's going on?"

"I called Jake this morning."

She raises her eyebrows. "That's a name from our past."

"I bumped into him in the Village last night and he asked me to."

"You're amazing. You've been in the city for three days and you've done more than I have in three weeks." She reaches for her cigarettes that are never far away. "So what happened?"

I pull back my long, curly red hair into a ponytail, twist it, and let it fall to my shoulders.

"Well?" Beth blows a puff of smoke.

"I called his office and spoke to his receptionist, then his secretary, then to him. He sounded frantic, busy. But he was so nice. Happy to hear from me." I giggle. "I was a wreck though, pacing around my folks' apartment. Other than the few minutes last night, it's been over three years since I saw him, just before he and Linda broke up."

"Oh, Linda," Beth's voice drops. She sits back against the armrest and folds her right leg under her body.

"Linda's with someone new," I say. "I was friends with both of them so why can't I go out with him?"

"Are you?"

"Lunch tomorrow." I close my eyes.

"Madd, aren't you asking for trouble?"

As I shift on the couch, the book next to me falls off. To avoid answering, I bend to pick it up. Beth knows all about Jake and his life-style. We all met the first summer I went to Fire Island.

"Forget the book, answer my question."

"I don't know," I lie. I can't keep a straight face. "Yeah, I'm interested. Always have been. I never would have done anything while he and Linda were dating or partially living together. But he's free now." I stare out the window. A bird feeder suspended from a wire on a neighbor's patio sways gently. Through the strands of an ivy plant, I watch the puffy clouds drift across the Hudson River.

"Maddy, I love you, but you're crazy," Beth shakes her head. "You're asking for trouble."

"Why?"

"Jacob Miller may be an adorable man." She pauses. "But you know him. You're going to get hurt."

"Maybe, maybe not." I toss my head back. "I could be the one to make the difference." We both know how many other women thought they would be the one to rein Jake in. I pictured Claudia with the haunting eyes.

"I hope you don't believe that." Beth refills her glass and takes a long drag on her cigarette. "Why, now? Do you think Jake has changed?"

I study my left hand and poke at my cuticles.

"No."

"So what are you doing? We've spent hours on the phone talking about how you want a relationship. But Jake is not the guy."

I tremble thinking about Howard and how once again that didn't work out. "Jake's not bad. He's creative and charming. He has this joie de vivre that translates into not wanting to settle down, but he did once before."

I get up and walk to the window. I look down at the busy street below packed with cars, cabs, and people walking in all directions. The sound of horns blaring, a jackhammer tearing up pavement and the screech of a truck braking add to the confusion.

"Maybe Jake will be a New York fling, maybe he'll be something more." I smile. "Don't burst my bubble. We're only having lunch. Unless his drafting table has a dual purpose, we'll just talk!"

"Cute," Beth says.

2

NEW YORK CITY
July 1979

I **stand outside Jake's office** surveying the lettering on the door. I take a deep breath before entering. The small reception area has a large floor to ceiling window that faces south to the Statue of Liberty. I walk over to the desk where a young woman doodles geometric figures. She reminds me of a dark-haired Grace Kelly.

"Good afternoon. Welcome to Miller, Smith & Walters," she says in a perfunctory manner. "May I help you?"

"I have an appointment with Jacob Miller. I'm Maddy Gold."

"I'll let him know you're here, Miss Gold."

I nod but don't stick around for the rest of the memorized speech about taking a seat and waiting. I scan the view west to the river and down to the Bowery. I never miss New York until I see the Manhattan skyline. The majesty of each steel structure stretching high toward the clear blue sky thrills me. I feel the same awe looking at man's technical excellence as I do watching a sunset in Hawaii, or seeing the snow capped peak of Mont Blanc in France.

I tug at my short red dress and adjust the bolero jacket Beth loaned me. We'd spent an hour coming up with this outfit, which gave me another opportunity to explain why I had called Jake. Beth and I are both in our early thirties and single. Each of us wants to find a man and fall in love even though Beth has already been married.

"Miss Gold?" The receptionist's voice startles me.

"Mr. Miller can see you now." She points. "Through that door."

"Thanks."

As I walk down the hall, it feels like fireworks erupting all around. Deadlines and panic permeate the air. A boisterous lunch conference is happening in the first room I pass, while in the smaller cubicles people are either talking on the phone or typing furiously. A man in a white, short-sleeve shirt runs down the hall and passes me with a drawing in his hand. He disappears into the conference room and slams the door shut.

When I get to Jake's office, I stand outside for a minute. Adrenaline pumps straight to my heart. It begins to flutter. I straighten my dress and jacket again, push open the door and step inside. Jake sits behind a long cluttered desk talking on the phone. He looks up and smiles. His full head of dirty blond hair appears thinner and grayer. His shirtsleeves are rolled up to his elbows and his blue tie hangs loose at the neck. I usually picture him in jeans or tennis shorts, or wearing his beret and galoshes, but he looks good in whatever he wears. The tingle in my belly lets me know he still has the same effect on me.

Jake nods for me to take a seat. Instead, I walk around the room noting the drafting table in the corner. I spent many nights here with Linda waiting for Jake to finish work so we could go to the opera, the ballet, or an expensive upscale restaurant I could never afford. I feel guilty seeing Jake without Linda. Even if they're no longer a couple, I detect Linda's influence on Jake's life all around the office. She chose the modern Scandinavian furniture and the blue and gold color scheme. She even selected the artwork. I go over to the bookcase and see several more Clio awards added to the collection. At least those are his.

I take a seat on the couch facing Jake's desk. He holds the phone to one ear, reading a storyboard for an advertising campaign and signs a paper lying on his desk. He flashes five fingers at me, then three. He hangs up the phone abruptly and grabs his jacket. "If we don't leave now, we never will." I follow him out of his office, scurrying after him like a baby bear cub. "I'm going to lunch," he calls out to anyone listening. When we reach the elevators, Jake pushes the button and puts his arm around my waist.

"I'm sorry. It's always like this. I made a reservation at a small fish restaurant around the corner. It's crowded, but we should be able to talk."

I smile but feel awkward.

"You look wonderful," he says, stroking my cheek with the back of his hand. "California agrees with you."

The elevator door opens before I can say a word. We squeeze inside the crowded space and stand quietly, Jake behind me. When he presses his body against mine, I take a deep breath and lean into him.

———

Leo, the maître d', guides us through a maze to a table at the back of the restaurant. The frenetic "time is money" energy overwhelms me. Waiters hustle to the ringing of silverware and glasses bouncing from the walls to the ceiling. In Los Angeles a lunch like this would be on an outdoor patio with hanging pots of fuchsia. "No rush, take your time," the waiters would say casually. "Enjoy."

After he seats us, Leo chats briefly with Jake. He recommends the Chef's Special with a bottle of Chenin Blanc. We take his suggestion.

"Nothing's changed," I say, commenting on our first half hour together. "Three years later and chaos still reigns."

"Probably." His blue eyes sparkle.

"I don't know how you do it. You thrive on tension and excitement." That's what makes him so damned sexy.

"This is my element," Jake says, as he scans the room.

A waiter brings the wine and fills our glasses.

"You already know that about me," he says. "Tell me about you." He raises his glass. "You look happy. In fact, glowing. Anything to do with Howard?"

"No, he's just a friend from college." I avoid looking at him.

"Good. Very good." He reaches across the table and strokes my hand. His touch sizzles like a bolt of lightening. "What's happening? It's been ages since I've seen you."

A cork pops at a table in front of us and the waiter pours champagne into two slender flutes. Watching a young couple toast each other, I hold my glass up to them, envious. I turn back to Jake excited to share my dreams.

"I've quit teaching to write full time. Beth's coming to L.A. and we're going to write a teleplay. We did one last summer, a comedy. It didn't sell but we had the best time." I take a sip of wine. "And you? How are the kids? And Claudia? Is she anyone special?"

"She was." He withdraws his hand. "We all sort of went together — me, the kids and Claudia. She was my partner, my lover, and the kids fucked it up. Not so much Becky. She's away at school. But Kevin is fourteen. He hates everything — me, himself. I'm sick of it." He drains his wine glass and pours himself more.

"You're so angry."

"We were living together." He takes a sip. "I was out of town on business and one night Kevin didn't come home after school. He stayed out until four in the morning. Claudia was frantic. He never called. Didn't think there was anything wrong with that. She left me three days later."

"I'm sorry, Jake." I reach across the table and take his hand. He looks weary and defeated, and every bit his forty-five years.

"She was special and now she's gone." He rolls some breadcrumbs around the white cloth.

Claudia may have moved out of his apartment, but after seeing them at the theater last night, she didn't look gone to me. Beth might be right. I'm probably asking for trouble.

The waiter arrives with the food and ties bibs around our necks. "Bon appetite," he says and refills our glasses.

I peer down at the bright orange Maine lobster stuffed with shrimp and crabmeat. "All my favorites." We eat in silence. I search for words to fill the quiet and change Jake's mood. Selfishly I want the charming, quirky Jake. The man who can turn a tennis match into a Charlie Chaplin routine, or a trip to Balducci's into an exotic food expedition.

He speaks first. "You told me about your writing, but what's happening personally? I always pictured you married and a mother. Don't you want to meet someone? Have children? You're great with kids." He smiles. "Even after hearing my brilliant endorsement of mine?"

I gulp. "Yes, very much." I hadn't envisioned this conversation. "I grew up believing I would be married by now and have three to five kids." I giggle. "I guess that translates to four."

"What's stopping you?"

"I could be conventional and say the man I haven't met yet, but I won't." I shrug. "Actually, I've been thinking about it a lot more lately. I'm almost thirty-four. Still single and there are no guarantees that will change." I think of Aunt Renee alone her whole life. "I'd like a baby. I want to be part of a family."

"You aren't pregnant are you?" He tips his head to one side. A broad grin crinkles his eyes. "Is that why you're glowing?"

"No, but I've been struggling with this for years. My clock is loudly ticking. What if I don't meet someone?" I sigh. "It's not my first choice, but I want a baby even if I'm not married."

"Well, that's rather Auntie Mame-ish. And brave." He sits back in his chair.

"There is that small, unconventional part of me." I laugh.

"But this would be big!" He picks up his wine glass and swirls the liquid around. "Have you discussed this with anyone else?"

"On and off." I study his face. He seems intrigued. I'd gone this far. "I guess you don't remember?"

"What?" He looks perplexed. "You told me?"

"I asked you! You were having a Christmas party at your place after I moved to California. I came back for a visit. Linda and I were setting the table and talking about kids. The subject of sperm donors came up. You walked in and I asked you to volunteer." My face burns.

"What happened?"

"I got embarrassed, Linda changed the subject."

"I must have been drunk. I have no recollection of that. I'm sure I was flattered." He pushes his hair off his forehead but it doesn't stay. "This is mind-boggling, Maddy. What do your friends think?

"Some people think I'm crazy. They say it's hard enough with two parents. And some people think it's just talk."

"You'd make a wonderful mother," he says. "But being almost solely responsible for two kids, I'm telling you it's not easy." He peppers his asparagus. "Have you chosen anyone else?" His look and voice are flirtatious.

"No." I shake my head. "I've thought about artificial insemination, I've thought about a stranger. Neither feels right."

Jake laughs. "You're beautiful and intelligent. I can't figure out why you're still single. It doesn't make sense."

"That makes two of us." My throat tightens, my stomach flips.

"This is ironic," he says. "You're contemplating the joys of parenting and tying yourself down for the next eighteen years, and I'm counting the hours till my burden is over."

"We're at different points in our lives."

I notice lines and wrinkles in his face I haven't seen before. We finish lunch in silence. I wipe my mouth with my napkin, wishing I'd kept it shut. I tried to be open with Jake, more than I have with any other man. It backfired.

He leans forward and reaches for my hand. "Let's not end this on such a serious note. It's our first date and I'm hoping there will be more."

His gaze makes me feel like I am in the spotlight and the only woman in the room.

"How long will you be in town?"

"Through next weekend." A thrill surges inside me.

"That's not much time. How about dinner tonight? At my place."

"That sounds nice," I say calmly, my heart pounding. I struggle to contain my grin.

He looks at his watch. "After we finish here, I want to stop at a record store. A friend just had a baby boy, and I want to get this jazz record of lullabies, so when mama gets up to nurse in the middle of the night, she can soothe her soul too." He brings my hand to his lips and kisses it. "I'll get you one, too. When you're ready."

———

I ring Beth's doorbell. When she doesn't answer, I use her spare key, glad to have the place to myself. I loved being with Jake, but trying to be perfect so he likes me, is emotionally exhausting. As I walk to Beth's room to change into my jeans and oversized blue work shirt, I stop to look at the photographs and book jackets on the wall. I find the picture of Brian and Beth, the happy, hippie couple at their wedding in 1969. He died two years later from cancer and although Beth was moving on, her wounds were still open. Her claustrophobic fear of trains and buses, any enclosed place like a theater or department store, stemmed from rushing Brian to a San Francisco hospital in the middle of many nights. She'd drive terrified, across the Bay Bridge with her delirious husband curled up in the back, while she was suspended between a blackened sky above and dark, cold water below. Those experiences, from diagnosis to death, still had a hold on her.

At the end of the narrow hallway, I come face to face with the head shot of Jonathan Kaplan, her "moving on" guy, a Los Angeles based Hollywood industry type, recently divorced. His dark brooding eyes and half-smile beckon. I'm not convinced he deserves a place up there, but he's the reason Beth is coming to L.A. this summer, so maybe it is. I change clothes and go into the kitchen for some water. I discover a note posted on the refrigerator.

Madd,
I'll be home around six. We'll have dinner here.
Love, B.

Oh shit. We never talked about dinner and I don't want to disappoint her. I lie down on the couch. I don't want Beth to feel I'm choosing a date with a guy over being with her. But I am. And not just any guy. Jake is intelligent, commanding and successful, yet he has that vulnerable quality that makes me want to take care of him. I shiver. I turn over and close my eyes.

I wake up to the door rattling and get up to open it. Beth comes in pulling a shopping cart filled with groceries. She kisses me on the cheek.

"I figure you had a big lunch so I bought rare roast beef, rye bread and coleslaw. You always complain about L.A. delis."

I follow her through the living room into the kitchen, not knowing how to tell her.

"I'm not going to be home for dinner," I blurt out. "I'm sorry."

"Jake, I suppose?" She glares at me. "Should I leave a light on?"

I bite my lower lip. For a few seconds she looks annoyed, then smiles.

"All right. You put the food away. I'll wash up and then you tell me EV-ER-Y-THING."

The air, stuck in my lungs, leaves my body. Before I know it, Beth reappears.

"I told Jake I'm thinking of having a baby."

"You said what?" She slaps the dining room table. Her pinky ring pings against it. "You're thinking of having a baby?" She stares at me as if I'm from the red planet. "How could you tell him that? I didn't even know you were still thinking about it."

"Always. It never goes away. Whether this is a first date conversation is another issue," I say. "It just popped out of my mouth. The point is I want a baby. I don't know if you understand. I never hear you talk about kids."

She sips her soda and fidgets with her napkin. "When we found out Brian had cancer, I wanted to get pregnant. I didn't want him to die without leaving a part of himself behind — something I could hold and love. But he wouldn't do it. And most of the time he couldn't. Chemo made him impotent." She fiddles with the crumpled napkin. "Before and even after he died, I hated any pregnant woman or any woman with a baby. Other people's joy made me angry. Mine had been ripped away." She pauses. "How do I feel now? If I got married again, I would like to have a baby. But alone? That's crazy."

"I don't care. I want a baby more than anything. I always have. But look at me. I never thought I'd be single and childless at thirty-three."

"What about the baby, growing up without a father? And your family? How will they feel?"

"The baby will be okay." I want to sound strong. "I'll make a good parent, better than most." I sip some water. "As for my folks, I can't live my life for them. I'm tired of being alone and feeling crummy. I told you about last Thanksgiving at my cousin Ruth's house. All my West Coast family in attendance with everyone in nice, neat family units. And I was alone. When we were cleaning up after dinner, I told Ruth about wanting to have a baby. And she pipes up, 'if you really wanted one, you'd have one. Simple.' I was flabbergasted. You know Ruth, my personal Emily Post. Proper, dignified, traditional. She called my bluff."

"For Christ's sake, Maddy, it's not simple. It's not like buying a goldfish. What about the father? Where does he fit in?"

"I don't know. I don't know a lot of things. I'm just telling you what's going on. I haven't done anything yet."

"Good to know. And Jake, what about him? What did he say?"

"That I'll make a great mother."

"That's all?"

"You know Jake. He'd support something like that because it's an adventure. I reminded him I'd asked him before."

"You did? Oh, Maddy. When?"

"Four or five years ago. The point is he didn't say no then, and the idea certainly doesn't seem to scare him now."

"What? Is that why you called him yesterday?"

"No." I sit up straight. "I didn't even think about Jake until I saw him at the theater. And he suggested lunch."

The phone rings. We freeze.

"Saved by the bell." She goes to get the telephone and I put our glasses in the sink.

"It's for you, it's Linda."

Beth gives one of those "now what are you going to do" looks and passes the receiver to me.

———

A few blocks from Jake's house, I buy some flowers. I think about wine, but Jake always chooses the right wine for the right occasion. I don't want to look foolish.

He rents the second floor of a converted brownstone he sometimes shares with his kids, friends or lovers. I have no idea who might be there. I push the buzzer and wait.

I climb the wood stairs. The creaking sound makes me cringe. Instead of my usual loose fitting clothes, I had poured myself into white jeans and a hot pink silk blouse to look sexy. My mother always told me it's painful to be beautiful.

"Hey, down there. You look great."

I silently thank my mom. I look up and stop mid-step. Jake leans over a rickety banister dressed in an extra large tattered brown T-shirt over faded jean cutoffs. I hide my dismay with a smile and continue to the top of the stairs. I hand him the bouquet of irises and daffodils. He puts his face into the floral mix and takes a deep breath.

"Thank you. I don't remember getting flowers before." He puts his arm around me and kisses me lightly on the lips. "Welcome." He kisses me again. "Come in, but be careful. This place is an obstacle course."

I step into the living room. Stacks of newspapers and packing cartons cover the hardwood floors.

"What's going on?"

"I'm moving. Didn't I tell you?"

"No." I'm stunned.

"I guess we had other things to talk about. I bought a loft in lower Manhattan."

"That's wonderful."

"It will be by January." He grimaces. "Long story. Tell you later. In the meantime, it's a real bitch. I have to pack up this four-bedroom place by next week."

I look around. Except for empty cartons and newspapers, the room is perfect. Nothing has been touched.

"Jake, that's impossible."

"You haven't heard the worst. I'm leaving for Detroit in the morning for two days on business. I couldn't get it postponed."

I sit down. "What are you going to do?"

"I left Kevin on Fire Island for a few weeks, so I don't have to worry about him. And while I'm gone, some friends are coming in to pack. When I get back, I'll finish up before the movers come."

"There's so much to do."

"I know." He kneels beside the chair and puts his hands gently on my shoulders. "Maybe you'll help tonight? I promise it won't be all work."

I hide my disappointment. "What can I say to an offer like that?"

Holding out his hand, he gently pulls me up. He kisses me again, this time parting my lips and toying with my tongue. A pleasure filled tingle rises in the pit of my belly.

"Mmm," he says. "Lots to look forward to. Let's get some wine and put these flowers in water, then we can work for an hour. After that, I faithfully vow to feed you the best turkey sandwich you've ever had."

"That will not get you my best efforts." I follow him into the kitchen.

"How about an IOU? After the move we'll do something special."

I want to raise my arms to the ceiling and rail at the Gods. Instead, I reach out and take the glass of wine he offers me.

"With you going out of town, I think tonight's it. I go home next week so I won't see you again this trip."

He looks into my eyes and raises his glass. "Who knows? New York, California, the future."

"The future. I like that." I smile and clink his glass. "Come on. Where do we start?"

"If we dismantle and pack the things in the den, that will be great. Kevin did his room before he left. I'll do my room when I get back. This will get done."

We walk out of the kitchen down a dark hallway into the den.

"All this is going into storage," he explains. "I bought a quarter of a warehouse that's being converted into four lofts. It'll be gutted and totally rebuilt. I'm staying at a friend's place in the Village until they come back from Europe. Then Kevin and I will live in the loft as it's being constructed."

"You couldn't have made this more complicated. Ever hear of planning?"

"My lease was up, and I couldn't get an extension. It was now or never."

I sigh, surveying the den. Every knickknack is in place. Nothing has been touched in here either.

"You pack the books," Jake says. "I'll get going on something else."

I walk toward the three large mahogany bookcases and we both set to work in silence. Comfortable.

"What's next?" I ask, after closing and labeling the last carton.

"Sit here while I go through these old photos. You may find them interesting."

I head to the black leather couch and hold up a picture that had fallen on the floor.

"Who's she?"

"That's Kathy, my ex-wife. You never met her?"

"Uh-uh." I look at Kathy closely. Petite, slender, dark hair and dark eyes. "She's pretty. Your kids look like her."

"I know, there's not much resemblance to me."

I sift through the box of photos. "There are so many in here. You might think about organizing them. It'll be a treasure for your kids."

"You think they'd care about old photos?" he snaps.

"Not now. Kids are too self-centered. Maybe when they're older. My family has pictures of my grandparents and parents from childhood up. They date back to the late 1800s. Everyone looks young and vibrant."

"Hey." He hands me another one. "Remember this?"

"Linda, in front of your beach house."

"The first summer I owned it. Same time I met you."

"All of us met that summer. Beth, too."

Beth's mother-in-law had convinced her to stop mourning and start living again. Beth and I called it our coming of age summer. We'd shared a house with a group of strangers who loved to eat, drink and have sex with anyone who passed within sight. Fragile and withdrawn, Beth lasted two tortured weekends. Not willing to waste my prepaid rent money, I stayed.

"Have you seen her? Linda?" Jake looks at the picture and then at me.

I shake my head trying to understand Jake's question. "We're having lunch on Thursday."

"We broke up a long time ago. She wanted a monogamous relationship and that wasn't me." He takes back the photo. His fingers trace the edge of the picture. "I was one hundred percent faithful to my wife for fifteen years. I never looked at another woman. I didn't even know how to talk to women. Now, I enjoy them. All of them. Different sizes, shapes and personalities."

"What about Claudia? Weren't you faithful to her?" I listen closely.

"I met Claudia a year after Linda. I fell madly in love with her, but I dated other women. It bothered her."

"I can't imagine why."

I feel his eyes on me. I look up.

"It was easier for both of us to blame it on Kevin when he didn't come home that night, but I know he wasn't the sole reason she left."

"I'm sorry, Jake. Maybe in the future you'll want a commitment. The women in your life certainly do."

My stomach lets out a growl. "Ooh, did you hear that? I'm starving." I'm relieved to change the subject away from Jake's infidelities and their implications.

He gets up from his chair and holds out his hand to me. "Let's go eat."

After dinner, when I get up to clear the table I have to steady myself. Two glasses of wine, Miles Davis and Jake, and I'm woozy. "You did well," I say, trying to be cool, "delicious turkey sandwich."

"I'm glad. Don't clean up. My maid's coming tomorrow to pack the kitchen. She'll do it."

He takes our glasses and leads me down the long hallway. The silence gives me too much time to think. I flash on Howard. I don't want another disappointment, another embarrassing failure.

"Are you into pot?" Jake asks.

"Not really."

"It's relaxing."

"I've smoked a few times, but I'm not into it. I feel like the cops will raid the place any minute. Stupid, I know."

"You can check under the bed or in the closets if you like." With a playful smile, he kisses my forehead. "You're really sweet. Come on, I feel like a joint."

I follow him into his bedroom. He places the wine glasses on the night table and turns on the lamp beside his carelessly made bed. He walks over to his dresser and takes a small plastic bag of marijuana and a package of Zigzags out of the top drawer. I straighten the sheets and curl up on the bed. Leaning on one elbow, I watch him wander around the room collecting his paraphernalia. His walk has a bounce to it, his weight mostly on the ball of each foot. He sits next to me to roll the joint.

"You're so focused. Is it hard to do?"

"I'm just learning. I'm not very good, yet."

"With all the wine I've had, if I smoke that thing I'll probably fall asleep." I lie back on the bed.

"I'd rather you be wide awake." He smiles. "There are so many wonderful things I want to do with you."

Everything becomes still. Jake leans over and kisses me passionately. I put my arms around him and pull him closer.

"Wait." He lights a candle and turns off the lamp. "I want to smoke this." He takes the joint and inhales deeply. Exhaling, he hands it to me. "I promise it won't make you pass out."

The sweet pungent smell fills my nose and the grass fills my lungs. My body tingles — alive and demanding. Jake strokes my hair as he sits up against the headboard. He plucks the joint from my fingers and takes two long drags. I don't want him smoking that. I want him inhaling me. I roll over and put my head on his belly. He reaches for the ashtray then slides down next to me. His mouth opens under mine and our tongues touch. I feel tiny shocks all over my skin. He moves on top of me and opens the buttons of my blouse. I want to lie there and feel every nuance of his touch on my body. We kiss as he undresses me. The candlelight flickers across my body. It makes me feel beautiful. I watch as he lifts off me to disrobe, everything in slow motion heightening my urgency.

"Come on, Jake. I want to feel you." I reach out my arms.

"You feel so good, Maddy. You're body is so . . ."

"Show me, Jake."

He traces his fingers around my breasts. Each nipple rises to meet his touch. His lips and tongue circle them, one at a time, making them taller and harder with each kiss. My body pulsates. I want him to go farther down but at the same time want him to stay where he is. I wrap my legs around him, moving up and down, back and forth so I can feel him.

Slowly he slides down my body. He kisses and licks every part of me along the way. My legs open wider to receive him and a guttural sound comes from the deep recesses of my throat. My nails grip his shoulders as I press against his mouth and tongue. Every part of me wants more. I don't know if I'm speaking out loud or Jake just understands my body. He gives me everything I have always imagined until my body can no longer respond.

"Wow," he says.

We both breathe heavily. Our bodies glisten in the candlelight. Jake stays on top, inside me as our breathing slows and our bodies rest.

"That was the best it's ever been for me." I'm embarrassed admitting it. I look into his eyes. "I never knew it could be like that, so tender yet so explosive. Thank you."

He lies by my side, still holding me close. He kisses my nose. "And thank you, too." He stays silent for a few seconds. "Is there any way you're free for the weekend? I can pack on Thursday and Friday after I get home and then we can spend the weekend in the Village at my friend's place."

I throw my arms around him and almost squeal, but kiss him instead. "Sounds wonderful." I know I'll have to switch my plans.

He looks over at his alarm clock. "It's one-thirty, honey. I have to get up at six. Are you sleepy?"

"Uh huh. Just keep holding me, okay?"

We settle into a comfortable spoon position. Feeling content, I close my eyes. We hadn't used anything — nothing to protect me, nothing to protect him. I wonder if Jake even thought about it? If he'd asked, I would have told him. A chill runs down my body.

———

In the morning, I tiptoe into Beth's apartment.

"I thought I heard you," Beth says, coming out of her bedroom. "What are you doing home so early?"

"Jake dropped me off on his way to La Guardia." I yawn and make my way to the sofa bed.

"Oh, no you don't. You have to talk to me. Give me all the details. But I want some coffee first. If I'm keeping your strange hours, I need my fix."

We go into the kitchen. I prop myself against the wall while Beth makes a cup of instant coffee.

"I wish I had a camera. You have a grin on your face like a kid who's just been to Disneyland."

My grin widens.

"Okay," Beth says walking back to the living room. She plunks down into her chair and wraps a blue wool blanket around her shoulders. Her short blonde hair stands up like porcupine quills. "Coffee's ready, cigarettes ready. Let's hear it."

"There's not much to say." I sit on a chair facing her. "Jake was sweet and caring and we had a good time."

"That's it? Are you going to see him again?"

"Yes." I lower my eyes and feel the heat in my cheeks. "This weekend. I'll rearrange everything so I can."

Beth sips her coffee. "Madd, did you use anything?"

A door in the hallway slams followed by footsteps. My euphoria evaporates. I can't lie to her, but I don't want to have this discussion now.

"No."

"Shit, Maddy. What are you doing?"

"I'm almost positive I can't get pregnant now," I say calmly.

"Excuse me. Have you been pregnant so many times that you know that?" Her voice rises. "Or do you have a special crystal ball? You know there's no safe time." She runs her fingers through her hair. "I have a friend who had her period and got pregnant and another got pregnant while nursing."

"I'm not ovulating. Trust me."

"Maddy, it's not my life, but have you really thought this through?"

"I've thought it through as far as anyone can when they make decisions that involve the unknown." I get up and walk to the window. I turn back to face my friend. "I know how complicated this is. I even know how selfish I sound. I can argue every side of this conundrum all by myself." I laugh. "I'd be a great lawyer for the prosecution and the defense."

"Did you tell Jake you've chosen him?"

"I haven't chosen him, Beth." I sit back down. "I just haven't eliminated him."

"Not cute and not fair."

"Fair?" I soften my tone. "You should know there is no fair. I want something for me. Now. There are no guarantees. I'm not trying to use Jake or hurt him, but he's got some responsibility in this. I couldn't get pregnant alone and he knows what I've been thinking. He didn't ask if I was using anything. I wouldn't have lied if he did, and if he doesn't, well that's that."

Beth stands up and the blanket falls from her shoulders. "I need some more coffee. What about you?"

"You have any fruit?"

She checks the refrigerator. "Oranges, plums or peaches? I bought a lot of stuff in your honor."

"I know and I'm sorry. I haven't been around much." I kiss her on the cheek. "I'll get an orange. You get your coffee."

I peel the orange while Beth boils some water.

"I know I'm jumping way ahead, but I'm trying to understand. Let's say you get pregnant."

I nod. We sit at the kitchen table across from each other.

"What about money, Maddy? How are you going to raise this child alone? Who will give you emotional support?"

"I still have a job. I only took a year's leave. I won't be thrilled going back to teaching, but as my father drilled into me, 'Being a teacher is the best profession for a woman.'" I laugh. "And for support, I have a great group of friends in L.A. I can't vouch for their reaction but I don't believe they'll abandon me." I pop an orange wedge into my mouth. "Look around, Beth. How many others are doing it all alone and they didn't opt for it? Most of them expected a life of wedded bliss, family, and joy into the sunset."

She sips her coffee and lights another cigarette. "Are you in love with him?"

I toy with a piece of orange peel.

"I don't think so. I could probably get there, though." I smile. "I really like Jake and last night I felt something I never felt before." I stop, suddenly understanding Beth's intent. I shake my head. "I'm not trying to trap him if that's what you mean. These are two very separate issues. Wanting a relationship with Jake is separate from wanting a baby."

Beth inhales smoke deep into her throat.

"This conversation is purely hypothetical," I continue. "I'm sure I'm not pregnant, so let's drop it. I had a good time last night. I want to savor it. And I don't want you to be angry at me."

"I'm not angry. Sorry if I sound that way." She reaches across the table and pats my hand. "I do think you're making a big mistake, but I'm also playing devil's advocate. You're my friend and I love you no matter what."

3

—

NEW YORK CITY

July 1979

*M*y **week in Manhattan** has been a mixture of activity and day-dreaming. I couldn't focus on the Guggenheim and the Frick museums. Images of making love with Jake replaced the framed masterpieces hanging in front of me. I get off the subway at 42nd St. to meet Linda for lunch in a midtown coffee shop.

Older, wiser and more sophisticated, Linda had become my mentor after the Peace Corps. Faced with free love, drugs, sex and the escalation of the Vietnam war, I was overwhelmed when I returned to the States. After two years of living in a village with no electricity or running water, wearing dresses that covered my knees, I even forgot about paying fifteen percent tips in restaurants. Linda helped me adjust to a new and changed world.

During lunch we talk about everything, except what is really on my mind — Jake. As I pay the bill, Linda waits outside. I watch her through the window. I count each man who passes by her and does a double take. Five, so far. She has a way about her that attracts male attention. With dark hair and porcelain skin, Linda's colorful style belies her age. Tall, regal, and elegant, she appears closer to twenty than forty-five. She looks like the women in my key dream.

"I love watching your impact on men," I say to her outside.

She laughs. "The same thing can happen to you, if you'd relax. You're beautiful. You just don't know it. You give men power. Imagine them wearing skirts, then you'll do fine." She rubs her upper eyelid, careful not to smudge her eye make-up. "Want to walk? I have fifteen minutes before my next appointment."

"Perfect. I ate too much." I'm always concerned about my weight.

Linda picks the direction. It's a sunny, summer day.

"There are things I miss about New York," I say, "and the best days of each season are on my list."

"Let's walk to the library," she suggests. "We can sit and talk in the park."

We head west on 42nd Street. Linda stops by a jewelry store and points to an oval stone set in gold, surrounded by diamonds. "Isn't it magnificent?"

I peek in the window. "What is it?"

"A black opal. I walk here often, so I can look at it."

"How much?"

"I don't want reality." She laughs. "My dream would become ludicrous."

I smile. I know about dreams. As we continue walking, I study her profile and small upturned nose. She says it's her Swedish ancestry that keeps her young, but she works at it the way she works at everything — her interior design company, raising two daughters, being a gourmet cook.

"I saw Jake the other night." I blurt out. "I had dinner at his place and helped him pack."

"Did you have a nice evening?" she asks, her voice calm.

"Yes. Is that a problem for you?" I touch her arm. "I know you're not seeing him, but I wasn't sure."

"There's a bench over there," she points.

My gut tightens. We sit at one end of the bench. A young couple stands next to an oak tree.

"Maddy, you lived through my relationship with Jake. You know what it was like, what he's like. Other than protecting you, I don't care."

"If things were reversed, I'd have a hard time."

"Maybe you'll be right for Jake — better than I was." She shades her eyes with her hand and looks straight at me. "But I'm reminding you, he's still busy and involved with a million things. If it's a relationship you want, forget it. If you can take Jake as he is, enjoy."

"You sound pissed."

"We were together a long time," she says, her voice wistful. "Jake is appealing. But he can be difficult too. I'm over him."

I watch the couple feed the pigeons. "Are you sure this isn't going to hurt our friendship?"

"Why should it? You forget. You're not the first friend of mine that Jake has dated and bedded. And you won't be the last."

That comment smarts. I don't want it to be true.

"Sorry. I know that hurt," she says. "You need to know what you're up against going into this. It'll be easier on the way out." She glances at her watch. "Gotta go." She hugs me. "Jake won't get in our way. Just take care of yourself."

With her head held high, she walks away. The wind ruffles her cotton skirt. Linda may be speaking the truth, but like her opal, I want my dream.

———

It's seven-thirty Friday night and Jake is an hour late. He hasn't called. Beth is out, so I pace every inch of the apartment. I'm crazed. This is just like Jake. He gets caught in the moment and forgets about time. It has never bothered me before. I find it part of his quirky charm. When the telephone rings, I run to answer but wait for the third ring to pick up.

"Sorry, Madd. I know I'm late. I'll explain. I'm just leaving a meeting. Be there in fifteen minutes. Can you meet me downstairs, so I don't have to find a parking space?"

"I was worried, Jake."

"I know. I'll make it up to you."

"Are you a man of your word?"

"Absolutely. See you in fifteen."

I write Beth a note:

> B.
>
> *Miss you already. Glad you'll be on my side of the country soon.*
>
> *Love,*
>
> M.

I put her keys on the table, gather my things, and leave.

When I get to the lobby, Jake is already waiting in the circular driveway of the building. He leans against his weathered black VW, with his collar open, his tie hanging loosely around his neck. His blue linen slacks look like he's slept in them. He smiles when he sees me and reaches for my suitcases.

"You're looking good."

"I wish I could say the same about you Jake. You look exhausted."

"I am. Sorry, I'm late." He tosses my luggage in the trunk, takes my arm and guides me around the car. "Let's get out of here. I want to change these clothes and have a drink." He looks out the side window and pulls away from the curb.

"What happened at work?" I ask.

"My office is a madhouse. I'm the only fucking person who makes decisions. Besides the new General Motors contract, we got three more today and every time I think I've solved something, someone else needs me. I wonder why I have partners." He slams his hand on the horn and holds it. "Idiot! The light turned green."

"Jake." I pat his thigh. "We'll get there."

He swerves around the car in front and passes on the right. I clutch the dashboard. My foot automatically hits the nonexistent brake.

He laughs. "Okay, I'll slow down."

We drive in silence. At first it feels natural but then my mind bounces around like a tennis ball. Why can't I think of anything to say? I'm totally tongued-tied. I run through a list of topics — the kids, the move, the office, but they're boring. I look at Jake. The quiet doesn't seem to bother him.

"Madd, wait till you see where we're staying. It's a four-story, brick house. Very Dutch, minus the canal."

"Whose house is it?"

"People from the agency. They're in Europe for the summer. Last fling before a baby."

I stare straight ahead, wide-eyed.

"We're almost there. Then we'll unwind. Anything special you want to do this weekend?"

"Have fun! Relax, be with you."

"We'll take it as it comes," he says. "We're near Little Italy. We can have Italian one night and there are great jazz clubs around." His face comes alive. "And while I'm living there, I can hang out at a different club every night."

I love his exuberance. I want it to rub off on me. Tone down my seriousness.

"We're here," he says. He turns left onto a side street and parks the car.

"Which one?"

"Right there."

He points to a lovely red brick building nestled between two others. Trees line the cobblestone street, and flower boxes filled with pink peonies and purple pansies line the window ledges. Down the street I see a grocery store, a fruit and vegetable market and a delicatessen.

We unpack the car and carry my luggage into the house. The hallway is a tight squeeze. We decide to leave my things in the living room.

"Do you want to look around first, or go upstairs?"

"Upstairs. I'm hot and sticky. I want to wash up."

A spiral staircase, steep and narrow, leads to the second floor. Jake's bedroom is the size of a matchbox with a single bed, a four-drawer dresser, a bookcase and three pieces of luggage stacked in the corner.

"Glad we left my stuff downstairs," I say. "When you go for unique and rare, you give up other luxuries."

"You'll get used to it. We'll shift some things around and it'll be cozy."

The room feels oppressive. The windows have been closed all day and the sun and humidity make it feel like an oven. I walk to the window to open it. I need air and space.

"Let me do that," Jake says. "It can stick."

After a few tugs he opens it and we wait for a breeze. The air outside matches the air inside. We stand next to each other, watching the buildings and the street below. He slips his arms around my waist.

"You're tense," he whispers.

I close my eyes and lean against him.

"I'm glad you're here," he says.

That's all it takes, a few words, a touch. My shyness disappears and what remains is suspended time. Our clothes lie in a heap on the floor. Jake's eyes roam all over my body — my face, my breasts, my belly. He reaches out his hand and pulls me toward the bed.

Our lovemaking is passionate and tender. I don't second-guess myself and wonder if I'm pretty enough or doing it right. I let Jake show me with his touch, his kiss, his urgency. He leads and I follow, I lead and he follows. And then we come together. We hold each other tightly, savoring every moment. We don't speak until our breathing slows.

"That was without booze or grass," he says. "I didn't think I could." He kisses my hand. "Come on, let's take a bath. It's down the hall. I'll get it started." He sings as he gets up.

I feel like singing too. If I were Julie Andrews, I'd be twirling on a mountaintop, bursting forth with "The Sound of Music". If I were

Doris Day, in *Calamity Jane*, I'd be shouting my secret love to a daffodil. But I'm only Maddy Gold, in a strange townhouse, in New York City.

"Ready?" he asks, as I enter the bathroom.

"Yup." I start toward the tub and catch sight of myself in the mirror. "Look at me," I groan. My hair is matted, my eyeliner smeared and dripping down my cheeks.

"You look wonderful."

"Lovemaking's blinded you. Let me clean up," I plead.

"Not necessary, trust me." With the water running, he helps me into the tub first. Facing each other, we adjust ourselves until he can stretch out his legs and lay them on top of mine.

"What are you writing about?" he asks, grabbing a bar of soap. "Have you thought about a single woman who decides to have a baby?"

I'm stunned. "Yes, I have," I answer slowly, "but I don't know the ending." He obviously didn't forget about my wanting a baby. "Why haven't you asked if I'm using anything?"

"That's a woman's responsibility."

He raises his eyebrow. "You don't agree?"

"Never. If I knew I could create a life, and didn't want to, I wouldn't leave that decision up to someone else."

"Well, I don't think that's my role." He pats my leg. "Is this enough water?"

"Yes," I mumble.

He shuts off the faucets and holds up the soap. "Slide closer. I'll wash your back."

When dawn breaks, a cool breeze wafts through the room. Jake and I sleep with a sheet over us. After only a weekend together, I'm used to sleeping with him in the single bed and making love in every other part of the house. It will be hard to go home and be alone again. I roll over onto my side, not wanting to wake him. His breathing quickens and he pulls me closer.

"You didn't sleep much, did you?" He nuzzles my ear.

"Did I keep you awake?"

"No."

I turn to face him. "I had a wonderful time, Jake." Other words stick in my throat.

He raises his head and rests it on his hand. "It's hard to read you sometimes. I want to know how you're feeling."

"I'm practical Jake. You live here. I live three thousand miles away. How should I feel?"

"It was a great weekend, Maddy, but —"

I put my fingers on his lips. "Don't say anything. No speeches. It's okay."

He strokes my hair. "When's your plane?"

"I have to be at the airport by ten."

He glances at the clock. "We have time," he says, kissing my neck.

I put my arms above my head and let him come to me.

4

MARINA DEL REY

August 1979

$\mathcal{B}$ack in California for almost a month, I drive along Admiralty Way to meet Beth. The Marina, a singles playground on the Westside of Los Angeles, attracts successful men and women looking for a relaxed, upscale environment for their boats or Mercedes. It also draws the hopeful — people who haven't yet arrived. I rented an apartment here two years ago to put myself in the middle of where *it* was supposed to happen. And while I love the Marina, the sun and salt air, and easy access to tennis and beach volleyball, I feel isolated and empty. I could easily pack up and move out of my complex, and not say goodbye to one person in this shallow singles paradise.

I park in the underground structure of Beth's building and climb to the first floor. I knock on the door of the one-bedroom, furnished apartment Jonathan leased for them, so Beth could be near me. So far their living together experiment isn't working so well. Beth answers the door in her blue bathrobe with a new cigarette burn on the front. She has dark circles under her eyes and her face looks puffy.

"God, you look like hell." I walk inside. "I'm taking you out to breakfast."

"What about our script?"

"You couldn't concentrate on the trials and tribulations of Jennifer Dalton. You have enough of your own."

She attempts a smile. "I'll get dressed."

"Bring your writing stuff and a bathing suit," I call out. "We'll go to my place after."

I sit on the couch and survey the living room furnished in Formica and plastic, with pea green shag carpets, and orange plaid fabric. Beth returns wearing white shorts and a rose floral blouse. It doesn't add any color to her face.

"I'm ready," she says, "let's go."

"How about the Brown Bagger? We can walk there."

"Fine. Anywhere."

We saunter along Washington Boulevard in silence. Beth and Jonathan's relationship has been rocky since Beth arrived. Neither one is willing to compromise, so it's going to be a long six weeks living together. She'll talk when she's ready.

The restaurant is empty for a Wednesday morning. Clear with sunny skies and none of the usual fog, I figure everyone is at the beach. We choose a table on the patio and scan the paper bag menu. After the waitress takes our order, Beth sits back and lights a cigarette. "This is one of the things we're fighting about." She points to the pack. "Jonathan is allergic to smoke and I'm not ready to quit. He takes it personally, as if I continue to smoke just to get him." She frowns and inhales. "He didn't come home until nine last night. It was supposed to be seven. He called every half hour to tell me he was leaving, but something always came up."

"Are you taking that personally?"

She glares at me as if I'm betraying her. "Probably." Then she smiles. "I've only been in L.A. two weeks and I've threatened to leave him three times."

"You want to be number one and you don't feel that way."

"You're right."

The waitress interrupts with our food. I'm hungry for the first time in weeks. My usually hearty appetite has been on vacation. "It looks delicious." I cut into my omelet and take a bite. "Jonathan's got obligations here and you're only one of them. California is his life, his world. When he goes to New York, most of his business doesn't go along with him. There you can be numero uno."

"What are you telling me?"

"The time you spend together in New York isn't real. He's a very busy person here and if you marry him, the only thing that will change is your name."

"Not funny, Maddy."

"I'm not trying to be funny. You're attracted to a creative, high-powered man. You can't expect a normal life."

"I'm not comfortable here. Everything in L.A. feels artificial." She sweeps her arm around in an arc. "Where are my tall buildings, subways, garbage trucks?"

I laugh. "It's hard to uproot yourself."

"You did it, right?"

"I did, but there are trade-offs."

She lets out a deep sigh. "Jonathan and I have a lot to talk about. I expected these few weeks to be a mini-version of our life together, but I'm just visiting. Maybe if I look at it that way, it'll work better." She smiles the first genuine smile of the morning. "I won't stop smoking, but at least I'll do it outdoors."

"That's a good compromise. And don't forget the mouthwash."

I take a small bite out of my sourdough toast. It tastes like sawdust.

"What did you do last night?" Beth inquires.

"I went to Fran's for a barbecue. I don't think my L.A. friends are thrilled with me right now. I haven't been around much this summer. They're hurt."

"Did they say something?"

"Just the 'we haven't seen you in a long time!' greeting. Anyway, when I got home I worked on our teleplay and crashed. I've been tired lately."

I leave most of the eggs and some of the toast on my plate. Only a twisted orange slice remains on Beth's glistening white dish. "I don't know, even when I think I'm hungry, I can't eat." I'm antsy. "Let's get the check. Are you ready?" I stand up without waiting for a response. "We'll work on our script. We've solved your problems, at least temporarily, now we can create some for Jennifer Dalton."

Five days later, I roll over in bed, not ready to get up. It's just after eight in the morning and my routine with Beth begins when I pick her up at ten. We write for a few hours, then sit by the pool and work on our tans. Sometimes we go out to lunch, but mostly we skip it and go back to work for a few more hours. We're making progress in the art of script writing and love the character we've created for our envisioned television series. By late afternoon, I drive Beth back to her place so she can relax before Jonathan arrives home. Beth says their relationship has improved and she's not as critical and demanding of him. She's even started exploring the Marina to do research for the Cosmo article she's working on, "East Coast/West Coast Lovemaking."

I swing my legs across my bed and get up slowly. I look in the mirror, massage my cheeks, then pull them back toward my ears. I walk to the front door to get the newspaper. As I bend down, the phone rings. Yesterday, I willed my heart to stop skipping every time I heard it ring, hoping it might be Jake. If he'd been interested, he would have called more than twice. I answer it on the fourth ring.

"Are you up?"

That wakes me. "Hi, Jake."

"I just got back to the office. I've been away on business."

"You work too hard." I walk around the kitchen on the cool linoleum floor, twisting and untwisting the curlicue phone line around my index finger.

"I know. How are you and Beth doing?"

"Fine, really great. Things were up and down at first for Beth and Jonathan but they're better now, and we're making progress with our writing. I love our heroine, Jennifer Dalton — J.D. for short. We've got to get her out of the pickle we put her in."

"Sounds good. Listen, honey I want to remind you I'm moving into the loft next week. Well, Kevin and I are."

"It's finished?"

"God, no. They haven't begun. It'll be a mess for months, but what choice do I have?"

"Better planning?"

"Yeah, well you know me. Anyway gotta go. Just wanted to touch base and tell you I had a great time. My bed feels empty."

"I miss you too, Jake." I close my eyes. I love hearing his voice but wish he didn't have to go so soon. I hold onto the receiver long after he hangs up.

———

The next morning, I sit at the dining room table with my calendar in front of me. I've already been up and down three times and walked around the apartment in circles. My period is late. But how late? Part of me wants to know, and part of me doesn't.

I left my pencil on the counter the last time I visited the refrigerator. I opened the door, checked the contents, pushed things around and then shut it. Food numbs my feelings — positive, negative, and neutral. I'm feeling up, down and scared. Unmarried women don't choose to get pregnant.

I find the pencil and sit down. Determined this time, I pick up the calendar. A red star in the middle of June stands out. I begin counting. I calculate my cycle for May through July. Sometimes I get my period every four weeks, sometimes five. It's a significant difference in terms of ovulation. My finger keeps landing right in the middle of my weekend with Jake in New York. I hold my breath.

I go into the bathroom. The wall facing the huge mirror is papered in a jungle print of bright reds, blues, yellows and greens. I love bold colors because they cheer me up. But I only see my pale reflection. I poke at my red hair without its usual sheen. I open my bathrobe and turn sideways to see if my belly has changed. I touch my breasts. They're tender, but that doesn't necessarily mean anything.

I can't ignore the other signs though, the dizziness and nausea. And feeling like I have my period when I don't.

I want answers. I stare at the phone next to me. Who should I call for support? Beth has never been pregnant. What about my cousin Ruth, my friends Fran and Deborah? They each have three, almost-grown children. And what about my parents? How would they deal with this? I go out to the patio to think. I lean against the wooden railing and look down over the garden. The tennis court is empty and no one is at the pool. My robe billows in the gentle breeze. "Beth first," I whisper.

Earlier in the week, I saw a flyer announcing a Fundraising Fair for the Cancer Society at Burton Chace Park in the Marina tomorrow. I assume Beth will want to go and support the event in memory of her husband. It will be a good place to tell her about the *maybe baby*.

The Marina is perfect on a summer day. The green grass, blue sky and white sailboats, create a sense of both calm and excitement. The channel breeze and sun balance the temperature as people of all ages wander through the park. Beth and I stroll by the water. I have my hair in a ponytail but Beth's silky blonde hair blows all over her face.

"Thanks for picking this place," she says, stopping to watch the boats sail in the bay. She combs her hair with her fingers to get it out of her eyes.

"Are you thinking about Brian?"

"We were so young when we got married. And I was so young when he died. I wonder if we would have been another divorce statistic if he'd lived."

"Is this connected to Jonathan? You've been quiet on the subject."

Beth gives a pursed-lip smile. "You were right about me, us. And things have been a lot better, but I'm not sure there's anything more."

"What happened?"

"It's nothing specific. I just can't be in another traditional marriage and Jonathan wants that." She starts walking. "He'll make a suggestion, but it's really an order. He wants a stay-at-home wife who will be available on his schedule." She folds her arms across her chest. "He's nice about it, but there's this tone in his voice. He says I'm too sensitive and critical. He jokingly calls me his women's libber, but he means it and not in a funny way."

"What are you going to do?"

"I'm stuck. It's hard to love someone and think you can't live with them. We'll talk on the phone after I go home and he'll come to New York in late October. We'll make a final decision then. If we're not going to be together, I want to think about dating again."

"Wow, I didn't know about all this."

She bites her bottom lip. "I haven't said anything because, to be honest, I've been a little worried about you. You've been so tired and distant. But you seem better today."

"Better? I guess."

This would be the perfect time to tell her but I can't. Instead I point to the sky. "Look at the kites."

"Did you ever fly one? It always seems so easy when someone else is doing it."

"On Fire Island. Jake took his kids and I went along. My first time. It's not hard if you have help and once it's up, it's easy." Tears well in my eyes. "Come on," I say, hoping to hide them, "let's walk around and see what we can buy." People in the park are selling paintings, ceramics, wood sculptures and glassware. "Do you want to shop together or meet at a certain time?"

"Let's try to stay together and keep an eye out for each other. It's more fun."

That plan lasts ten minutes. Beth stops at every table and buys T-shirts for friends and knickknacks for herself. I'm too anxious to be attentive. I wander off and buy a glass of ice-cold lemonade from two nine-year-old boys in business to make money for their soccer uniforms. I tell them I'll be back for two more and continue exploring the park. Under a big eucalyptus tree, three children watch over an open, wriggling carton. I walk over and peer down at four cute, calico kittens. I sit down on the grass and with the boys' help I'm soon covered in orange, black, and white furry balls of noses and tails. The kids work on me to take one home, but I decline.

When I get up to leave, I see Beth on a bench surrounded by packages. I say my goodbyes, buy two more lemonades and take them over to her.

"That's it?" Beth takes one of the cups. "This is all you bought? I finally ran out of money."

I smile.

"What were you doing?" She takes a sip.

"Walking around, playing with kittens. I'm tempted, but I can't have pets in the apartment."

"They're way too much responsibility anyway. You have to be home, feed them, care for them."

"There is a payoff," I counter. "You have something to love."

We're quiet.

"Beth, I think I'm pregnant."

She whirls around. Lemonade flies out of her cup, onto her lap and some of the packages. "Oh, my god. That's why you've been so tired. And your stomach flu — that's morning sickness!"

I nod and hand her some napkins. She wipes herself off and sops up the liquid on her gifts.

"What are you going to do? Are you going to have it?"

"One step at a time. I'm not even sure I'm pregnant. But of course I'll have it."

"Oh, wow. A baby." She shakes her head. "So much for not being able to get pregnant."

"I know," I say softly.

"You haven't talked about Jake and I've been so wrapped up in me." She scrunches up the soggy napkins in her hand. I hold out my empty cup and she deposits them in it. I toss the cup in a nearby trashcan.

"Did he use a condom? Did it break?"

I shake my head. I imagine what's coming.

"What? He didn't use anything?" Incredulous, her voice rises. "And you never told him to?"

I shake my head again.

"Did he ask? Did you lie to him?"

"No! He never asked. I was the one who brought up contraception, and he said it was the woman's responsibility. We disagreed." I pause. "We both played Russian Roulette." I don't like being flippant, but I'm defensive.

"I didn't mean to attack you. Will you tell him?" She softens her tone. "How are you going to tell your folks?"

"Whoa!" I hold up my hand. "You're going too fast. I don't even know if I'm pregnant yet."

"When can you find out?"

"I think I can go now. It's around six weeks and I haven't had my period."

"Does anyone else know?" She creases her brow. "Don't handle this by yourself, Maddy."

I smile. "You're the first. I'll tell Ruth and my L.A. friends tonight. They'll be there for me, if I have any friends left. We've been working so hard, I've hardly seen or talked to anyone since you came. And honestly, I'm ready to get back to a normal life."

"Normal?"

"You're right." I laugh and reach into my purse. I pull out a gift-wrapped box tied with a red ribbon and hand it to her. "This is as good a time as any."

"For me? What is it?"

"Something I bought for myself in June. I won't be needing it. You might as well enjoy!"

Beth looks at me suspiciously and unties the bow. She opens the box and pulls out a tube of Ortho Spermicidal Jelly. "You really do have a sick sense of humor."

"At least it proves I was prepared if Jake had asked. I swear I would have used it if he told me he didn't want any part of my dream."

Beth fiddles with the ribbon. I pick at a cuticle on my thumb. "I'd like you to go to Planned Parenthood with me to get the pregnancy test." I let out a deep sigh. "I don't want to go alone."

———

I've been awake for an hour thinking about the test. Today's the day. Am I pregnant or not? And if I am, can I pull this off by myself?

The phone interrupts my obsessing. I answer.

"You up?" my cousin Ruth asks.

"What's sleep?"

Today Ruth is the representative of my L.A. support group. Our families call us *The Gang of Four*. We share everything — marriages, divorces, affairs, kids, and now my possible pregnancy. I glide my hand across my bed smoothing out the blue and green striped sheet.

"When are you going?"

"Beth's picking me up at nine-thirty. The clinic opens at ten. Hopefully we'll be the first ones there."

"How are you doing?"

"Great," I lie.

"You'll feel a lot better knowing for sure."

"How come everyone knows what I'm going to feel?"

"You're right. We just think." She pauses. "Knowing is better than this limbo you're in."

"Maybe."

I'm stunned by what I've done, even though I did it on purpose.

"I'm scared, Ruth. I don't know if I'm prepared for this. This is another life I'll be responsible for."

"Once you've had the test you'll have something to work with. You'll have time to make a decision."

"A decision?" I bolt upright. "You mean an abortion? No, I want this baby."

"I'm only reminding you it's an option."

"If I'm pregnant, I don't want an option." I take a sip of water from the glass on my night table. "I'm just scared. I'm making myself crazy worrying about everything."

"I called to calm you, not upset you. Take a shower, get dressed, eat something."

The mention of food makes my insides churn. I swing my feet over the side of the bed ready to run to the bathroom.

"I'll call when I get home."

"Call before, if you need to."

"Thanks." I hang up.

I swallow, praying the nausea will pass. Before standing up I wait a few seconds and then walk into the bathroom. I step into the shower thinking about Jake. Every night I pour my heart out in a journal. I write about him and the *maybe baby*, and about the part of me that wants a relationship and the part that wants a baby. I explore my body with my hands, looking and feeling for any changes. I dry myself and check my breasts in the mirror. Are they bigger? I look closer and see a vein I've never noticed before. A sign. I wrap myself in a towel. How am I going to feel in a few hours, one way or the other? I check the time. I better get going. Beth will be prompt.

In the car on the way to the clinic, Beth chatters, but I'm not very talkative.

We're first on the list for the walk-in appointments. The receptionist hands me a clipboard with a form to fill out and a plastic specimen container with my name on it. She points to the bathroom and tells me to get a urine sample. I follow her directions and place the cup in a cubbyhole.

I return to the now full waiting room. I sit next to Beth and force a smile. One solemn, young couple sit arm in arm across from us. No wedding bands. What's their story? I try to read a magazine, but I can't concentrate. I hear my name called. A slightly overweight, gray haired lady ushers us into an exam room.

"You're Maddy Gold?" She looks at me. "My name is Harriet."

"Yes, and this is my friend, Beth."

They nod at each other.

"Please have a seat on the exam table."

I sit next to the specimen that has been placed on a metal tray. Beth and I both check the label to make sure it's mine. Beth backs away, but stands by my side. Harriet launches into a clinical, step-by-step commentary. First she holds up a small square of black cardboard with a white outlined circle in the center.

"Now, I take a drop of urine," she explains, "and put it in the circle. Then I add various chemicals. See? It turns milky white." She shows it to me. "Now I set the timer and swish around the liquid. If it's still milky when the timer goes off," she flashes a Mary Poppins' smile, "you're pregnant."

I stare at her grin, then at her hand holding the cardboard. All I can hear is the sound of the timer clicking. I don't breathe.

The bell dings. The liquid is still milky. I gasp.

"Are you happy?" Harriet asks.

"I don't know," I mumble.

Fear kicks in. This is really happening. Why do I feel confused? I want this baby.

I place my hands under my thighs to stop them from shaking. Beth puts her arm around me.

"Do you have any pamphlets on pregnancy?" Beth asks.

"No, sorry. Only birth control." Harriet chuckles. "And you're too late for that."

We don't respond.

"I'm sorry, if this isn't what you want."

"It's okay," I say. "I just have to get used to the idea." I wiggle off the table. "Let's go."

Beth takes me by the arm and guides me outside. I don't resist. I'm not sure I can make it on my own. My rubbery legs nearly buckle at the knees. I'm pregnant. I did it. Wow! I'm scared. Terrified. Vulnerable. Alone. I wanted to get pregnant. Yes? I can't speak.

Beth drives me home in silence giving me the space I need. She pulls up in front of the apartment and offers to come in, but I want to be by myself.

As promised I call my cousin, but we don't talk long. I take some milk from the fridge and go out to the patio. I look at the empty tennis court. Tears pour down my cheeks, blurring the flowers and the palm trees in front of me. The phone rings as I reach for a tissue. I walk inside, hesitant to answer. I stand up straight. Whatever my feelings are, I'm determined to present a positive view to the world. I blow my nose and pick up the receiver.

"Hey, Maddy. It's me."

"Jake!"

"Yeah, hon. I've been so fucking busy. I didn't want you to forget me."

"Trust me, I could never do that."

Such irony. I picture him in his office, buried under papers, barely looking out the window at the New York skyline.

"How are you? Did you get the photos? You look great with the wind blowing through your hair and the Hudson River in the background. I kept a set for myself. They remind me what life should be. But it's the same old rat race."

"You love it, Jake."

"Sometimes. Most of the time, but that doesn't change the fact I hate it too."

"But you don't do anything to change it."

He doesn't respond. I hear papers being shuffled.

"What about you?" he asks. "Still writing?"

"Yes. Beth moved on to other projects, so it's up to me to finish ours."

"What's the heroine's name? Jennifer Dalton?"

"You remember." I'm surprised. "Now she's in really deep shit. I have to figure a way to get her out of it. It's a feminist script so she's got to do it herself — no knight in shining armor to rescue her."

"You'll work it out. I have faith."

I hear a woman in the background. His secretary? Oh, Jake, are you even at the office? I can't bring myself to ask.

"Gotta run," he says. "Just wanted to hear your voice and let you know I haven't forgotten you. Take care."

I place the receiver in its cradle and slowly walk out to the patio. I sit in my chair and take a sip of milk. What are the odds of a thirty-three-year-old woman getting pregnant the first time she tries? I shake my head. Timing. Everything is timing. And why did he call, just now, this day? He doesn't even know yet. And I'm not sure I'm going to tell him.

For some crazy reason I feel different. I stroke my belly. You just rest in there, and grow strong and healthy. I promise I'll take care of everything else. I love you.

5

NEW YORK CITY

October 1979

*T*wo **months later,** I pace around my apartment, all packed. The down jacket I borrowed for New York's unpredictable fall weather lays across my suitcase. My sixty-seven-year-old father is having emergency bypass surgery. There is nothing I can do from Los Angeles except wait for my mother's call. I imagine myself in the operating room next to the doctor, encouraging him to do a good job.

The phone rings. The operation has been a success and my mother and I cry from relief. Crying isn't unusual for me, anymore. For the past three and a half months, I've cried everyday for good things and bad, for happy and scared. I don't discriminate. My doctor tells me it's hormonal, but I'm terrified. Family and friends, on both coasts, are supportive, yet I'm still alone in this. How am I going to raise a child by myself? Am I as strong as I think? Will my baby grow up and understand?

At ten o'clock, Ruth picks me up and takes me to the airport for the red-eye to New York.

I exit JFK and hail a cab. Four months ago, single and unattached, I made this same trip. And now, with my flat belly belying the truth of my pregnancy, I am still single, but definitely attached.

The taxi weaves in and out of traffic. I look at the small, brick, single-family houses lining the streets of the middle class Queens neighborhood. The maple trees in the yards have a mixture of summer and fall foliage. Piles of brown, yellow and orange leaves, raked over the weekend, lie on lawns waiting to be picked up and thrown away.

The cab stops at a red light. I watch a woman push an elderly man in a wheelchair. She struggles to get the wheels off the curb and into the street. The man is hunched over and buried under a worn Tartan blanket. He doesn't look stable. I stare at him. He reminds me of Anna's husband, Anthony, at the Bar Mitzvah — old, crippled, dependent. I picture him trapped by my father's rage and jabbing finger. I still don't understand the strange incident and my parents' unwillingness to answer my questions. With everything that has happened these past few months, I haven't given it a thought, but if my father is well enough, I will ask. I don't want secrets. That isn't a good way to start a new life.

But I have a secret, too. And until yesterday I wasn't sure what I would do. Then I find a message from Jake on my answering machine.

"Maddy. You're never home. Aren't you writing? I've been running around like a mad man. How're you doing?" Click.

I listen to the message twice. I'm not sure if I hear something in his voice or if I have an epiphany. But whatever it is, Jake doesn't need to be protected. I'm going to tell him.

I look out the window of the taxi. Through the early morning haze, I see the faint outline of the Manhattan skyline. I pray for the strength and sensitivity to survive the next few days.

———

My mother meets me at the elevator. As we hug, her muscles relax and she collapses against my chest. We back away to arms length. Her stiff upper lip and stoic approach to life has disappeared. Her green eyes that usually twinkle look sad and tired. I'm glad to be here for her.

By the time we're ready to leave for the hospital, I've showered, brushed my teeth and called Jake and Beth. I plan to see Jake tonight and ask Beth to be flexible. Linda is on my list, but that can wait until after I tell Jake.

We hail a cab on Third Avenue and ride in silence. I think about my parents and their forty-year marriage, living in their two-bed-room Eastside co-op. My father, a judge, and my mother, a part-time secretary at a furniture store on Fifth Avenue, are such opposites. My mother is short and round, while my father is tall and lean. She is friendly and outgoing, while he is guarded and reserved. They both love telling funny stories but have their own styles. My mother's whole body gets into the act. Her sunny, freckled face laughs from the beginning, straight through to the end. I'm never sure if people are laughing at the joke or at her pleasure in telling it. My father is more of a raconteur and loves the limelight. He is in complete control when he tells a tale and knows it's good.

I look across the seat of the cab at my mom. She is bundled up in a black wool coat even though it isn't that cold. I reach out and take her hand. She turns toward me. "I know you spoke to Jake and I know I'm not supposed to ask questions, but have you told him?" Her voice is strained.

In the letter I'd written to my parents to tell them I'm pregnant, I told them not to ask about the baby's father. I stare at her and then smile.

"We're not stupid, Maddy. You told us about Jake in July and we can count."

"I don't want you to be angry at him. This was my doing."

"Does he know?"

"No. I'm seeing him tonight. I'll tell him then." I see the concern in her eyes. "Don't get your hopes up, Mom. It's not going to be what you want."

"What do you want?"

"I want to stay friends, at least."

"Don't you want him to marry you?"

"He's not going to. That's not what this is about. I know it would be easier for you. But it's not going to happen."

"I'm worried. It's going to be hard for you and the baby. You can't imagine."

"The baby and I are going to be just fine. I promise."

The cab stops in front of the hospital. I get out and pay the driver. I feel cold inside and out and pull my jacket around me. The baby and I are going to be just fine. Stoicism runs in the family. I take my mom's hand and help her out of the cab. I place a kiss on her freckled cheek. I know she doesn't believe me any more than I believe myself.

My mother leads the way to the nurses' station in the Intensive Care Unit. She takes small, hurried steps. I follow behind like a duckling. I hate hospitals, mostly their smells. I remind myself to breathe. Standing quietly by her side, my mother checks with the nurse about my father. The report is good, but I need to see him with my own eyes.

I follow my mother through the electronic doors into the ICU. Patients are in cubicles that open to a main area. I stare straight ahead not wanting to appear a voyeur, but like the pull of the sun to the planets, I peek at each patient and at each piece of machinery that beeps and whirrs.

"Oh, my God," my mother cries out.

I hurry into the room. My father lies small and shrunken in his bed. His face is grayish-yellow with gray and black stubble growing on his cheeks and chin. An oxygen mask covers his nose and mouth. Clear liquid drips into his arm intravenously, yellow liquid drips out of him into a bag hanging from the bed. I look from my father to his monitor. Everything is lit up, but the beeps are rhythmic and the squiggly peaks and valleys give no indication of a flat line emergency. I relax and put my arm around my mom's slumped shoulders. I can feel her bones through her silk blouse and share her anguish. "He's not dying, Mom. He just looks awful."

The tears in her eyes make mine well up too. We watch him. My mother and I each take one of his hands and she strokes his forehead. He twitches and whimpers in his sleep. To see him so weak and vulnerable heightens my own fears. I want to be a little girl, protected and sheltered, not all grown up facing his pain and suffering. I walk back around the bed. "Come on. He's sleeping. We'll come back in a little while." She kisses his forehead. I pat his hand.

"Rest, Daddy. You'll have a grandchild to meet soon."

———

Our evening get together is typical Jake. First we take a couple from Jake's office uptown — "They're going in our direction." Then we go to an apartment theater where inept actors perform uninspired plays in someone's home. Now we are chauffeuring Peter, a friend, who is "going in our direction."

I pull my jacket closed and wrap my mother's blue cashmere scarf around the collar. Jake speeds and weaves down Park Avenue as he had in July, but this time Peter is folded up in the back seat, and I'm fuming in the front. What's going on, Jake? If you were so fucking busy, why did you make a date with me?

On West 45th Street and Broadway, in the middle of the Great White Way, Jake slams on the brakes and the car screeches to a halt so Peter can get out. Shaken, I jump out of the car and pull the seat forward. Peter slowly, and with great effort, unfolds his tall, rail-thin body from the tiny back seat. Once on the sidewalk, he shakes himself out, one limb at a time, and grunts.

"Ready to go," he says. "Thanks." He salutes us and leaves.

I hurry back into the car and slide the seat as far back as I can. I'm pissed. My body is rigid. I fold my arms across the bulky jacket and stare out the window at the throngs of strangers on the street. I'm no longer used to the hustle and bustle here, so different from L.A. The sex clubs, the bars, and the sleazy people walking the streets depress me. Yet the bright lights of Broadway are still tantalizing. The marquees sparkle and I yearn to be a tourist on my way to see, *Cabaret* or *Annie* or *Sweeney Todd*.

"Sorry, Madd," Jake says. "I didn't expect it to be so hectic. We'll go down to my place and then out to dinner." He pulls away from the curb. "Are you hungry?"

"Starved." I work hard not to sound peeved. We have a big conversation ahead of us and I don't want to start an argument. "I haven't eaten since noon."

He checks his watch. "My God, it's nine o'clock. Didn't realize it was so late. By the way, how's your father? Were you at the hospital all day?"

I hoped he'd ask hours ago.

"They say he's okay, but you'd never know by looking at him. The nurse assured us he'd be better tomorrow, once the anesthetic wears off."

Jake reaches over and touches my leg. "Sorry you had to come in for that reason, but I'm glad you're here." He sounds weary. I glance at the lines across his brow and around his smile.

"We're going to the loft? It's finished already?"

"No, but I'm living there anyway, with Kevin. I need to check on him. It's a mess, Madd. Really awful, I'm warning you. There are rats and roaches and all kinds of undesirable things."

I shudder and question his sanity — and mine. He makes a right turn on Canal Street and parks. I follow him into a building that looks like a bombed-out tenement in London during the blitz. We start up the stairs.

"I own a quarter of this old warehouse. When my section is done, it'll be four bedrooms with two decks, and a large open kitchen plus dining area. Right now, Kevin and I live in a small part of it. I sleep in the main area and Kevin sleeps behind it. The bathroom is a toilet and a sink. We shower at the club." He sounds almost proud. "Oh, there's no heat either."

He opens the door and I walk inside. I'm horrified. His description didn't do it justice. My eyes are as big and round as an owl's. I stand in the middle of a room covered with a thick layer of dust from all the construction. A piece of plastic covers Jake's bed, I assume to protect it from all the debris. Jake's and Kevin's books and papers are strewn all over and huge pieces of plaster, torn from the ceilings and the walls, lie on the floor. I shiver. A cold wind blows through the rafters. I need long underwear and a full-length coat.

"I know it looks bad, but it will be great."

"Hard to believe," I say.

He reaches over and kisses me on the cheek.

"You just need an imagination!"

"I don't understand, Jake. Why are you and Kevin living like this? Why didn't you sublet a place for a few months?"

He looks surprised. Had no one asked him before?

"Cash flow problems. Between this place, the house on Fire Island, school for the kids . . ." He shrugs. "I borrowed funds from my mother rather than the business, but it isn't enough. Anyway, it's just temporary." He scans the room and takes some books and a blue sweater off a chair. "Sit down," he offers. "I need to use the john. We'll go after that. I'll leave Kevin some money so he can get dinner."

I watch him walk around his bed and disappear behind a beige curtain I hadn't noticed. That's the bathroom? I cover myself with the sweater and am about to sit down when I realize I'm not alone. Kevin is standing quietly by the entranceway, partially hidden in the shadows.

"Hello," I say, and walk over to hug him. I stop midway. I haven't seen Kevin since he was a little boy, and there is no resemblance to that carefree child. Dressed in old, torn army fatigues, is an awkward young waif. Dirty stringy hair frames his face. His beautiful dark brown eyes are vacant. He hunches up his shoulders and shoves his hands deep into his pockets. I feel his disappointment and anger. Kevin hadn't expected company.

"It feels like forever, Kevin." I smile and hold out my arm about waist high. "You were a little guy then."

He raises his head to look at me.

"Remember Disneyland?" I wag my finger at him. "I'll forever hold you responsible for getting me on my first rollercoaster since the Cyclone at Coney Island. I screamed my head off. But I dragged you back three times."

He gives me a thumbs up.

"You're late, Kevin." Jake's tone is harsh.

Kevin's smile disappears. I turn around. Jake stands by his bed.

"There's nothing to eat here," Jake says. "I'll give you some cash. Maddy and I are going out to dinner. You'll have to buy something."

I step back. Kevin shuffles around waiting for Jake to give him money.

"Be home by ten-thirty. I don't want you out late."

"But tomorrow's a holiday. There's no school."

"I don't care. I don't like you wandering around with nothing to do."

I look from one to the other and feel so sad. He's a kid being pushed around and pushed away simultaneously. Kevin slips the ten-dollar bill in his pocket.

"Why don't you come with us?" I blurt out.

Father and son look at me as if they suddenly remember I'm there.

"No thanks. He doesn't want me around." Kevin turns and walks out.

My heart breaks. I clutch my belly. That won't be you, sweetie. No way. I don't know what Jake sees on my face, but he frowns and shakes his head.

"There's nothing I can do. He's a city kid. He looks older than his age and that gets him into situations beyond his years." His defenses are in full gear. "He's sharp, though. He can handle himself. I know he's into drugs. Sometimes we smoke dope together. I just hope it's nothing heavier."

I hate what he is saying. I can't look at him.

"I worry about him," Jake adds. "But what can I do?"

I want to yell at him, but instead I stay silent, keeping everything inside.

"Let's go," I say, "I'm hungry."

Lower Manhattan at night, especially around Canal Street, is not a tourist attraction. Jake and I hopscotch around shattered glass from broken streetlights and windows, and debris from overturned trash cans. Cars are stripped so you can't even identify the model.

It's ten o'clock New York time and I've been awake for twenty-four hours. My stomach growls, my shoulders feel like cement weights and whatever emotional and physical strength I came into the city with has been spent at the hospital and the loft.

We round a corner and Jake quickens his gait. "Can you hear it?" I raise my head and listen to the wail of a saxophone and the soft throb of a bass. "I hang out here every chance I get. Sometimes, after midnight, they'll let me jam with them. It's my escape."

He puts his hand on my back and guides me down four steps and through a door with a treble clef handle. The room is big enough for a five-stool bar, a raised stage with a four-piece jazz combo — a piano, sax, bass and drums — and ten tables around a small dance floor. Sweet sounds of melody and harmony waft through smoky air.

I stop at the door to take it all in. This is all about Jake. I want to eat and talk but nothing about this place is conducive to any of my needs. All the tables are taken. Jake leads me toward the one empty stool at the bar. A man behind the counter approaches us. "Good evening, Maestro Jake. You're early tonight."

Jake shakes hands with the man.

"Maddy, this is Cosmo, the owner of this jewel."

Jake puts his arm around my shoulder. "Maddy's originally from New York, but she's never been here before." He pauses making sure the compliment registers. "She's hungry. Please bring us some shrimp while we wait for a table. Also a double Chivas on the rocks and a Chardonnay."

"No, thanks," I say. "Just some hot tea, please."

Cosmo nods and disappears.

"No wine? Are you okay?"

"I'm fine."

"What do you think of this place? Isn't it great?" His eyes open wide, sparkling in the dim lighting.

I smile, hiding my disappointment. "I was hoping we'd have a chance to talk."

He squints at his watch. "They'll take a break soon and some people will go home. We'll have plenty of time to talk and dance when they play their next set." He nuzzles my ear and gently nips my neck. "We can pick up where we left off last summer."

Cosmo brings our drinks over and ushers us to a newly vacated table. He tells us the specials, Prime Rib and fresh Lake Superior white-fish. We decide on the whitefish. I dive into the breadbasket and the shrimp cocktail as soon as they appear.

"So," Jake says, holding up his scotch glass, "we can finally relax. I'm glad you're here." He clinks his glass against my teacup. "How come you're not drinking? On the wagon?"

"I'm pregnant."

He sets his glass down, his head cocked to one side.

"Mine?"

I nod. We study each other.

"Well." He looks bemused. "That's interesting. You're the second woman who's told me that. Both from last summer."

"What?" My head fills with questions, sarcastic ones.

"She miscarried. But you didn't. And you want it."

My head feels detached from my body.

"It's okay, Maddy." He takes my hand.

"I'm glad I'm pregnant, Jake." The words come out between gasps. I remind myself to breathe.

The food arrives with a clanging of dishes. I look at broiled fish, mixed vegetables and rice pilaf. The sight and smells make me want to throw up. I push my plate aside and gulp down the stinging bile in the back of my throat. Jake looks up from buttering his bread.

"Come on, Madd. You have to eat. You need to stay strong for both of you."

I work hard to get a handle on what he just said. "What's going on with you, Jake? You're so calm."

He looks away. The musicians put their instruments on stands to take a break. They light cigarettes and laugh amongst themselves. They tidy up and walk off the stage. The bass player crosses in front of us and disappears. Jake stabs at a piece of fish and chews his food slowly. He picks his words carefully.

"I'm not sure how I feel." He grabs his glass and downs his drink. His face breaks into a big grin. "Actually, I'm flattered. You chose me and I came through. But I've done it twice before, Maddy, and I can't take on any more responsibilities."

"I'm not asking you for anything, Jake. I want no more than you're willing to take on. If that's nothing, I understand. I expect to do this alone."

"Do your parents know?"

"Yes."

"Do they know it's mine?"

"I didn't tell them, but they figured it out."

"Oh, great. They probably think I'm a heel."

His choice of the word heel doesn't escape me, but I need to put the other woman out of my mind and take care of myself.

"They know it was my idea. Anyway, what they think isn't the issue."

There is a long pause.

"Aren't you going to eat anything, Maddy? You said you were hungry."

"I lost my appetite."

He takes my hand. His brow is furrowed and he looks concerned.

"I'm guessing this isn't easy for you."

"Yes and no." I hold on to his hand wanting to convey what I feel through my touch and words. "Jake, I want this baby more than I want anything. I haven't had a single regret. Lots of fears, but no regrets." I squeeze his hand. "My concern is you. I was selfish. I wanted a baby and now its reality impacts you, too." Tears rim my eyes. "I didn't mean to hurt you."

Jake orders another Chivas on the rocks when the waiter passes by. He finishes his dinner and some of mine while the musicians walk back on stage and set up. They start to play as he soaks up the remaining sauce with the last piece of bread.

"Let's dance."

He pulls me to my feet and gathers me in his arms. I will myself to relax. It's been a long time. The music and dancing rekindle the memories of our summer weekend. Jake holds me close with his right hand pressing into the small of my back. Our hips slowly rotate in unison — Jake's against me, then away, then against me again. I slip my hand down his leg. The crowded dance floor and the dim lights hide my actions. My boldness surprises me. It's like being born again with no past. A small gasp escapes from deep in my throat. I look into his eyes and he bends down to kiss me.

"We better get out of here," he whispers. "I'm about to come in my Jockeys and I'd much rather come inside you."

We leave the club holding hands, and walk the three short blocks back through the quiet, empty streets of lower Manhattan. Our safety doesn't seem to concern Jake, so I ignore it too. I don't want anything to ruin this moment. I even push away the thought, lurking in my mind, that Jake's calm reaction to my pregnancy might be temporary. I will deal with it, if and when I have to. Right now I ache for his touch and I don't care about anything else. I am overwhelmed by my sexuality and desire — something I'm not used to feeling. Twice he stops to kiss me, continuing the passion we stirred up on the dance floor.

We arrive at his building. Jake leads me upstairs. In spite of my desire, I recoil. Facing the hellhole we're about to enter and realizing Kevin will be there, makes me halt on the top step.

"What about Kevin?" I ask.

"Knowing him, he's fast asleep. A foghorn in his ear wouldn't wake him. He's been like that since he was born." Jake puts his arms around me allowing the full length of his body to meet mine. "Come on, it's been a long time. I want to do all sorts of wild and lovely things to you."

We enter the freezing cold room. Sheets of flapping plastic can't block the wind that penetrates the open sections of the wall. And the dim light of a small desk lamp can't hide where we are. Jake opens, then closes a door to the left of his bed.

"Kevin's sound asleep, just as I said." He smiles. "Do you need the bathroom?"

I shake my head.

"Why don't you get under the covers?" He rolls up the piece of plastic protecting his bed. "You look frozen. I'll light some candles and then work on heating you up."

I take off my shoes and coat. Fully dressed, I burrow under the down quilt. Jake walks around the room lighting candles strategically placed for making love.

"Be right back." He bends down and kisses my lips.

The candlelight flickers across the ceiling. The depressing mood of the room, the cold and emptiness fill my body. During dinner he told me he was going to Fire Island for the weekend. I wanted to ask, "With whom?" But I didn't want to know. Now I am curious. The ghosts of all his women jump on the bed, dance through the holes in the wall, and laugh at my naiveté.

The toilet flushes. Jake appears in the shadows. He is unabashedly naked. I've spent months dreaming and remembering what he looks like, feels like, smells like. I spent months wanting him inside me again. My mind and my body are at odds. He glides across the room. His strong muscular legs, his well-defined, hairy chest, blow my confusion to the wind. I will deal with reality later. I want him.

I unfurl my body as he crawls into bed beside me. I'm not the only one who is cold. Our teeth chatter in unison and we laugh. He begins unbuttoning and unzipping.

"It'll take forever to get through all these layers."

"It'll be worth it." I smile coyly and relax as he removes each piece of clothing. The candlelight dances and I feel his touch.

After making love and quieting the beat of my heart, I fall asleep in Jake's arms.

Contentment doesn't last long. I wake in the darkness with tears rolling down my face. The cold loft chills me inside and out. In my head, Frank Sinatra sings his haunting refrain, "In the wee small hours of the morning," from his *Only the Lonely* album. As an unhappy teen I listened to those sad words and melody, over and over.

I replay my night with Jake and don't like my behavior. I harangue myself about being passive from the Avant Garde theater disaster, to Jake's dismissive attitude toward Kevin, and then to his cavalier reaction to getting two women pregnant in one month. Why didn't I speak up? Am I so desperate for love that I've become a cipher?

A tear runs down my nose. Ever since I was a little girl, it was only after something was said or done that I knew what my response should have been, that I should have stood up for myself, but by then the moment had passed. Once a college friend called me enigmatic because I was so private and kept things deep inside. And she was right. Trusting people with the real me is too hard.

Jake is enigmatic too, but in a different way. He is a complex man. I am in love with the smart, funny, quirky man who has a joyful, carefree approach. But he also has a dark, angry side born out of frustration for living a life he didn't choose. Instead of being a jazz musician and composer, he took over his father's advertising agency. I've seen his wrath a few times at his office, and directed at Linda when they dated. And last night with Kevin.

The sun finally peeps through the cracked, broken windows and I wonder what the day will bring. A shiver tells me Jake's sanguine response to my pregnancy is going to be left on the dance floor. I roll over to see the clock.

"What time is it?" Jake whispers, caressing my breast. "Kevin's asleep."

I ignore the implication. "Seven. When are you leaving for Fire Island?"

"Around nine. You?"

"I told my mother I'd meet her at the hospital."

"I can drop you at the bus on First Avenue. You'll be there in no time." He pulls me closer. "Did you sleep?"

"No."

He kisses my neck. "Are you too tired?"

I feel him hard against my leg.

"We have to talk, Jake. We don't have much time."

"I know. I want to clarify things too. There's a restaurant on the way to the bus. We'll stop there for breakfast." His lips brush my shoulder. He slides his leg between mine. "You're wet."

So much feels wrong, yet my body keeps betraying me. He gets on top and slips inside me. I start moving with him, wanting him, not wanting him. I hear a noise. I stop.

"Shhh," Jake whispers. He keeps moving, but slows the pace. "It's Kevin. He's going to the john. He won't pay any attention to us."

"No. Stop!" I push against his shoulders. "You can't ignore Kevin anymore. And you'll never hurt our baby that way!"

Everything is dead quiet. There are no sounds inside or outside the room.

Jake lifts himself off of me and shoots up to a sitting position. I look around. Kevin isn't in the bathroom. He is dressed and standing by the bed, his mouth agape.

"Why did you say that?" Jake yells.

I look from Jake to Kevin.

"You're having another baby?" Kevin speaks through clenched teeth. "You fucker. I'm outta here."

He grabs his army jacket from a chair and storms out the door. His footsteps echo down the stairs. Jake whirls around, glares at me and springs out of bed. He rams one leg, then the other, into the pants he wore last night. He throws on a T-shirt and stomps across the floor. I pull the quilt up under my chin.

"What the hell did you do, Maddy? Telling him about the baby."

"I'm sorry." I cover my mouth. "I couldn't make love knowing he was awake." I close my eyes.

"That wasn't making love. We were fucking."

I swallow. "Where will he go?"

"He's staying with friends for the weekend." His eyes drill into me.

"I hope they're kind and loving," I whisper.

"And what's that supposed to mean?" he yells. "You don't think I love him? You don't think I pay enough attention to him? I sure as hell do." He backs away from me. "Why do you think I work so fucking hard if it's not for my kids? You think it's so easy?"

I look up but don't respond.

"He's sucking the life out of me." His face is red. "And now you tell me I could be having another one? I don't want another kid. They're always needy, demanding, complaining. Then they turn around and hate you for whatever you do."

He walks over to the bed, puts one sock on his right foot, balancing like a flamingo.

"It's not things he wants, Jake. It's you."

"I don't have anymore to give." He pulls his other sock on. "And I certainly have nothing for your baby." His jaw pulsates, his icy blue eyes small, piercing, scary. "You keep this to yourself for over three months. And it's perfect timing to tell me now. Isn't it?"

I know where this is going. I wait. He sits on the dusty floor and puts on his shoes.

"You want this baby. I don't. And it's probably too late for you to have an abortion. Right? But I want you to. I'll pay for it."

I just stare at him. The words I want to say ricochet through my mind, but I can't spew them out of my mouth. I've got to get out of here. I jump up, wrap the quilt around my back and riffle around the bed and floor for my clothes. I gather my things and go into the bathroom, dragging the quilt behind me. I look in the mirror. A dazed face looks back. My eyeliner and mascara smeared.

I come out of the bathroom dressed and ready to go. Jake sits at the desk, staring outside, through a hole, at a cement wall.

"I'm leaving," I say. "I didn't mean — I didn't want this to play out this way."

He twirls around in the chair. "The pregnancy or telling me? Because you did plan it." He is seething. "You wanted a baby and you used me."

"I did want — I do want a baby. But you knew that. You never asked me if I was on the pill or had a diaphragm. For god's sake, I'm the second woman you got pregnant last summer. Doesn't that suggest something to you?"

"You used me plain and simple."

"No." I have my hand under my coat, shielding my baby.

"So, now you think I'm going to marry you?"

"What? I told you last night I don't want anything from you." I hold up my hand like a cop at a crosswalk. "Stop! We better do this at another time." I grab my purse and start to walk away. "I'll be here for another week or two. We'll talk later." I exit the door Kevin left wide open.

"Does Linda know?" He calls after me.

"No. I wanted to tell you first." I don't turn around.

––––

Three days later, a waiter calls my name at the Kung Foo Palace restaurant in Manhattan. I pick up my take-out order and pay the bill. My parents and I are dining in my dad's hospital room. I button my jacket and quickly walk the two short city blocks back to the hospital. It's a cool night and the warmth of the hot food coming through the bag feels good against my body. I salivate from the smell of shrimp in lobster sauce and moo shu pork.

Everyday, my father improves. Each time I walk him down the long corridor, beyond the nurses' station, his gait gets faster and more sure-footed. My mother also looks better. Less tired, less tense. We laugh together playing our daily gin rummy games. I usually lose because she keeps track of every card and I don't.

My parents never mention Jake. I am relieved. What could I tell them? I left Jake two messages, but he hasn't called back. I'm determined to talk to him before I go home. After dinner, I walk around the hospital room picking up empty cartons of Chinese food and putting everything into a big plastic bag. I pass my father sitting in an arm chair. He reaches out for me.

"I know it isn't easy for you to travel," he says, holding my arm. "Mother and I really appreciate your being here. She would have a harder time without you."

"It's important for me, too. We're family." I twist the bag, tie a knot, and squeeze it into the trashcan. "This will be the only time you get to see me pregnant." I turn sideways and stick out my belly. "There's not much to see, but my clothes are getting tight."

"No more morning sickness?" my father asks.

"It went away as soon as I started my third month."

I help my mother get my father into bed.

"Your mother was sick everyday for nine months." He looks over and smiles at her. "If our grandchild is anything like you, we'll be very happy and thankful."

Tears fill my eyes. It's unusual for my father to be sentimental.

"What kind of grandchild do you want?" I ask. "They can tell now, although I don't need to have the test. I wouldn't want to know, anyway. Would you?"

My parents exchange glances.

"A healthy girl or boy will be perfect," my mother says.

"I want to be surprised," I declare, "but I guess I could be surprised now or later. Anyway the doctor said I don't need amniocentesis."

My father lowers his bed so he is lying almost flat.

"Have you thought about names?" my mother asks. She straightens the covers and rearranges my father's pillows.

"Not really. I like Robert. Maybe Robert as a middle name if it's a boy."

My mother suddenly signals me with a finger to her lips. My father is fast asleep. We chuckle and grab our coats. We tiptoe out of the room.

6

—

NEW YORK CITY
October 1979

Linda and I decide to get together for dinner at her place on the Westside. It's a direct shot across the park from my parents' apartment to her old rent-controlled building. Her two-bedroom, with a den and eat-in kitchen is a New Yorker's dream. We spend the first hour dining and catching up on the events of the past few months. We talk about the Fifth Avenue penthouse she's decorating and the teleplay Beth and I are writing. We talk about everything except my pregnancy. No time feels right, but after dinner seems best. I dry the last plate and put it away.

"Let's go into the living room, Lin. We need to talk."

We sit on her couch covered in a peach velvet floral print. I grab a lime green throw pillow and hug it for support.

"This is hard, but there's no easy way." I inhale. "I'm pregnant. And it's Jake's." My breath escapes like a gust of wind into the chasm of the room. I try to read her reaction as I focus on her alabaster skin, as smooth as a mannequin's.

"I suppose that's difficult, " she says, her voice strained. "Are you having it?"

"Yes."

"When?"

"Middle of April."

"Does Jake know?"

I nod.

"What was his reaction?"

"Anger. Rage, actually."

"Did he know you were trying to have a baby?"

"We'd discussed it. He said I'd make a good parent." I ignore the implication that I'm 100% percent responsible. "Jake knew. He never asked if I was using any form of birth control."

Linda gets up and heads to the kitchen. "I need some wine. Do you want anything?" Her steps reverberate on the hardwood floor.

"No." I stretch my back and try to find a comfortable position on the couch. I put a magazine on the coffee table to rest my feet on. Linda returns and this time sits in a chair across the table. She puts down her glass of wine and lights a cigarette.

"I thought you quit."

"I did. I just keep them around for such occasions." She exhales and blows smoke into the air. "You know, I think you're crazy. You have no idea what this project entails. I did it alone and it's damn hard work."

"I've made up my mind Lin. That isn't the issue between us."

"That's direct. What should I say? You set out to deceive him. You got what you want. He got used."

I put my feet on the floor. "No. He's not poor Jake, the victim. He didn't protect himself. Jake rarely thinks of any consequences and you know that."

"You should have asked him," she says firmly.

I stand up. "I'm getting some water."

"Does he know you're telling me?" she calls out.

"Yes."

I go back and sit on the couch. "We finally talked on the phone. We're meeting tomorrow." I take a sip of my water and look at her. "I know what I did. It was selfish. But I didn't dupe Jake, or take advantage of him." Cool, condensed water from my glass drips on my slacks. I place it on a coaster. "This wasn't premeditated. I didn't come to New York last summer planning to hook Jake, or anyone else, into fathering my child."

I stand and walk over to the credenza, turn and face her. "Things conflated. I was thinking a lot about wanting a baby. Most of the men I dated were divorced fathers and adamant about not having more kids. Then a few weeks before I came here, my IUD literally and painfully began to fall out and had to be removed. The doctor told me to wait to have another one put in." I toy with the orange poppies in a vase. "Without getting too woo-woo, I thought it might be a sign."

Linda watches me as I wander around the living room. "Bumping into Jake was unexpected. Having feelings for him was not." I sit on the couch next to her chair. "Everything from there is a jumble. My insecurities, wanting a relationship, Jake being so casual, almost supportive, about my getting pregnant and being a single parent — all these things got mixed-up." I clear my throat. "I could blame it on passion, but I knew I was gambling." I take another sip of water. "I know all this isn't easy for you. I can imagine how I'd feel in your place."

She runs her fingers through her hair. "It's not my place to be hurt or angry. I'm not sure what I'm feeling. Jake isn't my possession, just an ex-lover."

The phone rings and she picks it up. Tired of excusing and defending myself, I think about making an exit. She hangs up.

"It's late, I need to go home." I head to the hall closet and get my coat. At the door, we stand face to face and I don't know what to say. She reaches out and gives me a hug.

"We've been friends for a long time Maddy, you're special and I wish you luck."

I hold her tight, clinging to the warmth of her embrace.

———

I wait for Jake at the Central Park tennis courts between West 94th and West 96th Streets. Jake, Linda, another friend, and I had spent many early, bleary-eyed Saturday mornings playing mixed doubles here. When I spoke with him earlier, he'd been superficial. "How are you? How's your father?" Then he asked about date, time, and place. I'm not sure what this meeting will accomplish. At least, I want to be friends.

I sit on a bench and watch a match between two men in warm-up suits trying to kill the ball and each other. I feel a peck on top of my head and look up. Jake peers down at me looking lost and vacant. It's the first time I've seen him with a scruffy beard and his pores reek from too many Chivas Regals. I feel responsible. He sits next to me.

"My men's group met last night. I told them you're pregnant. It opened a whole range of things we'd never discussed. We've been meeting for five years and this was our best session."

"What did they say?" I brace myself.

"They raked you over the coals."

"That was sweet of them." I watch the guy on the far side of the court lob the ball deep over the head of his opponent at the net. "Didn't they think you had any part in it?"

"No. We agreed it's the woman's responsibility to protect herself."

It doesn't surprise me that Jake would receive validation from his male friends, but I didn't realize I'd be this furious. An intense pain burns through my body.

"Did you tell them about the other woman, Jake? How in one month two women were at fault?"

Jake blanches, but I continue my assault.

"Think they'd still feel the same way? Like only the woman is responsible? Do you think maybe a man does have a role in creating all these bambinos running around the world?"

"You deceived me. The guys told me to send you back to California and forget about you."

"Is that what you want to do?"

"No. But if we stay in touch, I don't want to know anything about your baby. I don't want to see it, hear about it, and I don't want it to know who I am. I'll be your friend, but not your child's father."

"I'm going home soon. I promise not to share the details of my pregnancy with you. But I won't lie to my child. If you're in my life, he or she will know who you are."

Two bicyclists fly past our bench. Jake whirls around.

"You fucking don't get it. I'm forty-five. My kids need me, my ex-wife needs me, my mother needs me, and now you. They hate me. You will too."

My heart races as I reach out and touch his shoulder.

"Jake, I want this baby. I'll take care of it on my own. I'll raise a healthy, well-adjusted child." I grab his hand. "I don't mean to hurt you. I can't separate the two things happening to me — wanting a baby and falling in love with you."

"I'm not in love with you, Maddy."

His statement is like a punch in my gut. Hearing his truth out loud, hurts more than the lies I tell myself. I bury his truth under my dreams and desire. I speak so softly I hardly hear myself.

"I know." I swallow my tears and gather my strength. "I'm not expecting you to love me or marry me, or declare the baby as yours. I wrestled about telling you, but you have a right to know. I don't want anything from you."

"You will."

"You're bitter, Jake."

"You've no idea what you're getting into. Cute little babies grow into selfish, demanding kids."

"The battle between you and your other kids has nothing to do with me. That's your war. Your experience isn't going to be mine."

The tennis court is empty now. Birds chirp and dogs bark. With their game over, the players can just walk away and celebrate with a beer, no matter the outcome. That isn't going to be us. Sadness and confusion overwhelm me. I'm pregnant. And I've created a problem for someone I love. I kiss Jake on the cheek and walk out of the park.

———

Aunt Margy and I approach Katz's, my favorite deli in New York. There is no waiting line outside, which is unusual. Every time I go there, it's packed. We're both famished after our shopping spree for maternity clothes. Margy has done it four times before with her daughter, my cousin Arlene.

We walk into the restaurant, our arms filled with packages, and dodge around a few tables and chairs. Exhausted from traipsing all over Manhattan, I find a table next to the wood paneled wall covered with celebrity photos. I collapse and order my usual colossal corned beef on rye with a cream soda. With my morning sickness over, I relish eating for two. Margy chooses a lox and onion omelet.

Looking across at her reminds me of the strength of the Gold family genes. I see both my father and Aunt Renee in her smile, her voice, and the wave of her hand. We haven't seen each other since Robbie's Bar Mitzvah last summer and I want to ask her about Anthony and my father. I'm bewildered by my parents' refusal to tell me anything about that encounter.

We wait for our food, munching on sour pickles. Resting my elbows on the table, I lean toward her. "Do you know anything about Anna's husband and my dad. Are you aware my father exploded at him after Robbie's ceremony? Do you know what that was about?"

She shakes her head. "It was a misunderstanding. My fault. Arlene and Robbie wanted to invite just Anna, but Anthony turned up. They were there and then they weren't." Her straight salt-and-pepper hair falls across one eye. She ignores it.

"Why couldn't he come? Because of my father?"

"I'm not sure. I just knew it wasn't a good idea."

"You never asked? You two are so close."

"There are things I don't press him on."

"And that's one of them?"

She turns away.

"Then please answer this. Do you know anything about Dad's depression when I was a little girl? My mother says he withdrew and stopped talking to everyone."

She shakes her head and frowns. "You need to talk to your parents, Maddy. I wish I could help. Your father's a private man. He can get angry and freeze you out. I'd let this go if I were you."

I have no intention of doing that. Margy changes the subject to the baby and I go along with it so we can get through lunch. I can deal with my parents later. My father has been home from the hospital for a week with no restrictions on his diet or activities, so he is strong enough for me to confront him. I'll tread carefully but I'm done with secrets and want some answers.

By the time I get into the elevator at my parents' building, I'm too tired to put down my packages. I slouch against the wall. I exit the elevator and walk along the hallway to the apartment. Tissue paper rustles in the bags. I juggle things to get out my key and open the door.

My mother comes out of the kitchen wiping one hand on her apron. She signals for me to be quiet and points to my father asleep in his chair, with a book balanced over one knee. She takes two of my shopping bags.

"Did you buy out the stores?" She leads me into my bedroom. "You must be exhausted."

"I'm wiped." I plop into a chair. "Aunt Margy is too. My feet are so sore. We walked and walked." I take off my shoes and squish my feet into the carpet. "I hope she doesn't fall asleep on the train and miss her stop. I did that when I was fifteen. I woke up at the last stop." I laugh.

"I didn't have any money to get back to Aunt Margy's house, so the conductor let me ride for free." I smile. "Wanna see what I bought?"

"I thought you were tired? We can wait until Dad wakes up. Give us a fashion show after dinner."

"But I'm excited. I bought enough for two pregnancies."

A look of anguish crosses my mother's face.

"Mom, just joking. Please, let's enjoy this. You're going to be a grandmother." I let that sink in. "You'll come out to L.A. when the baby's born?"

She hesitates. "I wouldn't miss it, Maddy. You'll need help."

I ignore the warning. "Good, that's settled. Now look at what you bought me." I dig through the bags and show her three outfits. Then I find the special emerald green silk dress wrapped in purple tissue paper. I unwrap it, hold it against my body and twirl. "Aunt Margy insisted on buying it for me, although I can't imagine when I'll wear it." I grin. "But who knows?"

I lay out the slacks, tops, nursing bras, and dresses all around the room. My father calls my mother's name. Immediately she stands. "We'll finish this later, Daddy will want to see everything too." She turns to leave, but comes back and kisses my cheek.

———

Dinner and the fashion show are over. My father sits in his chair reading, and my mother sits on the sofa knitting a mint green baby sweater with yellow ducks on it. I sit cross-legged on the floor folding all my new clothes. An occasional horn or siren blares from the streets below. It's a good time to bring up Anthony.

I look up prepared to open the conversation, but before I say a word, my father peers over the rim of his glasses. "Mother and I wonder what you're planning to tell the baby. We think it's important to get our stories straight."

I place a pile of folded clothes into my lap and hold myself ramrod straight.

"What do you mean?"

"About its father," my mother adds. "What should family and friends say?"

"The truth!" My voice rises an octave. "That I couldn't imagine my life without a child. That I wanted a baby."

"Calm down, Maddy." My mother pats the air. "Lower your voice. We're trying to understand."

I comply and soften my tone. "I plan to tell the child that he or she is wanted. Not an accident or a mistake." I clear my throat. "I won't lie. That's the surest way not to get the stories straight. People here and in L.A. know I'm pregnant out of wedlock. What story do you want to create? That he died? Killed in a car accident or a non-existent war?"

"We don't want the baby to feel different," my father says, "or angry because there's no father. You can't be angry if your father is dead."

"I wish that were true Dad, but children do get angry after a divorce or a death. And he or she is going to feel different. Kids know about mommies and daddies. I can't raise my child in a vacuum." I smooth out the dark blue maternity blouse on my lap. "I want to be truthful. Always. Imagine lying to your child, whatever the intention, and then the truth comes out years later?" I shift my position. "Speaking of truth and secrets, why are you so angry with Anthony? And don't dodge the subject."

The wall clock ticks near the dining area. My parents look uncomfortable. A door slams in the hallway followed by a clatter of garbage hitting the sides of the trash chute.

"Why do you need to do this?" my father asks.

"I told you, I don't want secrets. After the Bar Mitzvah, I thought there was something between you and Anthony. Now I'm not sure. When I was a kid I sometimes had weird pictures flash in my head of a dark room and of our kitchen in Brooklyn with Anna making pancakes. The images scared me. They never made sense. Do they to you?"

My parents look directly at each other.

"What?" I cry out. "Did Anthony do something?"

"Must we go there now, Maddy?"

"When would be a good time, Mom? Did Anthony hurt me?"

My father lowers his head. He glances at my mother then turns to me. "I thought you were too young to remember." His voice sounds flat. "I thought I could protect you."

"From what? What did he do?" I shift from my sitting position and kneel. My clothes fall on the carpet around me.

"You were almost four," he says. "Mother and I went away overnight and Anna stayed with you. When we came home, you started sucking your thumb. You stopped playing with your toys, your dolls, and you spent hours sitting in the windowsill in your room."

"That windowsill was my favorite place. I'd watch Anna iron and wait there every night until you came home. I loved that windowsill."

"We'd never left you before," my mother adds. "We thought you were sad because we didn't take you with us."

My father pulls at his beard. "Slowly you came out of your shell and things seemed fine. Then a year later, you went to spend Christmas Eve and Christmas Day with Anna and her family. She called us in the middle of the night when you woke up screaming. She said we should come get you so I took a cab and picked you up. You cried all the way home."

"I don't remember that."

"You were a little girl, Maddy. Finally you told me Anthony once played a game with you and you didn't want to play it again."

"What game?"

He lowers his eyes. "A touching game."

"What?" I gasp.

He clears his throat. "I think it was just touching, nothing more."

"Just touching! You think?" I yell, shaking.

My father looks up and shoots out of his chair. The recliner crashes to the floor and his book lands beside it. "What did you want me to do?" he shouts. "No one spoke about those things then." His shoulders droop. "I did the best I could."

"What was that exactly? What did you do?"

"I went over to his house when Anna wasn't home. I took a baseball bat to scare him, but when I came face to face with him, it took every ounce of self-control not to smash that son-of-a-bitch to pieces. I promised he'd never get near you again."

My insides shiver. "Did Anna know about him?" I whisper, afraid to ask.

"No, impossible. Anna loved you like her own child. She would have risked her life for you."

I roll a button between my fingers and look up. "Mom said you were depressed when I was little. Was it after that?"

"Yes." He walks away from me, shoeless. A brown sock slips down his ankle as he paces.

"Daddy withdrew from you, me, everyone. He never said a word. He only worked."

"He kept it from you?"

My mother nods. "For years."

I'm bewildered and conflicted. I can't process this.

My father stops pacing and turns to me. Tears pool in the corners of his eyes. "I betrayed you, Maddy," he gasps. "But not because I lied, because I didn't protect you."

"Simon, you couldn't have known." My mother tries to console him.

"That doesn't matter."

"Yes, it does." My emotions run the gamut but I feel a sense of relief just knowing the truth. "I don't hold you responsible for Anthony. There was nothing you could have done until I told you. And then,

I don't know, we should have talked about it. It's the silence and the secrets." I take a breath. "I hope he never hurt another child."

I struggle to get up and gather my clothes. "I'm very confused." I go over to my mother and give her a hug. Standing on my tiptoes, I kiss my father. "I need to think." I walk away, but then stop and turn around. "Thank you. I needed to know. It's not your fault."

I go into my room, alone.

———

It's my last night in New York and it's turning out to be the most fun. If I can be carefree and silly with anyone, it's Beth.

"I haven't laughed this hard in months." I straighten my body against Beth's headboard. "My stomach hurts."

"Remember the *Mary Tyler Moore* script we wrote?" Beth ignores my discomfort. "With Ted using chocolate for brown shoe polish." We finish the line together, "so that way every time he puts his foot in his mouth, he can eat it too." We double over with giggles and pound the mattress with our fists.

"It's good to laugh," I gasp. Then I get quiet. "I was more disappointed than you when things didn't work out with Jonathan. We could've had so much fun in California."

"He called the other night. It's not completely over for him. He blames me for being rigid and critical. He's angry I'm dating, and thinks I came out to California with that in mind, so I never gave us a chance."

"What do you say?" I turn on my side and lean on my elbow

"That's not how it was." She shrugs. "We just weren't the people we thought we were. Does that make sense?"

"To me?" I chuckle. "That's what I did with Jake."

Beth leans over and takes a cigarette from the night table.

"Blow it that way." I point to the door.

"Right." She lights it and follows my request. "I'm listening."

"I'm the number one fantasy maker. It took a while, but I finally admitted I lied to myself." I frown. "Desperation can do that. I created a fake persona for Jake. I didn't see who he really is. I wanted him to be the man of my dreams, exciting, romantic and witty, so I ignored his frenetic, disjointed behavior." I close my eyes. "The way he treats his family didn't fit my scenario, so I ignored it." I'm ashamed when I hear myself say it out loud. "Jake never made himself out to be anyone else."

"What about the baby?"

I close my eyes again, my body weighed down with sadness. "It's separate. Complicated. I didn't set out to con Jake and I didn't mean to hurt him. I gambled not thinking of his consequences. I went for my gold ring on the carousel." I shake my head in disbelief that I'm actually pregnant from the first time I tried. "I didn't count on falling in love. I thought I could change him and make him into what I want. But if we were to get married, then all the reasons I got pregnant, being part of a loving family, going to soccer games, recitals, picnics, would be destroyed. It would be awful. Jake saved me from myself."

Beth sighs. "I guess we're both lucky." She puts her hand on my arm. "Do you realize I won't get to see you hugely pregnant?"

"I'll send pictures." Excitement courses through me. "I can't imagine what I'll look and feel like, big and fat and lumbering."

"I'm envious. I couldn't do what you're doing, but with Jonathan out of the picture, I wonder whether I'll ever have a baby." She crushes her cigarette into the ashtray. "You force me to think about having a child. I understand more now why you did it."

I pick up a piece of lint on the bedspread and toy with it. "Never having a child if you want one is difficult. A friend describes it as a wound that never heals. She can go along and everything is fine and then suddenly it starts bleeding."

"Will you see Jake again?"

"He'd have to come to California. And that's not happening. He called this morning though. My mom answered the phone. Imagine winter at the South Pole."

"What'd he want?" Beth smiles.

My chest muscles cramp and I put my hand on the pain. "He gave me one last warning about having kids." I look at her. "Kevin ran away from home last Thursday."

"He what?"

"He didn't come home. Jake thought he was at a friend's. He didn't realize Kevin was gone until he got a call from Kevin's school the next day."

"Where'd he go?"

"He had some cash, took a bus as far as he could, then hitched the rest of the way to his mother's house in Georgia. His stepfather called to tell Jake he was safe." I pull my fingers through my hair to untangle my ponytail. "It must have been a nightmare."

"Why'd he do it?"

I look at her askance. "We both know why." My anger pours out. "Jake treats Kevin like an annoyance, a burden. He doesn't want to be a parent. That would require him to be at home more. Not live like some workaholic, alcoholic, womanizer." I stop and take in a huge breath of air. My eyes widen and I start to laugh.

"Tell me how you really feel," Beth teases. "So what's happening now?"

"Kevin will stay in Georgia and they'll see. It's depressing. What I refused to realize even yesterday is so clear today."

"Did you tell any of this to Jake?"

"I made a few comments about Kevin, but I didn't say anything about him or me. I'm finished. If he changes his mind about the baby, we'll work something out. He is the baby's father."

I'm exhausted. My body wants to sink into a soft cloud and float over a green field of clover. "This has been a rough visit, between my father and Jake, telling Linda, then finding out about Anthony. I feel like a handball slapped from one wall to another. I want to put everything behind me, go home and start over."

"Just like that?" She snaps her fingers. "That's impossible." She reaches for her Coke on the nightstand and takes a sip. "You can't put Anthony and Jake, and your father for that matter, in some little box and hide them away."

I close my eyes and sift through all my hurts and disappointments. I think about my date with Howard and how I left his home feeling empty and cold. I open my eyes. "Do you remember me telling you about my dream and the gold key? How every woman wore one around her neck but me? How every woman had the secret to being loved, but me?" I pat my heart. "I still don't have the secret, and I'm tired of trying to get it."

Tears drop one by one until a stream careens down my face, under my chin and soaks into my blouse. Beth hands me some tissues and puts her arm around me. She lets me cry. I finally stop, blow my nose and straighten my back.

"And that box you referred to, the one for Anthony, Jake and my father? I can lock them in it with my special gold key and hide it in the back of my brain. I'm moving on."

"These things had a huge impact on you, Maddy. You have to deal with them."

"I'm done dealing. I'm going home Beth. I have my friends there and you here. I'm about to start a new life." I touch my belly. "This is all I want to think about now."

1980 – 1997

PART TWO

7

SANTA MONICA
1980–1981

S**ix months later** and two weeks past my due date, I'm twenty pounds heavier. Clumsy and forgetful, I can hardly fit behind the wheel of my little yellow Fiat. In my quiet, scared moments, I feel like I'm sitting on top of a gigantic slide waiting for someone to sneak up from behind and give me a push.

On Thursday, with my mother here to help, we shop for the baby, for me, and for the house. We buy food and cook, so I'll have meals I can dig out of the freezer in case I'm housebound. Things are relaxed between us until we begin to feel the crunch of time. She'd planned to visit for two weeks, but we're already one week into it and there is no baby. She will be flying home before the end of April, because of my dad, and then I'll be on my own.

I read everything about babies and motherhood I can get my hands on. I'm determined to do it right. Stacks of expensive books pile up on the floor near my bed, but at least my money supports the local bookstore.

After dinner, I'm resting on the couch when my water breaks without a warning. No big pop, just a warm wetness. I jump up and run past my mother to the bathroom. "It's time!" I yell.

I have no control of the milky amniotic fluid gushing out of my body. I grab a hand towel, bunch it up, and put it between my legs. I waddle around the house in one direction while my mother flies the opposite way. We locate my pre-packed suitcase, my car keys, our purses and house keys.

I have twelve hours of light natural labor, followed by twelve hours of heavy induced labor. Eventually I need a C-section. Terrified, I hyperventilate until a nurse, standing by my head, instructs me to breathe. The doctor gets into a tug of war with my baby and my womb. He pulls, relaxes, pulls and relaxes. He finally yanks a screaming baby out of my body. Already panicked and in pain, I want to bolt off the operating table and run. My body trembles.

When the nurse suggests I hold my baby, I vehemently shake my head, too afraid I'll drop him. But the nurse doesn't listen. Instead she places a tiny bundle with a perfectly shaped head and peaches-and-cream complexion into my arms. At the sound of my voice, he stops crying and gazes into my eyes. As tears roll down my cheeks, all the pain and fear evaporate. I hold him tightly to my breast. "Welcome, Ethan Robert Gold. You are amazing!" Bursting with love for this perfect little being, I kiss his forehead. "I am your mother. I will protect you, always."

For the first week, my mother stays with Ethan and me. She helps me through the healing process and I am able to share my bliss with someone who is equally in love with my baby. We both coo over him, laugh at the little squeaking sounds he makes when he nurses, and take turns walking the floor when he needs calming. The bond between my mother and me is stronger than any other time in my life. And when it's time for her to leave, it's like I have a hole in my soul.

———

Our first year isn't always easy, but we make it. Colic, clogged tear ducts, sleepless nights, earaches, and separation anxiety are hard, but we thrive. My giggling alarm wakes me every morning. His smile greets me as I drag myself into his room to get him from his crib. When Ethan gets his first tooth, I drive through Santa Monica to my cousin's house beeping my horn to announce its arrival. I share every milestone — his first bath, his first kiss, first word, first sentence — with everyone.

When Ethan's first birthday arrives on April 25, my friend Deborah offers her house for the party so I can invite a lot of guests. I am *gung ho* to celebrate Ethan and thank all my friends and family who opened their minds and hearts to embrace us. On the big day, I stand in Deborah's backyard listening to the music, enveloped by bright colored balloons and Happy Birthday signs. I have a Piñata for the older kids and Deborah bakes her Omaha chocolate cake in the form of the number 1 outlined with red, blue, yellow, green, and orange M&Ms. At the side of the yard, a metal folding table is piled high with gifts for Ethan. At the end of the party, we sing "Happy Birthday" as I hold firmly to my squiggly year old bundle of joy and energy. All I can do is grin.

Ethan and I are exhausted by the time I drive the ten minutes to our home in Santa Monica. He almost falls asleep in his bowl of "paghetti", so I wash his face, change him, and skip the story. He is out before the lights are.

I settle down on the living room floor of the small, two-bedroom rent-controlled apartment I've called home since three months before Ethan arrived. I'm surrounded by his birthday gifts — boxes with multi-colored ribbons containing overalls, bathing suits, Superman pajamas, blocks, pull toys and stuffed animals. The "Happy Birthday" refrain plays in my head as I figure out what to return, and where to put everything I keep. Ethan's room is bursting with more possessions than any one-year-old should have.

I lean against the couch and hold up a navy and white sailor outfit. I yawn and put it back in its box. I look at my watch and it's seven-thirty. Ethan's asleep, perfect. Now it's my turn. I switch off the lights, walk into his room and hear his baby snorts. I go in to check him three or four times a night, sometimes in a panic because I haven't heard him breathe, or just because I love to look at him.

I gaze into his crib. His thumb is in his mouth with his well-worn blankie under his head. His little legs are tucked under his body so his tush sticks up in the air. I brush some wet hair off his forehead and happily watch him sleep.

When the phone rings, it startles me. I squint from the hall light as I walk to my bedroom. It must be Beth calling to find out how the party went.

"It was wonderful," I say.

"What was?"

My heart pounds.

"You were expecting someone else?" Jake asks.

"Yes."

"I've been thinking about you. How are you?"

"Fine."

"Good. I know this is a surprise but I'm ready to move on. I thought we should talk, maybe be friends."

I switch the receiver to my other ear. "What does that mean?"

I retrieve my red corduroy backrest from the floor and place it against the headboard of my bed. My temples throb.

"I want to know how you are. How Ethan is."

I absorb his words and their implications, but I don't trust him. When Ethan was born, he sent two-dozen long-stemmed red roses to the hospital with a card signed, *Love, Jake and Linda.* It felt like a double edge knife stabbed and twisted in my gut. I gave the roses to the nurses.

"Your timing is incredible. Today's Ethan's birthday."

"I know."

I pick up the cloth storybook of *Little Red Riding Hood* on my bed. I roll and unroll one of the pages.

"Maddy, I know this is a surprise. I understand you have questions about why I'm calling. I'm not sure. I've been thinking about you, though. And Ethan. Maybe we can talk. See each other. I'm going to Arizona in a few weeks. I'll come to see you both, if you want."

"I'll think about it," I say, confused.

"I'll call before I finalize my plans. That'll give you time."

"Okay. In a few days."

I hang up and drift into Ethan's room. I peer into his crib. I don't understand Jake's olive branch, but Ethan is my priority. Whatever decisions I make must be best for him.

Three weeks later, my chaotic mind is full of questions. Why is Jake coming? Is Ethan important to him? Am I? Do I want to be? Is he ready to be a loving parent? Involved? Has he changed? One minute I feel strong, the next minute insecure.

———

Jake's plane is on time, and with no nighttime traffic, his cab will arrive soon. I worry my lovely Santa Monica apartment is too paltry and crowded for three. I wander around my living room waiting to hear his footsteps on the stairs. To show off my figure, I wear a new magenta jumpsuit that contrasts with my long red hair.

Sitting in a chair across from the open screen door, I try to read the last ten pages of a novel, but I can't concentrate. Snippets of conversations with my friends over the last few weeks intrude. "Tell him to get a hotel room," one advises. "You're not going to sleep with him, are you?" another one asks. "Why is he coming? Be careful."

I agreed to allow Jake to visit because he is Ethan's father and he has rights. But I also need to protect my son. I hear his footsteps and the wheels of a suitcase along the cement walkway, then on the staircase. I put my book on the end table and walk out the door to see Jake struggling with his luggage. I meet him halfway and reach for his briefcase.

"You look beautiful," he says. "Having a baby agrees with you."

"I've never been happier, Jake."

His compliment about my body gives me confidence. I turn and walk inside ahead of him. He gives my living room a quick once over.

"Cute place."

I study his face, trying to read it.

"Sorry it's late," he says. "It's been a rough week." He takes my hand and kisses me on the cheek. "I'm tired, but glad I'm here."

"I'm tired too. That's normal."

"Right, I guess so."

"I'll make you a drink or something to eat if you want."

He shakes his head.

"Do you want to see him?"

"Sure."

I turn on the hall light and lead Jake into Ethan's room. We walk to his crib and I step aside. He stares at his son.

"He's big, a towhead."

I laugh. "He must get that from your family."

Jake touches Ethan's back. He is so gentle with him that I drop my guard. He turns and reaches for me. He cups my face and kisses me lightly on the lips. I don't want to kiss him back, but his mouth opens and his tongue explores mine. As he pulls me to him, a moan escapes from my throat. I put my hands on his chest and push him away.

"Let's be clear about this, Jake. I won't sleep with you. We talked about you getting a hotel room, but you said you'd sleep on the bed in the living room."

"I know what we said." He strokes my hair. "But we were always good together. Being here, I hoped you'd change your mind."

"Not until I understand what you want and what's best for Ethan." I look at his face. The hall light reflects off his glasses.

He strokes my arm tenderly. "All right. I'll get ready for bed." Without giving Ethan another glance, he walks out of the room. "Maybe we can play some tennis in the morning. I brought my sneakers figuring you'd have an extra racket." I don't respond. I look at my sleeping child, innocent and trusting.

Knowing Jake is in the next room makes it difficult on many levels. Why would I bring a man into my life? My days and nights are full of Ethan, work and friends. Dating isn't a priority. And being with a man is stressful for me, not loving and supportive. I don't fall asleep until after 3 a.m.

I awake to a couple arguing in the alley outside my bedroom window. I stretch, pop a vertebra and glance sideways at the clock. 8:15! I jump out of bed. Where's Ethan? Seeing my door closed, I guess Jake got up with him. The only other times I've slept late were when Ethan and I visited my parents in their new home in Florida. The proud grandparents would take over so I could relax and enjoy a break.

I come out of my room and find father and son on the floor of the living room, surrounded by books and puzzles. I watch for a few minutes. Ethan looks up at me and his whole body bounces.

"Mama," he squeals. He raises his hands and crawls to me.

I pick him up and rub his nose with mine. "Good morning pumpkin.

I smile at Jake. "And good morning to you. Thanks for letting me sleep."

"I forget how exhausting a baby is," Jake says. "He's so active and curious. He crawls so damn fast. You gotta watch him every second."

"The house gets baby proofed every day as he does more and more things," I say as I step over some puzzle pieces. "You both must be starved. Do you want some coffee, breakfast?" I walk into the kitchen and put Ethan into his highchair. "The paper's outside if you want it."

I hand Ethan a piece of banana and stand in the archway that separates the kitchen and living room. "I've been thinking about the tennis thing. We can pack a picnic and go to one of the parks with a court. While Ethan naps, we can play. I only have a sitter tonight."

Jake does push-ups while I wait for a response. The phone rings. I pick up the receiver.

"Yes?"

"Is he there?" my cousin Ruth asks.

"Yes."

"Everything all right?"

"Yes."

"Can you talk?"

"No."

I hang up. Telephones will ring around Santa Monica as Ruth relays the cryptic exchange to our friends.

I check on Ethan and put some Cheerios and more banana in his bowl. I fill a Superman cup with milk and put it on his tray. "You aren't used to me not sitting with you, are you?" I kiss him on top of his head. "I'll be right back."

I walk into the living room, sit on the gold carpet and lean against the love seat I inherited from Aunt Renee. Jake lies on his back, his bathrobe open. He lifts his left knee to his chest. His body is firm and sexy — so tempting.

"Was that a friend wondering about you?" His breathing is irregular. "Do your friends hate me?"

"I don't know that hate is the word."

"What is?"

"They don't want to see me hurt. Or Ethan. He's their baby, he's a group project."

"What about your parents?"

"We don't talk about you. They like their life in Florida and love their grandson. They think I'm doing a good job, so they're happy. If they're concerned about me, they don't say."

"Let's get a baby sitter for the day. I'll pay for it."

"No!" My head jerks back and I straighten up. "He's with a sitter all week. The weekends are our time together."

Jake looks at me. "You really enjoy it, don't you?"

"I love it. I love him." I stretch out my legs. "He's like a little vacuum cleaner sucking up life with giggles." I chuckle. "I could do with more sleep and more help, but I'm happier than I could ever imagine."

Jake stands up. "I'm taking a shower. Whatever you want is fine with me." He leaves the room.

I go to check on Ethan.

————

It is almost a perfect day with ideal weather. Even with the sun shining, a cool breeze drifts through the park by the ocean so playing tennis in mid-afternoon is pleasant. I haven't played in two years. I'm not as fast as I used to be, but my long legs still cover the court and my forehand and backhand are accurate.

Ethan does what he is supposed to do. I wear him out on the colorful plastic swings and slides for toddlers and after lunch he conks out in his stroller, right on cue. He sleeps in the corner of the tennis court while his mother and father play.

At Fire Island or in Central Park, Jake and I were evenly matched opponents. What advantage Jake had in power, I made up with a mixed bag of shots. I was comfortable at the base line, the net, or lobbing the ball where Jake wasn't. Today's set is the same until Jake breaks my serve. The score is now five games to four. He looks pleased and teases me from across the net. "Gotcha!" He puts one ball in his pocket and sends a bullet flying across the court, acing his serve.

"That was great. Dare you to do it again."

"Watch me!"

He throws the ball high in the air as Ethan starts to cry. I return the serve with a backhand shot that drops just over the net. Ethan's wail gets louder. He isn't happy being ignored. I watch Jake run to meet the ball, torn between wanting him to miss because my shot is so good or just quitting. But he slams the ball back.

I don't run for it. "Good return," I call, my breathing shallow. "We've got to stop. Ethan's awake."

I turn to get my son.

"You're quitting?" Jake yells. "Now?" He stands at the net, red-faced and fuming.

I walk back to him with Ethan in my arms.

"You're angry?"

"We're in the middle of a game!"

"And he is crying."

We pack the picnic basket, Ethan's toys and blanket, and drive to the market on the way home. We don't speak. The silence is deadly.

Once we're out of the car and on my turf, I relax. Ethan climbs the stairs to our apartment. Gently, I swat his behind. "You're taking a long time today." We are on step five out of twelve. Jake has already made three trips carrying the cooler, three bags of groceries and Ethan's red, white, and blue horse on wheels. He loves to ride it everywhere.

Ethan sits on a step and covers his eyes with his hands.

"Peek-a-Boo, see you."

He has advanced language skills for a one-year-old. Aside from the usual Mama, he began saying words at nine months and sentences soon after. That makes our communication easier because he can tell me what he wants and we are both less frustrated.

"I'll give you a Peek-a-Boo." I swoop him in my arms, nibble his neck and give him a big kiss, producing the giggles I love. "Come on, you."

I walk into the kitchen as Jake empties the cooler. "Sorry about the tennis. We can play tomorrow. Maybe my cousin will watch Ethan."

"I need to make a few phone calls. I'll use the phone in your bedroom."

"Sure."

I put Ethan on the floor and give him some wooden spoons and plastic containers to play with while I put the groceries away. "Jake's not happy," I whisper. "This isn't what he had in mind." After I stack the last can of tuna in the cabinet, I ruffle Ethan's hair. "Okay, baby." I pick him up and walk into the bathroom. "It's time for your bath. I'll get you all cleaned up for Randi and she'll give you supper."

I turn on the faucets, adjust the water temperature and sit down on the floor to undress him. Jake comes out of my bedroom and stands in the doorway. He stares at his feet looking embarrassed.

"I'm sorry, Maddy."

"It's okay. I'm used to doing it by myself. You were a big help carrying all that stuff upstairs." I smile. "We'll have time together once Randi gets here."

"I can't do this." He makes a sweeping motion with his hand that includes everything in the tiny bathroom.

"You don't have to give him a bath." I shut off the water. "Oh," I say, suddenly getting it. "This whole thing, Ethan, and me."

"I changed my ticket. I'm leaving tonight. I thought I could do it. Be loving and friendly to you, to him, but I'm not. I can't. It's not you or him. He's a sweet, pleasant baby."

"Then what is it? I'm not asking you for anything. Have I ever put pressure on you?" My throat closes, my gut tightens.

"Only by having him."

It's like a slap across the face.

"But that's not it," he continues. "He's here. You're happy with him, with this."

"You keep saying 'this.'" I imitate his sweeping arm motion. "But what's 'this?'" I do it again.

"Your life, motherhood. I'm suffocating."

"Wow!" I blink and swallow. "We wouldn't want that." I strap Ethan into his bathtub seat. "I assume you called a cab. Why aren't you leaving?"

"I thought with Kevin settled and Becky calming down from college angst, it might be nice to have a second chance."

"You know Jake, it's always about you." I think about Kevin and how he'd needed to run away to get attention. "What did you expect?

115

That kids raise themselves? Their needs come first Jake. A tennis game isn't more important than your child."

Ethan sings as he pushes his blue plastic boat through the water. "Row, row, row your boat…"

"I'm glad you got this experiment out of the way before he's older." I take a breath. "By the way, did you bring any condoms?"

"What?"

"In case we slept together. Were you prepared this time?"

He glares at me, his blue eyes blazing. I glare back. I turn away and squeeze baby shampoo into my hand.

"Come on E., let's wash your hair."

Jake walks into the living room.

8

SANTA MONICA

Summer 1995

*E*than and I stand at the United Airlines gate at LAX. A woman announces the boarding of his flight over the PA system. He is flying to New York to spend the summer with my cousin Arlene and her family. He's fifteen now and responsible, but I'm shattered into a million pieces. Even though he's been to sleep-away camp several times and gone to Hawaii for a basketball tournament, this is different. He is flying alone, far away, for a long time.

I hover and fidget. Ethan remains calm, reassuring me over and over. He tolerates my pestering with little annoyance.

"I have my ticket." He holds it up. "See? I have Arlene's information, just in case they're not at the airport." He smiles. "And yes, I have the cash you gave me this morning."

"Okay, I'll stop." I bite my tongue. "One last hug, though."

He wraps his arms around me and kisses me on the cheek. He gives me a thumbs up and turns to leave.

"Have a fabulous time," I call after him.

He waves and walks through the door.

I retrieve my car from the parking lot and drive to my mechanic's to get an oil change and tune-up. I turn up the radio hoping to drown out the jumbled thoughts whipping around in my head. I'm alone. Ethan's gone. He's growing up and independent. Will he be okay? But the summer is all mine, no responsibilities except for the dog. I'm done with school so I can sleep late, take some art, writing and yoga classes, and maybe even go away for a few days.

I sit alone in my mechanic's waiting room while they do the oil change and tune-up. My thoughts still collide. I need to stop. Ethan is gone and I can be happy on my own. I sit up straight to prove my point.

A tall, slender, gray-haired man comes into the room. He looks like he stepped out of *GQ* magazine. At ten in the morning at a garage, he wears perfectly pressed tan cotton slacks, a light blue Oxford button-down and a pair of brown Gucci loafers. He is hard to ignore. Every seat is vacant except mine. He chooses a chair diagonally across from me. I look into a pair of brown eyes flecked with gold. His smile brightens the dreary, overcast morning.

"You do crossword puzzles in pen," he says, "I'm impressed."

I look down at the newspaper in my lap and the pen in my hand. "I don't have a pencil. I'm not very good at them, but I forgot to bring a book."

"Want some help?"

I smile, why not? He crosses over to sit next to me. I shift in my seat to share the newspaper with the attractive stranger. I'm embarrassed when I look at the many empty squares. "I'm good at the ones about weekly television or from *People* magazine."

"My name's Phil Stewart," he says, and holds out his hand.

I can't remember the last time anyone flirted with me. I shake his hand.

"Yours?" He has a glint in his eye.

"Mine? Oh, my name?" I roll my eyes. "Maddy Gold."

We work on the puzzle together. Phil does most of it, but he is pleasant and positive, and not at all condescending when I show my ignorance. He gets my sarcasm and wry sense of humor. That's a big plus.

Our mechanic Conrad enters the room wiping his hands on his overalls. "Your car's ready, Phil. It's in great shape." He turns to me. "Your car will be done in about ten, Maddy."

When Conrad leaves, I feel a little sad. I don't want this to be over. It's nice to know a romantic side of me is still alive. I sit immobile.

"I'm sorry to leave you with no book, and now no puzzle," Phil says. His eyes twinkle, his grin a little crooked. "I'm meeting some friends for golf, but if you're free Saturday night, we could do something."

"I'd like that."

He gives me his card, writes down my phone number on the back of another one, and leaves. I glance at his card. Phil Stewart, a law partner in Stewart, Frank and Irving. Sounds impressive. I'm glad I don't have a book or the puzzle. My thoughts are more than enough.

As soon as I get home I call Julia, my West Coast Beth, my confidant and partner in laughter, as well as serious matters. We met at a synagogue seminar with out kids on Bar and Bat Mitzvah protocol. It turned out that Julia's daughter, Katie, a year older than Ethan, went to the same school with him.

She answers on the first ring. I'm like a giddy teenager going out on her first date and I need every bit of support I can garner. I don't want to be this way. I'm setting myself up for disappointment. Every insecurity and past rejection occupy every waking moment. The two days until Saturday drag on. I speak to Ethan twice and he's fine. I'm glad he's not around to witness my crazy.

Julia comes over at six o'clock on Saturday. She keeps me grounded and helps me find something to wear. Few people can create style like Julia. She checks me out when I'm all dressed. Just before eight, she leaves the apartment.

When Phil arrives at the door, we both stare and laugh. I assumed based on his dress at our first meeting, his black Mercedes sedan, and being a senior partner in a Century City law firm, that he would be fairly conservative. But he is wearing jeans, a blue plaid shirt and sneakers. I'm in a purple silk dress and heels.

"Very nice," he says, looking at me admiringly, "but I guess I forgot to tell you what we're doing. I've been out of the dating loop for so long. If you put on comfortable shoes, you'll be perfect."

I change shoes and we end up at the Santa Monica Pier. It's a happening place with so many activities that if we run out of things to talk about, the carnival atmosphere on the pier will provide inspiration. There is the merry-go-round, the Ferris wheel, the arcades, an abundance of restaurants, and throngs of people on a balmy summer night walking along a boardwalk above the Pacific Ocean. I want to put my arm through his as we walk, but I hold back.

We decide to get hotdogs and ice-cold beers to go, instead of waiting for a table at one of the crowded restaurants. When I pop the last bit of a hotdog into my mouth, Phil wipes some mustard off my cheek with a napkin. It feels sweet, natural. We check out the arcades, play a few games, and walk along the boardwalk.

"Whatever made you choose this place?" I ask.

"You. Something tells me we both work very hard. I wanted to let our 'kids' out to play."

"I used to bring my son here and he was the one who played, not me. Except for the carousel. We'd go on that together because I'm a sucker for merry-go-rounds."

"We can go on the way out."

We stop walking and lean on the guardrail and stare out at the black ocean. Waves lap against the pylons. Phil turns to me.

"It must have been hard raising him on your own."

I shake my head. I tell him about Ethan and a little about Jake, and he tells me about his deceased wife and nursing her through an illness.

"I can't imagine walking away from a child of mine, no matter what the circumstances," he says.

"I didn't think Jake would either. Not totally."

"How does Ethan feel about having an absentee father?"

"Angry. He doesn't want to talk about it when I bring it up, so I assume he's buried his feelings. I don't believe he doesn't have any."

"And you never met anyone else?"

"No. Gun shy, very gun shy."

"Then I'm flattered." He leans over and kisses my cheek. "I haven't been dating either. Taking care of my wife took time away from my kids and my practice. I've been playing catch-up ever since."

We stand side by side silently watching the dark waves below. A cool wind blows in from the ocean. I shiver. Phil reaches over and puts his arm around me.

"You're cold. We'll go on the carousel, if you want. Then I'll take you home."

I nod readily and like the natural force of a wave pulled to the shore, I snuggle into his warmth and protection.

Weeks later, I lie in Phil's arms while he sleeps. It's the last night of my carefree days of summer. Ethan is coming home tomorrow and our schools start in a few days. I'm concerned about Ethan. His voice has a different tone with an edge to it. Maybe he's homesick and soon he'll be back to normal. Maybe I'm imagining his sadness.

Things will be different for Ethan, for us, with Phil in the picture. I look forward to their meeting, but I'm aware of potential jealousies and resentments that can happen when someone new is added into a relationship. It has always been just the two of us. But Phil is a perfect role model for Ethan, a man he can admire and learn from. They share similar interests in sports, politics, and even video games. Rap music, though, is a TBD. I want everyone to be happy. I plan to pick Ethan up at the airport in the afternoon and Phil will come for dinner later.

Phil and I lie together like two spoons, his warm body presses against my back, his arm wraps around me. A generous lover, he is patient, giving me time to open up physically and emotionally. I never feel rushed or pushed. We care about each other.

"Why aren't you asleep?" I feel his breath on my shoulder.

"How'd you know?"

"You're body is tense."

I wiggle against him. "Do you want to do something about that?"

"Don't deflect with me, Maddy. I want to know what's going on with you."

"Everything's about to change and I don't know how," I say into the air. "I feel out of control."

He strokes my arm. "Change can be good. We've been great for each other. I'm happier than I've been in a long time and so are you. Your friends like me, Ethan will too. Whatever happens, we can work on it together."

I turn over and with the help of an early ray of sunshine, I look into his warm, brown eyes. "You are so positive. So lovely." I wrap my leg around him to get as close as possible. I want to absorb his confidence. I want to be one with this man who is changing me, expanding my world, allowing me to believe I can finally have that gold key.

He straddles me, grabbing each of my hands in his. He smiles as he looks down at my face. He kisses my eyes, my nose. My lips open with the touch of his tongue, probing and strong. His kisses move down my body. I arch up to meet him and wrap my legs around his hips.

"Please, now," I moan.

He enters me with a slow, taunting back and forth rhythm. He smiles, toying with me, playing. I want no part of that right now. I want his power. I want his love. And I want to give myself completely to him.

I put my hands on his buttocks and pull him deeper into me. His pace quickens. Tears roll down my cheeks from the exquisiteness of our connection. Our bodies shudder as we come together. We stay entwined. Our breathing slows and our sweat cools us. Eventually we fall asleep.

9

SANTA MONICA

Winter 1996

*I*t's **Friday morning and the school week is coming to an end.** I plan to celebrate tonight with Julia, but it's still a long time away. Arguing with teenagers in my special education classroom, in the school hallways, and then at home with my fifteen-year-old, exhausts me. Trying to teach and lead by example is a huge challenge.

Sarah, one of my students, and I are in the middle of an argument about why it's important to study the Roman Empire. I wait for her protestations. She is sometimes sweet but mostly oppositional. She leans her long, skinny body forward in her chair and looks ready to spring.

"Why do we have to learn about that?" she hisses. "I don't care about the past."

I refrain from smiling. "It's an old-fashioned idea that learning from the past helps us not to make the same mistakes in the future."

I pivot to include all of my students. "Everyone turn to page one-thirty-four." I heave around my copy of the four hundred page world history book. "That's the Roman Coliseum. You can all go to Rome one day and see it, in person. It's awesome."

Sarah grimaces without following directions. "Who'd want to go there?" She slams her book shut.

The faces of my other ten students say, "Here we go again."

"Sarah, don't you want to travel, see the world?"

"I don't care." She rolls her eyes.

I walk closer and pat her long black hair. "I know, honey. That's the problem."

The phone in my classroom rings and I give the kids a written assignment as I go to answer it. My heart sinks as I listen to the message. Ethan's counselor wants an after school meeting and now my day gets infinitely longer.

Hours later, I sit in a straight-back wooden chair. My feet, firmly planted on the floor, fit neatly on top of two beige linoleum tiles, toes and heels not touching the lines. My clenched hands stick to the armrests waiting for the executioner to strap me in and begin the electric shocks. This is not San Quentin, I remind myself. It's an office at Ethan's high school. I take deep breaths to calm myself.

The late afternoon sun drops toward the horizon through huge windows, highlighting a few personal items and lots of posters endorsing success, positive self-image, and perseverance. It reminds me of the decor in my classroom, where I'm the one trying to inspire troubled kids.

Ethan's counselor, Mrs. Castenada, is still on the phone. Her dark, curly hair, graying at the roots, covers part of her face even though she constantly hooks it around her right ear. She signals to me with five raised fingers. Behind her, on a bookcase, are photographs of happy students. Two girls stand with the mayor of Santa Monica and several boys hold tennis rackets and a large trophy. Everyone is smiling.

The receiver hits the cradle. I look at the petite woman behind the desk I'd met briefly a few times before, once at the ninth grade orientation, and again at a Back-to-School night. I like the way Mrs. Castenada talks about her kids. I'm glad Ethan is one of them. I smile and point to the photos.

"I have the feeling you're not going to tell me Ethan's won something."

"I wish I could. Maybe after we get him back on track. He has the ability." She picks up a paper and hands it to me. "This is Ethan's progress report for the third quarter. His grades have dropped dramatically."

I glance at it. I know the As and Bs from last semester, but I'm floored when I see an F in English and two Ds for Math and Spanish.

"He isn't easy to be around lately. Every time I ask about school, he gets testy." I'd heard this message many times before at my school. Here's another parent not in control of her kid. My face burns. I reach up to touch it, hide it. I'm a teacher. I've requested countless meetings like this. I shouldn't have one myself.

"We have plenty of time to turn this around." She coughs and clears her throat. "I called his teachers, and both his Math and Spanish teacher suggested the usual — more attention in class, completing his homework assignments, and some tutoring. His English teacher though, wants to meet with you and Ethan. They'll both be here soon."

The bell rings. I look at my watch and smile at Mrs. Castenada. It's Friday and it's been a long week. It's going to be a longer weekend. I want to bury my head in my hands. I imagine the fight we'll have later. Ethan's yelling has escalated and I'm more and more frightened. I'm not ready to tell anyone, I'm too embarrassed. How could this happen to us? Maybe his angry, aggressive behavior will go away as quickly as it appeared. I put on a brave face and make small talk.

"I appreciate your contacting me. I'm surprised you have time with such a large caseload."

There's a knock on the door so I turn. Ethan enters the office. He seems taller, and more muscular than this morning, although he is hidden inside his baggy clothes. I hate those sagging pants. They scream gang attire to me, but I have to pick my fights. His handsome face, with a strong jaw, button nose and hazel eyes, is framed by heavily jelled hair combed straight back. His charming smile, the one that always makes me melt, disappears when he sees me. I slide my chair back giving him more room. Ethan looks at Mrs. Castenada and then at me.

"What are you doing here?" His voice isn't quite contemptuous but it isn't friendly.

"Mrs. Castenada called me. We're concerned about your report card."

"Why don't you sit Ethan? Bring over a chair for Mrs. Levine, too. She'll be here shortly."

"Mrs. Levine?"

Ethan brings over two chairs and places them next to me, in front of Mrs. Castenada's desk. He sits, leaving the middle seat vacant. I watch my angry child get settled. Before I figure out what to say to him, Mrs. Levine knocks on the door and walks in. She is a tall, blonde ponytailed, twenty-something with bright, lavender blue eyes and a harried demeanor. She carries an armful of papers and a loaded briefcase. Her blouse hangs halfway out of her skirt. If I read her face correctly, it's been an exhausting day, and perhaps week. Most teachers avoid Friday afternoon meetings for just that reason.

Mrs. Levine lets go of her briefcase. The clunk on the floor makes me jump. She reaches over to shake hands with me, and then Ethan. With this gesture, Ethan appears contrite, even ashamed. He casts his eyes to the floor.

Mrs. Castenada straightens some papers on her desk as she looks toward Mrs. Levine. "I've already told Mrs. Gold about the drop in Ethan's grades and how concerned his teachers are. Why don't you go into the specifics for English?"

The young teacher faces Ethan. The setting sun weaves darker shadows along Mrs. Castenada's desk and the wall behind her.

"First off, I think you're a great kid, and up until a few weeks ago, a capable, above-average student."

She turns to face me. "I don't know what happened. The students had a major project due before their progress report. Ethan didn't do it. He began to forget his homework and make excuses for various things before that, but I thought it was a middle-of-the-year thing."

She looks straight at him. "You knew how important this report was."

Ethan keeps his head down and stares at a piece of purple gum ground into the beige linoleum. His nod is barely noticeable.

"What was the assignment?" I ask, intense heat burning my cheeks again.

"We've been doing a unit on *To Kill a Mockingbird.* Ethan needed to write a character study about Atticus Finch, the father, one of the most beloved characters in modern American literature. The students were supposed to compare and contrast Atticus with their own father."

I close my eyes. My heart beats wildly, painfully. I can imagine what's happening to Ethan's. I bite the inside of my lip. We've been lucky up until now. There has always been time to explain the single parent circumstances. I look over at my son. He doesn't seem to be moving or breathing. I want to protect him.

"Ethan doesn't know his father, Mrs. Levine. That's probably why he didn't do the report."

"Oh, I'm sorry. It could have been another male figure in his life."

She turns to Ethan. "I said that in class." She reaches out to touch Ethan's arm. "Why didn't you — ?"

"Why didn't I what?" He rips his arm out of her grasp. "Why didn't I tell you that I don't have a father? That I don't know very much about him?" His eyes fill with sadness, but he rages on. "Jake's never even been to a birthday party or one of my soccer games. No one in my life compares to perfect Atticus. Is that what you want me to announce to you and the class?"

"You could have told me in private. I would — "

"You would have understood?" He looks from Mrs. Levine to Mrs. Castenada, then to me. If contempt is a thick, sticky substance, it would drip out of him one drop at a time. "You — don't — understand — anything." He bolts up, pushing so hard against the chair that it topples over. He hesitates like he wants to pick it up, but doesn't. "I'm outta here."

With his exit, silence fills the room in the same deafening way as the crashing chair. The three of us sit motionless.

"I'm sorry. Ethan and I have a lot to talk about. This goes deeper than school." I bend to get my purse and pick up the chair. "I hope you have a good weekend," I mumble.

I leave the dead silence in the room and pray for dignity. I'm torn in a million shreds. I need to find Ethan, but I want to hide. I want to run away, to throw up, to crawl into a hole, to scream, to cry. But most of all I want to find someone else to blame. But I am the only one around.

The campus is large. I know Ethan can't be found if he doesn't want to be. I walk to the theater arts building, check the parking lot near there, and return to my car. Ethan can get home by himself, but the sinking feeling in my gut immobilizes me. His outbursts are more familiar, although this is the first one in a public venue. His anger is like a racecar driver going from zero to one hundred miles per hour in five seconds.

A few weeks ago, I reminded him that summer was coming and he needed to think about summer school and getting a job if he wanted to visit his relatives in New York. He had such a wonderful time in the Big Apple last summer I figured he'd want to do it again.

"I'll pay for the air fare," I tell him at the end of dinner one night. "You'll be responsible for your spending money. I already spoke to Arlene and — "

"I don't want to go. What's wrong with you? You should ask before you go ahead and plan my life."

"Plan your life?"

"Go to summer school, get a job, go to New York? What do you call that?"

"Planning ahead. I suppose I should have discussed it with you before I spoke to Arlene, but that's what we're doing now. Or at least I am."

I get up from the table. There is chicken and salad left over to make lunch for the two of us.

"Do you have to yell every time you don't agree with something I've said or done?"

He pushes the chair away from the table. "Yeah, I do. You don't listen. I don't like New York. I don't like the picture-perfect family. I don't want anything to do with them."

———

I get into my car shaking my head. I'm confused and bewildered. I work with adolescents. I know what this stage is all about. And yet I'm not handling this well. When I arrive home, the house is dark and empty except for our dog, Phanny. Lately, The Phantom, so named because half her face is white and the other brown, is the only living being who is consistently happy to see me. Her long basset hound body shakes every which way as she jumps up and licks me. I turn on the lights and put down my things. I give Phanny a peanut butter dog biscuit and check the house. Even though Ethan's backpack isn't on the kitchen table and the radio isn't blasting, I hope he is holed up on his bed, safely in his room.

The phone rings as I close his door. I run into my room, hoping it's him, and find the phone underneath my bed mixed in with socks and slippers.

"You're finally home," Julia says. "Why so late?"

"I was at the high school meeting with some teachers. Good old Sam-o-hi."

"Everything okay?"

"Yeah, wonderful," I answer. "Look, I might have to cancel tonight. Ethan's not home and I want to wait for him."

"No problem. I'll come over and wait with you," she offers. "We'll go out after, have a drink and listen to some music. Sounds like you need it."

"I'm not sure. We had a fight. I don't know how he'll respond if you're here."

"Who cares? With these kids, you're damned if you do and damned if you don't."

I know that truth, but the sinking feeling this is more than normal teen-age rebellion, gnaws at me. Ethan's problems have to do with Jake and I can't keep burying my head in the sand. The mention of New York, the picture-perfect family, the Atticus report, all point to Jake. I have to do something more than hope it will go away.

"Okay Jules." I look at my watch. "I need to shower. Give me forty-five minutes, maybe Ethan will be home by then."

I hang up the phone and go into the bathroom. I undress and avoid the mirror. Why make myself more miserable? I know what I look like at the end of the day, a fifty-year-old slightly overweight, very tired woman. The hot water relaxes me and I let a passionate Latin fantasy take me over.

The Santa Monica Beach Hotel overlooks the Pacific Ocean and caters to business executives, celebrities, and occasionally President Clinton. Julia and I sit side-by-side in the lobby quietly people watching and listening to the jazz combo playing in the piano bar nearby. We always have fun when we have an evening out together. We watch elegantly dressed, perfectly coifed and bejeweled wives or mistresses on their way to dinners or trysts, and make up stories about them. But tonight is different.

I lean my head back and glance up at the five story high ceiling. Ethan left a message on the answering machine while I was in the shower.

"I don't want you to worry, Mom. I'm all right. I'm not ready to come home. But I will, by curfew, I promise." His sweet voice reminds me of my once little boy.

"Sorry," I say. "I'm not great company."

"Don't apologize. I'm happy. I can make believe I'm in Cannes or Positano, instead of Santa Monica with a sink full of dirty dishes and three loads of wash waiting for me."

I sit up straight and look at my friend, her long slender body folded comfortably into the gray overstuffed chair. "I wonder how many people in this room want to run away from their life?"

Julia lifts her head, her chin points at a young couple making love with their eyes. "Not them, at least not now. Wait until they have kids and a mortgage. That'll change things."

I laugh. "I have a list of things I want to do, places to travel."

"Like?"

"I want to go to the Galapagos. I want to ride in a hot air balloon across the Serengeti. I'll even parachute out of a plane if someone pushes me."

"I always imagine myself a pioneer woman," she says, with a wistful expression.

"You? A part of *Little House on the Prairie*?"

"And *Wagon Train*. I love those books, so exciting and romantic."

I shift in my chair. "The last time I did something exciting, Ethan was two years old." I sip my wine. "We were at Mount Rushmore and I decided I wanted to go on a helicopter ride. Danger be damned. I kissed Ethan, handed him to my cousin Ruth and off I went." I lean back and stare at the balcony above. "Haven't done anything like that since."

"Was it worth it?"

I squint, debating with myself. "The ride was amazing. We got so close to the faces I could have planted a kiss on Lincoln's cheek." I brush some hair out of my eye. "I almost lost my cookies, though. The pilot dodged and weaved to give us a thrill. But if something had happened to me and I left Ethan without a mother, obviously not." I cross and uncross my legs trying to settle myself.

"What about romantic?" she asks.

"What do you mean?"

"I said the books are exciting AND romantic?" She sips her wine. "You haven't mentioned Phil in a while."

"Bad segue. There's nothing to mention. It was nice while it lasted. It's better this way."

"I hope you know how empty and banal that sounds."

"But it is better. He doesn't need me and all that entails."

"He wasn't the one that walked away." She unfolds her legs and leans closer. "It got sticky so you got scared."

"No. Yes." I picture that first dinner with Ethan and Phil. "When Ethan came home from New York last summer, he wasn't nice to me and he definitely wasn't nice to Phil. He was snarky." The memory makes me anxious. "Phil raised two kids. He doesn't need to do it again."

"Why don't you let Phil decide? Maybe you're worth it and maybe Ethan needs to do things differently."

Why are all roads leading to Rome today? I wipe the crimson lipstick off my wine glass.

"Ethan's grades have dropped so we had a meeting at school this afternoon. I always expected him to be angry with me for doing what I did, having him with no father, but in my head, I'd always say and do the right thing that would make everything okay."

"You're taking all the blame?"

"I am to blame. If I didn't choose to be a single parent, Ethan wouldn't be suffering now."

Julia laughs. "In fact, Ethan wouldn't — "

"I know. He wouldn't be here. That's a depressing thought." I sigh and begin humming, then sing along with the piano player, "Change partners and dance with me." At that moment I want to be Ginger Rogers dancing with Fred Astaire.

"Have you thought about therapy?" she blurts out.

"What?"

"I know you, Maddy," she says gently. "I know you don't talk until you think you've figured things out, and I know you don't want to hear what I have to say." She pauses. "But I don't think you see what's going on, and if you do, you're kind of paralyzed. Ethan's different, has been for a long time, and it's affecting you. You're sad. I see it with you, and Katie sees it with Ethan."

I'm stunned. I thought I hid things so well. What did Julia and her perfect daughter see that required therapy, I want to ask, but I stop myself. I know the answer. "Therapy is not what I'm dying to do. Just so you know!"

Julia winces. She doesn't deserve that. Hurt and angry, my statement came out more harshly than I meant.

"I'm sorry." I rub my eyes forgetting my make-up. "Shit." I look at the black smudges on my fingers. "Is it all smeared?" I take out a mirror from my purse and try to clean off the streaks. I break the silence. "Therapy has crossed my mind a time or two. I keep thinking I'll get a handle on what's happening, on Ethan's behavior. But I'm not." I grasp the armrests. "I'm supposed to be the kind but tough teacher with all the answers for everyone else's kid." I shake my head. "It's not just school, it's the way he dresses. He looks like a wannabe gangster. He buys size forty pants. He's being devoured by his jeans."

Julia chuckles. "I have to hold myself back from yanking them down and embarrassing the hell out of him."

"Right. And then he tells me about his new friend Victor, from his computer class." I pause. "Lucky me, the whole family, his brother, Mac, his mom and sister, they live a few blocks away from us."

"Why's that a problem?"

"They scare me. They have different values. I think the father belongs to some kind of mafia group back East," I whisper. "And the mom's on disability, but there's nothing wrong with her. Ethan says they fight a lot, even break things in the house. It's a one-eighty from us." I sip my wine. "I don't want to tell him he can't be with these people. You know, forbidden fruit. And yet I don't want to give my approval."

"Do you think he's using drugs?"

"I don't think so." I frown. "I check his eyes and smell his clothes for pot. But I haven't taken to going through his things, yet." My body sags. "I want to trust him, Julia. I want to trust myself."

"But you're not trusting either of you." She touches my arm. "Professional help might sort things out, Maddy. With Ethan and with Phil."

"You kinda just snuck him in there." I smile.

"Phil's a really good guy, Madd. Just think about it. Seriously."

"Ugh, God." I close my eyes and see myself as a child sucking my thumb, huddled in the windowsill. I picture that imaginary locked box I told Beth I would hide in an imaginary closet in my brain. I hear her admonish me, warn me that Anthony, my father, and Jake had a huge impact on me and I'd better deal with it. I shudder.

"I don't want to open myself up to all that stuff.'"

"But look at you. You're in the middle of it all. And you're dealing with it alone. Greg and I might be divorced, but he loves Katie and we work on whatever together. But you're it. That's harder for you and for Ethan."

Julia's right. And from our telephone conversations, Beth knows it too. I know my ostrich approach isn't working.

"I have a friend who's getting her PhD in psychology," Julia says. "I'll ask if she knows someone. Get some advice, Maddy. It doesn't have to be a long term thing."

"Right! Who're you kidding?" I smile at my friend then look at my watch. "Do you mind if we leave?" I know I have to get a handle on Ethan, on me. I can't pretend anymore.

Julia finishes her drink and we walk out of the hotel into the cool winter night.

Back home, I keep glancing from the television to the clock. Before bed every night, I watch the news at eleven. Tonight there's a shootout in a McDonald's in Carson, a carjacking near USC, and an attempted kidnapping of a Venice girl on her way home from the beach. Ethan is fifteen minutes late. I sit in bed with the same sinking feeling I've had all day. The dog stirs and perks up her ears. I listen, but when Phanny settles down, I know it isn't Ethan.

"Where is he, Phanny? Why doesn't he come home?" I scratch Phanny's long, silky ears. "I hate this." I walk through the dimly lit apartment into the kitchen. I open the refrigerator and look inside. I touch the Swiss cheese, shuffle the bread and a container of milk, toss out some overly ripe tomatoes and close the door.

As I meander my way back across the blue carpet to my bedroom, I hear Ethan walk up the path. Phanny does too. She comes running from my room. I let out a big breath through my mouth the way I learned in yoga class and open the door right before he knocks.

"What? Are you laying in wait for me? What's with you?" Ethan pushes past me, and bends down to pet the dog. My stomach twists. I thought his sweet message earlier meant we would avoid this.

"Nothing's with me. You were supposed to be home at eleven and you're late. I worry about you."

"That's your problem. It's Friday night and it's only eleven-twenty. You're acting like a bitch, you know that?"

My head snaps back like he just landed a punch in the middle of my face.

"Don't speak to me that way, Ethan. It's not acceptable."

"What's wrong with it? It's in the dictionary."

"There are a lot of things in the dictionary. I don't like it. I don't speak to you that way."

"I don't like it when you start yelling at me as soon as I get in the house. What do you do, write a list of things I do wrong so you can hit me with them as soon as I get in the door? I'm only twenty minutes late."

"I don't like you out alone, walking home from Victor's or wherever."

"For crying out loud, Maddy, it's only a few blocks away."

I know he is calling me Maddy to make me angrier. I'm not going to bite. "I know, but it's dangerous."

"It's not the barrio, Mom. The drive-bys don't happen on this block."

"That isn't the point. Twenty minutes late is late."

He rolls his fifteen-year-old eyes toward the ceiling. "Anything else?"

"Yes, actually, you didn't take your keys." I hold them out to him.

"I couldn't find them." He grabs them out of my hand. "So what? You were home."

"But what if I wasn't? What if I went out?"

"I'd wait." He grits his teeth. "You see what I mean? You've got this list."

"Start doing what you're supposed to do and my list will get shorter."

I think about what I'd told Julia earlier in the evening about checking his eyes for drugs, but I don't want to stare and give him another thing to go off on. He throws up his hands and walks away from me. I don't like being dismissed so I follow him. He is taller and his broad back means he is stronger too. He stops in the hallway in front of his bedroom and faces me.

"Why don't you look at what I do that's good? You're always nagging and telling me what's wrong with me. You have no idea what I could be doing. I don't steal or lie. I don't," his voice drops away, "do drugs."

"And I'm really glad. But you're not being responsible. You tell me you'll do things and then you don't. We're a family, Ethan, and I need you to — "

"We are NOT a family." He enunciates each word. "We. Are. You. And. Me."

I take a step backward but feel cornered. "We are a family, Ethan. I work very hard to make us one."

"You're not succeeding. Just get off my back."

"I will when you do what you're supposed to do."

He glares at me, then whirls around and slams his bedroom door. The full-length mirror on the outside rattles. One of the plastic holders falls off. He has slammed his door so many times with such force that I am constantly repositioning the holders. Six or seven holes frame the mirror from the old screws.

I take a deep breath and look at my pale, lined reflection. Vacant green eyes stare back at me. This is not the way it's supposed to be. I open Ethan's door and enter. The lights are out, but I can see him curled up on his bed. I force my jaw to relax. Whatever is wrong, I want to fix it. I sit on his blue and red duvet and touch his leg. He recoils.

"Ethan, what is going on? This isn't like you."

"You have no idea what I'm like." He turns over on his back. "I'm sixteen and I don't need you in my face, telling me anything. IT'S MY LIFE."

I've had enough. I stand and look at my son.

"NO, IT IS NOT. You are almost sixteen. You aren't eighteen. You are nowhere near being on your own." I take a breath. "You are out of control and there are consequences for your behavior." I muster as much strength as I can. "Right now I am tired. We'll finish this in the morning."

I walk out of his room and close the door. The mirror rattles. Ethan is not the only one spinning out of control. My loneliness wells up inside of me with a force I haven't experienced for a long time. I grope through the darkness to my room, lie down on top of my bed, and cry.

I toss around most of the night like I'm in a clothes dryer. When I wake up, my head pounds to a syncopated drumbeat. I take two aspirin. Avoiding the bathroom mirror, I don't bother to brush my teeth. I'm afraid to see my swollen red eyelids and the puffy bags underneath them. I sit at a picnic table on the patio with my sunglasses, the newspaper, a pad and pencil, and a cup of strawberry tea.

It is one of those quiet, balmy, mid-winter mornings. The kind that appear each New Year's Day for the Rose Parade when everyone in the nation has their eyes on Southern California and wish they lived here. The sky is blue, the swaying palm trees tower over the buildings, and the sun warms the air somewhere between seventy and eighty degrees.

I think about what Ethan said last night. Am I too critical? Always ready to pounce on him? But he is out of control and my job is to stop him and help him make the right choices. I'm on a seesaw, either up in the air or down on the ground, never in balance.

I pick up the pencil and move the pad closer. I want to be organized. The irony of making a list doesn't elude me, but I want to be ready for him in a calm way.

The window of his bedroom faces the patio. When I hear him cough and go into the bathroom, my stomach muscles tighten and the concept of fight or flight crosses my mind. I stay put. It's getting warm so I take off my sweater and sit in the white plastic chair placing both feet on the ground to center myself. I pick up the sports section of the *Los Angeles Times*, but my attempt to read is half-hearted.

Ethan comes out to the patio and sits down at the table. I look up. He shields his bloodshot, swollen eyes from the sun with both hands. It's like staring at my own image, the one I avoided in the bathroom.

"What are you reading?" he asks.

"An interview with Michael Jordan."

"What's it about?"

"His amazing comeback and how hard he worked. You certainly knew who to pick to emulate.

"Maybe I should read it when you're finished."

"Ok."

We sit quietly. Am I dealing with Dr. Jekyll or Mr. Hyde? Is he experimenting with drugs? The lights in the apartment were so dim last night I couldn't have checked his eyes even if I wanted to.

"I'm worried about you."

"I know."

"You've been so angry lately. What's going on?"

"Nothing," he says, with a touch of defiance.

"It can't be nothing. Your grades are bad and — "

"Not all of them."

"Right, not all of them. The good ones aren't what got us called into Mrs. Castenada's office yesterday."

"I'll make up the work and bring up my grades."

"Yes, you will. You're not going out of this house until you do."

"What do you mean? You can't do that, Mom. It's the weekend. I'm going to a party tonight."

"Whose party?"

"Uh, a friend of Victor's. It's this girl's birthday."

I shake my head. "You're going to work on your English essay and any other missing schoolwork you have to make up. And most of it will get turned in on Monday." I pause and sip my tea. "I don't like you hanging out with Victor and Mac. There's no supervision. Their mother sounds like she has no control over them."

"You can't do that. They're my friends. All we do is listen to music. Nothing bad."

"Are you doing drugs, Ethan?"

"No!" He shoots out of his chair like a missile. "Why are you asking me that?"

"Your eyes are bloodshot and your behavior is weird."

"Well, I'm not. Are you?"

"What?"

"Isn't that why you're wearing your sunglasses? Aren't your eyes bloodshot?"

"Cute, Ethan."

He sits back down and leans closer to me. "Look, Mom, I'm sorry about my grades and I'm sorry I yelled at you. I'll get my work done and I'll stop exploding. I was embarrassed yesterday and I blamed you. It's not your fault — I know that. I promise to do better."

I want to believe him. I study his face. Everyone says he looks just like me only with black hair. But his green eyes are darker than mine and he has a much squarer jaw. He does have the Gold button nose though. My mother used to lament that his soft baby cheeks would someday be covered with whiskers. That's just beginning to happen. I plan to get him an electric razor for one of his birthday presents.

"Ethan, do your moods have anything to do with your father?"

"My father? I don't have a father."

"Okay, Jake. Does this have anything to do with him? Or are you just angry with me?" I feel my tears sting and my throat tighten.

"Huh?"

"Last night you said we weren't a family. That I'm not successful at making us a family. Do you blame me for Jake not being around?"

"God Mom, he's a jerk. I don't want him around. I just said that last night. Don't take it so seriously. I told you, I'll do better."

"It's more than that."

He picks up my pencil and fiddles with it. I look at the pink, purple and white impatiens plants that line the fence around the patio. The plants are delicate but hardy.

"I was angry, Mom. It won't happen again. I promise." He comes around to my side of the table. He takes my hand and gently tugs at me. "I'm starving. How about if you make me some potatoes and eggs and I'll start my homework? I can get a lot done today and I'll finish the rest tomorrow. There's not that much."

I shake my head with a smile on my face. "You're still not going to the party tonight."

"Will you at least think about it? Please." His grin could con a grifter.

I kiss his soft, whiskerless cheek. "We'll see."

———

On Friday, I'm wiped-out from three contentious days at school. My students can't fathom or control the spurts of testosterone and estrogen in their maturing bodies, so emotions in my classroom are volatile. Kids poke each other behind my back and call one another "stupid" and worse. Two boys threaten lunchtime and after school retaliation. I need a whistle or a bell to short circuit potential melees. We have several circle discussions to calm things down and bring order back into the classroom.

Ethan has made up all his assignments and his behavior is thoughtful and respectful. Dinners include interesting discussions on politics and race relations in America. He tells me about a girl he likes in his Spanish class. Can I trust him or is he snowing me?

I go to sleep early with a promise from Ethan that he'll be home by midnight. The phone rings, jarring me awake from a deep sleep. My heart races. I glance at the clock. 12:25 am. Groggy, I pick up the receiver.

"No Officer, Ethan should be asleep in his room. Hold on, I'll check."

Ethan isn't in his room. When I talk to the officer he explains Ethan has been picked up a block away from our apartment. They are holding him at the Santa Monica Police Station. The officer suggests I come to the station immediately.

I hang up, stunned. Before getting dressed, I call the one person who can help me. I don't hesitate, although I suppose I should have. Phil doesn't hesitate either, although I suppose he could have.

My apartment is the last one before the carport and alley. Phil always picks me up and drops me off there. I lean against my car and wait for him. The overhead light bulb makes me feel safe. I wrap my lime green woolen jacket around me. Headlights light up the alley. I turn to my right as a car stops. Phil looks out the open window and reaches for my hand.

"It's good to see you." He smiles reassuringly. "You look scared and tired. It'll be all right, Maddy. I promise."

I want to believe him. If anyone can sort through Ethan's arrest, it's Phil. He's an expert in criminal law. I squeeze his hand and walk around the back of the car.

"Is it yours?" I buckle myself into the BMW. It has that new car smell.

"New toy. The firm is paying for the lease. It's been a good four months. Lots of acquittals."

"I'm sorry — "

"Don't say it. You don't have to apologize for the hour or the reason. I told you I'd be there for you anytime."

I nod.

As he drives to the police station, I glance at the perfect patrician profile of the silver haired man I'd fallen in love with last summer. Julia's right. Once Ethan came home from New York, I got scared and bolted.

The car hits a speed bump and then we pull into the parking lot behind the Santa Monica Police Department. Phil finds a space near the entrance. I turn toward him and put on a brave face.

"What are you thinking about?" he asks. "You look a million miles away."

"Oil changes and crossword puzzles."

"That's a good sign." He touches my knee. "When we get inside, I'll handle everything. I want to find out who brought him in, and why. I'll see if any of the cops I know are on duty. I'm hoping they're just trying to scare him and they'll be successful."

"You know he's not going to be happy to see you."

"You're still worried about what Ethan thinks or wants?" His anger at me, at Ethan, at what caused our break up four months ago, surges from just below the surface. He stares at me shaking his head. "Right now he wants me, needs me."

I don't know what to say. We walk down the corridor in silence to the sergeant's desk. Colors, patterns, designs blur. It all feels surreal, each step mired in quicksand.

I sit in a chair. Phil shakes hands with the sergeant and disappears into another room. The officer I spoke to at home mentioned drugs. Drugs? Why am I in such denial? I cover my mouth. I want to throw up. Questions bounce around in my head. Can Phil really handle this and make it go away? Can I handle it? Will I have to face the police too? I shudder. I calm myself by breathing slowly and deeply, staring at the clock that seems as stuck as I am.

I become intimately acquainted with the waiting room of the police station. I pace, sit, count floor tiles and pace some more. I walk in and out of the cool night air because I can. Eventually, I hear voices from behind the door. I stand as the door opens and Ethan and Phil enter the waiting room. They look grim. Ethan focuses on the floor when he sees me. I glance at Phil. There isn't much communication. A few words of acknowledgment, a nod of his head, and a hand in the small of my back to guide me out of the station. No mention of my needing to talk to any officers.

The three of us get into Phil's car. Ethan sits in the back. The soft churning of the engine and the defroster are the only sounds on the way home. No conversation, no music. Proof of breathing comes only from the condensation on the windows. I accept the silence and am willing to hear the details of this nightmare later. Phil's car approaches my carport and stops. Ethan opens the rear door.

"Not so fast," Phil says. He looks at Ethan through the rearview mirror. "You got off easy this time, partly because of me, partly because they didn't have a solid reason to hold you. But from what they told me about your friends Victor and Mac, and the activities they're involved in, that won't be true the next time."

I stare at Phil. What is he alluding to? I look at Ethan in the back seat. He is half in, half out of the car.

"But I didn't do anything."

"That's mistake number two. If all my clients who said 'I didn't do anything' really didn't do anything, I'd be out of business. Most of them started out like you Ethan, doing punk-ass, stupid things and getting away with it. The getting away with it is the problem. It allows them to graduate to bigger and less punk-ass things and then they need someone like me. This is your first and last chance. Keep hanging around with guys who steal, smoke dope and drink, and you'll graduate too. Only your mother won't be able to afford me."

Phil and Ethan stare at each other.

"Can I go now?" Ethan asks.

"Ethan!" I exclaim.

"It's okay," Phil puts his hand on my shoulder. "I don't have anything more to say."

"Well, I do." I turn to my son. "I'll meet you in your room in a few minutes."

Ethan bolts out of the car and slams the door.

I run my fingers through my hair. "What exactly did the police say?"

"They'd been patrolling the neighborhood looking for some kids who were breaking into cars. Ethan fit the description, dressed like that, so when they saw him stumbling down the street, they stopped him. The marijuana and stolen CDs in his backpack didn't help. Coincidentally, another patrol car picked up his friends who just happened to be the ones stealing the radios and CDs. It must have been an interesting reunion at the police station." Phil shakes his head, a look of disbelief on his face. "The boys admitted to putting the roach and CDs in Ethan's backpack." He rubs his chin. "After all, what are friends for?" He pauses. "Anyway, the police know Ethan wasn't a part of that, but they're aware of him now and have warned him."

I close my eyes and grab my abdomen. "I don't know what I'm going to do. I don't know this person. And I don't like him."

"Maybe you should wait until tomorrow to talk to him. You'll be calmer and things might be clearer."

"I don't want to be calmer." I lean over and kiss Phil on the cheek. "Thank you. I wish seeing you was for a different reason."

I turn to open the door and get out of the car. Phil gently pulls on my arm. He cups my face in his hands and lightly caresses my cheeks. "We can see each other through this, Maddy. You don't have to go it alone."

"I've always done it alone. I don't know any other way." I stare at his face and into his inviting eyes. "I'll try. I'll think about it. I'll call." I kiss him lightly on the lips and get out of the car.

I open Ethan's door without knocking and turn on the light. He is under the covers with Phanny at the foot of his bed, body and tail in full wiggle motion. I used to tell Ethan bedtime stories about a superhero dog who could turn herself into a helicopter and save the day. I pat the real dog and kiss her nose. She settles back down.

"Don't start," he says. "I smoked a joint while we were hanging out, but I didn't put any of their stuff in my backpack. And I didn't steal anything." He sits up. "Those cops had no right to stop me. I would have been home by midnight like I promised."

I pull the desk chair around and sit closer to his bed. I look at the planet and star stickers on the ceiling, then at the five Michael Jordan posters on the wall. Ethan's old, worn red shorts and T-shirts peek out from under his bed. This used to be a typical room for a typical boy, but nothing feels typical now.

I turn to my son. "Here's how things are going to change. First of all, I don't trust you. You'll have to earn that back. Second, you will not hang out with Victor and Mac anymore. Third, you're going to get a job after school and on the weekends or you'll join some after school clubs to occupy your time. Fourth, you will bring up your grades by the end of the semester if you ever plan to have a social life outside of this house again. And finally, you're going into therapy, or I'm going into therapy, or we both are. We are going to work through this. I'm not letting you screw up your life."

"You already have!" he screams. When he tries to put his feet on the ground they are tangled in his blankets. Phanny gets caught in the fray. She yelps and jumps down. He reaches over and pets her. He looks at me with rage in his eyes. "What makes you think I'll do any of those things?" His jaw pulsates as he towers over me. "You can't make me get a job or join a club. You can't keep me away from my friends." He steps back.

"You're right. I can't make you. But let me explain something to you, Ethan. You see this room? This apartment? All the things you have, all the choices and opportunities. You have them because I give them to you. But you are about to blow it. Phil wasn't kidding tonight."

"This is a ridiculous conversation."

"Maybe, but humor me. Whatever you're angry at, you're dealing with it in the wrong way. If you continue to get into trouble, if you continue to make bad decisions for yourself, you will land in jail. You will successfully have hurt yourself, and me. I'll still love you. I'll visit and bring you things, but . . . " I stop, picturing a juvie visitor center in my head. "But, you know what? After I cry, and you know I will, I get to go home. I get to call my friends and be comforted by them. I get to choose where to go for dinner, which movie I want to see, when I take a hot shower. And you'll be locked up in jail being told what to eat and when, where and how long to be outside, when to read, when to sleep. Ultimately, who will be hurt more, you or me?" I stand up not waiting for an answer. "You'll look for a job tomorrow. Be up by nine."

I turn off his light and go to my room. I climb into bed and position the red corduroy pillow against the brass headboard so I can sit comfortably. Adrenaline pumps through my system, but I refuse to toss and turn because of it.

My concerns for Ethan are foremost on my mind, but seeing Phil, being with him, relying on him, brings in a secondary consciousness. I cuddle a pillow across my body. I wish things were different for us. I wish I was different for us.

I settle back into the cushion. Phanny's metal collar clinks as she makes her way to my room. She jumps up on the foot of my bed, walks forward, and pushes her nose against the covers, ordering me to lift them. When I comply, she slides underneath lying against my legs, and goes to sleep.

10

SANTA MONICA

Winter 1996

I **spend sleepless nights worrying about Ethan.** I toss in bed, obsessing about his arrest, his trouble at school, his friends, and his explosive behavior with me. When I nod off in the middle of an after school teachers' meeting, and my friend has to kick me under the table to wake me, I know I'm a mess. I'm not taking care of my son, or my job, or myself. A neon THERAPY sign blinks in my brain. Who in their right mind wants to explore their failures? Who in their right mind wants to dig down deep and bring up things that are best kept buried? But I cave. I need help.

I walk down the street in my own world ignoring most of the sights and sounds around me, until the salmon-color office building on San Vicente Boulevard in Brentwood looms before me. I ride the elevator to the second floor office to consult with therapist number three, the other two were not the right fit.

I flip through the pages of an old *People* magazine. I hear my name and look up. An attractive middle-age woman elegantly dressed in a dark blue, tailored linen pantsuit with a red silk shell, stands in front of me. She wears silver chains around her neck and bracelets around her wrists. A large diamond engagement ring sparkles on her left hand. I've always wanted one like that, a Tiffany setting with a round stone and diamond baguettes on either side. A symbol of someone's love.

"I'm Carol Russell."

I stand and we shake hands.

"My office is the first door on the left." Carol points the way.

We sit facing each other. I check out the couch, the overstuffed chair I'm in and the ergonomically correct therapist's black leather chair that rolls between the patient and her desk. Framed diplomas hang on the wall near the door. Two vases brimming with sunflowers and huge purple spider mums brighten the room.

I wonder where to begin. Carol makes it easy.

"You were referred by Teri Hauser, right?"

"Teri knows my friend Julia. I wanted a woman therapist who has children, specifically teenagers. Do you have any of those?"

Carol smiles. "I have four children. Two of them are teens."

"Boys?"

"No. The girls are the teens."

"Four children, two teenagers, and you're still walking and talking?"

Carol laughs. "It is a challenge. Is that why you're here?"

I nod and settle back in my chair. "Ethan is my almost sixteen-year-old son. He's having trouble at school, has bad friends, and last week he was picked up by the police, although he wasn't charged with anything. His friends set him up."

"Are you the main disciplinarian in the house?"

I'm sure Carol has checked out my left ring finger. "I'm the only one. I'm a single parent, by choice. Ethan doesn't know his father."

I listen closely to Carol's tone and inflection, ready to be on my way to the next consultation if there is anything critical or judgmental in her voice.

"You decided to have a child on your own?"

"Yes."

"That must have been a difficult decision."

My jaw relaxes. I tell her about Jake and my promise that I would raise Ethan by myself. I take a sip from my water bottle.

"You never felt that marriage was an option for you?"

I lean back, close my eyes and fold my hands on top of my head wanting to keep everything together, inside. I see Phil on the night of Ethan's arrest, leaning over and kissing me on the cheek.

"I'm here about my son. Not to open up all this old crap again." The power behind the word crap surprises me. I'm embarrassed. "Suffice it to say, no, I never felt marriage was an option for me."

"This is painful for you," Carol says gently.

I nod. "I'll do it if it's relevant to what's going on with me and Ethan, but I don't have to like it."

"You have a lot of feelings on this subject that you may want to explore. Perhaps not now, but in the future." She pauses and lets things settle. "How has it been for Ethan growing up without a father?"

I cover my mouth and take a deep breath. Air puffs out between my fingers. "Ethan began talking when he was nine months old. By the time he was two, he wondered who his father was and why he wasn't there."

"What did you tell him?"

"I tried answering him in age appropriate ways. I told him how much I wanted him, how happy I was that he was in my life, and that his father lived far away and was busy. But he felt rejected and I never found the words to take away that hurt." I gulp and hold back my tears.

"Did you think about contacting his father?"

"What would be the point? You can't demand interest, or love. Ethan would really have had to deal with this man's rejection."

"Don't you think he's feeling the rejection now?"

"Jake rejected me and the idea of another child. It wasn't Ethan."

"I suspect it's very hard to separate the two. What does Ethan have to say about his father?"

"When I ask him, he brushes me off. It's like his father doesn't exist in his life, which he doesn't, so why talk about it?"

"Talking about this makes you angry." She leans forward in her chair. "Tell me what you and Ethan fight about?"

I describe the fight we had after the meeting with his school counselor and his English teacher, his coming home late, slamming doors, cursing at me.

"What consequences did you give him?"

I look out the window then back at her. "I didn't that night. I was upset and tired. I couldn't think of any consequences in the moment. Then in the morning, even though I grounded him and said he couldn't go to a party . . . " My voice drops off. I feel the heat in my cheeks. "When he apologized, and made up some of his schoolwork, I let him go and hoped it wouldn't happen again." I thought of his arrest. "I was wrong."

"So you have this list of troubling things he's doing and he keeps doing them." Carol tilts her head and her long silver hair falls on her shoulder. She raises an eyebrow. "Anything wrong with this picture?"

"I know, but I always feel like the bad one."

"Why is that?"

"We're fighting all the time. It's hard to find things that are good. That's not why I had him." I shift in my chair trying to find a comfortable position. "It started after he got back from New York last summer. We were meeting my cousin for dinner. She was late. We waited outside the restaurant. Ethan sat on a bench by the bus stop and I sat next to him. Without looking at me he muttered, 'Move. I don't want you sitting near me.' I thought he was kidding. So I slid to the other end of the bench and yodeled at him." I smiled at the memory. "I thought it was funny. He was furious."

"What's that like for you?"

"I've worked with teenagers my whole life. I believed I knew what to expect and how to handle their not yet ready for prime time brains."

Carol laughs. "They weren't your teens. No parent escapes their kid's raging hormones. Having said that, you're not helping Ethan by letting him be rude, and allowing behavior that isn't acceptable."

"I know. I'm so tired of fighting. It's easier to make peace when I can."

"No it's not, Maddy. If you start expecting Ethan to do things and stick to your consequences when he doesn't, your job will be easier."

I look at the bold sunflowers standing tall in their blue porcelain vase. "I get turned inside out when I deal with him. He keeps apologizing, promising he'll change, and I want to believe him. The morning after the school meeting, I made him his favorite breakfast while he did his schoolwork. Later, when he showed me the essay he'd written, I was effusive in my praise."

"Why?"

"What do you mean? Positive reinforcement."

"You used the word effusive. He was doing what he should have done weeks earlier."

"But he did a good job. He had to write an essay comparing and contrasting Atticus Finch in *To Kill a Mockingbird*, to his own father. Writing that essay would have been painful. That's why he didn't do it. He ended up substituting my friend Roger for his father, and he nailed it."

"And you felt sorry for him."

"Yes." Tears drop down my cheeks onto my blouse. I cross my foot on top of my knee and twirl the shoelace on my sneaker. I let it go and watch it spin.

"He gets failing grades, comes home late and fights with you, then you reward him? What happened to your resolve to ground him?"

I feel like a jerk. "I know, I know, I shouldn't have let him go to the birthday party that night. But he did keep his promise to finish all his homework on Sunday."

"And the next week he got picked up by the police."

"All right, I get it." I lean back and cross my arms.

"Probably not yet." Carol smiles and shakes her head. "It'll take time for both of you to get it. You've been doing this with him for a long time."

I flash on Ethan's new weekend job as a gopher at a business supply store, and the acting club he joined after school. I want to tell Carol to prove she's wrong about me, but she isn't.

"We can talk more about this next week, if you'd like to work with me." She looks at her watch.

I can't believe fifty-minutes are up. Carol isn't going to back away from things I don't want to deal with. It is both scary and comforting. I feel less alone.

"That went fast. It's hard knowing the right thing to do."

"Being a parent is a difficult job."

I pick up my purse. We walk to the door.

"Remember, it gets easier with consequences."

————

It is late afternoon when I leave Carol's office. Things seem so bleak lately that it's lovely to acknowledge the existence of sunshine. I've found someone to work with, to help me with Ethan. Life can be good again. I think of Ethan as a baby, as a young boy. As difficult as it was raising a little one on my own, there were major payoffs. Ethan was a trusting, loving soul who thought I was terrific. He'd run for me when I picked him up from pre-school and kindergarten squealing, "Mommy, Mommy." He'd jump in my arms with an infectious giggle, and wrap his body around me as though he hadn't seen me in a very long time. Then we'd sing silly songs as we drove on errands or adventures. I miss those times.

Thinking of Ethan as a baby reminds me of my parents. I miss them too. In the last years of my parents' lives, we made our peace with each other. Being a parent myself, I learned how hard it is, that everyone does their best. Having Ethan gave us all a common bond. My parents fell in love with their grandson. They doted on him during every visit to Florida and they gave me a much-needed respite from being a full-time, working, single parent. When Ethan was only ten, my father died of a heart attack. My mother died shortly after from cancer. It was a sad time.

The foot traffic on San Vicente Boulevard is busy and noisy. Groups of teens eat ice cream and chat as they stroll along. Outdoor cafes serve customers their late afternoon pick-me-ups to get them through the rest of the day. I walk quickly to my car but I don't want to go to my apartment yet. It's four o'clock and I have until six when Ethan gets home. In spite of some residual sadness from the session with Carol, I feel a resurgence of energy bubbling inside of me. What I want to do is to climb into a red BMW convertible, speed north on the Pacific Coast Highway, with long, straight blonde hair blowing behind me. I settle for my blue Toyota station wagon, my short, curly red hair, and drive within the speed limit, toward the beach.

I park the car and unlock the back of the wagon. I dig through piles of Ethan's sporting equipment, my books and teaching tools, and find my aluminum beach chair. The green and white nylon webbing is shredding from sitting at Ethan's soccer, baseball, and tennis events. I'd been there for every game. Ethan could look over and find me cheering, or screaming, whether he was five years old or fifteen.

The sun is setting as I find a peaceful spot on the beach. The water laps its way onto the shore. A few people play in the waves. The clouds and the sun are hypnotic. I let cool sand filter through my fingers.

I reach up and stretch my arms. My backbone pops and readjusts. I study other people nearby. I'm the only one alone. A couple walks away from me on the beach. Something about the man reminds me of Phil so I lean forward to get a better look. Maybe it's the way his Bermuda shorts hug his behind, or maybe it's the way he holds the woman's hand and swings it toward the sky. Maybe it's a desire to recapture what I threw away.

The wind blows off the ocean again. Where are Phil's arms now? I look around the beach. I've been in such a faraway place that present time doesn't exist. It's getting dark. I check my watch. Five-thirty. I have to get home. I gather my things and hurry to the car.

Maybe I'll call Phil tonight. Maybe I'll be brave enough to open the door I shut five months ago.

I'm late getting home from the beach. Walking to the apartment, I hear Phanny howling as if she's in pain and find Ethan on our doorstep.

"I forgot my keys," he says, moving to the side so I can open the door.

Phanny jumps on both of us as we walk inside. Ethan pets her.

"And don't get angry. I've been waiting for forty-five minutes listening to her cry. That's punishment enough."

"Why don't you find your keys and leave them by the door." I put my purse and books down on one end of the dining room table. "If you do that automatically, you'll always know where they are." I keep the 'how many times have I told you that' from my voice. I don't want a battle. A quiet, serene evening will do fine.

"Yes, Ma'am." He salutes and clicks his heels. "Are you making dinner? I'm starved."

My shoulders relax. "You make the salad and set the table. I'll make the spaghetti."

"Ok. Let me find my keys." He walks to his room with Phanny bounding behind him.

I'm not sure who I'm dealing with, the easygoing Ethan or the one with the short fuse, although things have been calmer since his run-in with the police. Ethan comes back into the kitchen humming and kisses me.

"You're happy. Did you have a good day?"

"I did." He takes some vegetables out of the refrigerator. "My health class was great and then a bunch of us rapped after school."

I look at him.

"Don't worry, Victor wasn't there. He's not around much anymore. I was with some other guys. Ones you'd like." He grabs a stalk of celery and holds it like a microphone. His body dances to a rhythm he creates.

"Yo, my man, listen to my plan. There ain't a rappa fina, from here to Carolina, in any local dina or that rockin' boat to China."

"If you have a day job, kid, I suggest you keep it." I giggle.

"No, Mom, really." His face radiates joy and enthusiasm. "I'm telling you, I'm going to make it and take care of you."

"Take care of yourself and I'll be happy."

"I know you don't believe me, but it will happen." He takes a bite of the celery. "And what'd you do today?" He walks to the dining room table taking the vegetables and a bowl with him.

I decide to tell him. "I had an appointment with a therapist and then I went to the beach for an hour."

"What'd she say about me?"

"How interesting that's your first question."

"Well you went because of me, right?"

I stare at him. "Mostly true. She asked how you felt about Jake."

"What should I feel about him?" He stops tearing the lettuce. The cutting board is filled with sliced cucumbers and quartered tomatoes.

"Maybe he's playing a part in your life even though he's not around."

"Part. No part. We're apart. Who needs him?"

"Maybe you do? Maybe you want to know more about him?"

"I know all there is to know about him. He didn't want to know me and now I don't want to know him. And, I don't want to talk about it." He dumps the veggies into the salad bowl, pushes it toward the middle of the table and shoves back his chair. I'm sure he dug two more grooves into the already marred parquet floor. "The salad's finished. I'm going to watch television. I'll set the table when dinner's ready."

"That shut me up," I mumble as he walks away. I sprinkle fresh garlic and basil into the tomato sauce and stir.

Ethan's reaction reminds me of when he was five. He'd asked so many questions about his father, I consulted a child psychologist. She suggested the best age to let Ethan make contact with his father was nine. So the next time he asked, I told him, "When you're nine." After that he never asked again until the fateful day four years later. I had picked him up from school and we went to the Brentwood Mart to get a snack. The mart, a barn like structure, was our favorite place. There were lots of different shops inside and an eating area outside surrounded by various fast food counters. We sat on a bench near the big fire pit. While Ethan ate his hamburger, I stole his fries, one by one. A special mother and son moment. The mart was filled with people, talking, laughing, reading books and newspapers. I pointed at the sign hanging across the stationery store announcing the coming of Father's Day. I thought of the card Ethan needed to get for my father.

"I can write to my father now. I'm nine." Ethan stated, simply and directly.

"Yes, you are." I spoke slowly, searching for the right words, any words. "You never talk about him, ask questions, but I guess you've been thinking about this."

"You told me nine and I'm nine. I want to buy a Father's Day card."

"Okay. When you're finished eating we'll do that. You need to get one for Grandpa too." My stomach gurgled. One fry at a time was no longer enough. I wanted my own. Stuffing down feelings was my way of coping, and we were about to open a can of worms, swirl around a kettle of fish, and dig into a jar of sour pickles. What would Jake do? Think only of himself? Hurt Ethan? I swallowed, but refrained from getting more fries.

Finding the right card for his grandfather had been a cinch, but the other one was hard. There were lots of cards professing love and gratitude, but no cards for estranged fathers. We searched the card racks. Ethan finally chose a Garfield postcard having nothing to do with Father's Day. It showed Garfield looking into an empty mailbox thinking, "Waiting to hear from you."

Three days later, he was ready to send the card. We sat in the car in front of a mailbox near our old apartment. The postcard was written in Ethan's innocent nine-year-old hand.

Dear Dad,
This is Ethan just saying hello. Please write back.
Love,
Ethan

I'd made him address it himself and was going to make him mail it himself. This had to be his and it was killing me. I cried, but only when I was alone. I was so proud of him and hurt so much for him.

"E, I know we've talked about this a lot, but Jake might not answer." I touched his arm. "I don't want you to be hurt or blame yourself."

"Mom, it's okay. I can handle it. I know he might not answer. I want to do it."

I leaned back against the headrest, holding back a sigh. "Okay," I said. "Go to it!"

At my command, he jumped out of the car and took an enormous leap toward growing up. I watched him pull down the mail slot and let go of the postcard. A sharp pain pierced my abdomen. It was a slice into my still attached umbilical cord.

Every day, Ethan ran to the mailbox after school. For two weeks, I watched him swallow his smile, then lose his joy. I didn't know what to do, how to help him. When I tried to talk about Jake, he refused and over time I stopped bringing it up. Until now, and he still won't talk about it.

After stirring the spaghetti, I drain it through a colander and lean away from the hot steam. Like the pasta, issues boil up inside of me, sloshing around with Carol, ready to be drained. Maybe I'm ready to make some new choices for Ethan and myself.

I call Ethan for dinner. Later, I will call Phil. I sent him a thank you gift for helping me get Ethan out of trouble. Now I want his help to move us forward, if he's still willing. With my history and trust issues, I'm asking a lot.

After dinner, when the dishes are done and Ethan is settled in the den watching television, I make the call. My heart pounds and my temples throb as I punch in Phil's number. He picks up immediately and we exchange polite phone etiquette. I take a deep breath.

"I refrained from calling you," he says. "You promised to call, so I waited."

"You're a patient man. I wanted to get some things straightened out."

"Did you?"

"Somewhat." I roll a breadcrumb around on the tablecloth. "I made a beginning. Ethan is grounded and isn't complaining. He can't see those boys anymore. He got a part-time job on the weekends so he has to be up and out by six Saturdays and Sundays. And he joined an after-school acting club on campus. Oh, and he's bringing up his grades."

"Are you his warden now?"

I laugh. "I suppose so, for a while."

Silence.

"Thank you for the leather folder. I received it today. It matches my briefcase perfectly, but you already knew that."

"I try to be observant. You can return it if you don't want it."

"Why would I do that?"

"My feelings won't be hurt. It might not be something you'll use."

"You are very funny."

"Practical."

"Okay, practical. So what about us?"

I don't expect this discussion so quickly. I gather more crumbs.

"I've missed you, but I don't know how to make it work. Ethan needs me to help him get through whatever's going on, and I feel torn between the two of you."

"I know that. I tried not to impose, but you've made him your whole life, without room for anyone else, not even yourself."

"I'm his mother. I'm responsible for him. I can't forget about him and go off and have a fling because it feels good." My voice rises. "I told you that's what Jake did with his son. I keep picturing Kevin at fourteen, fucked up and lost, and then I see Ethan standing next to him. I won't abandon him."

"I'm not a fling, Maddy, and I wasn't asking you to abandon him. I'm asking you to let me in. Let me be with you and help."

"I don't know how." The words catch in my throat. "I only know how to do it by myself, and I certainly haven't done a good job."

"I'm not used to 'poor me' from you."

I smile. "I have my moments."

"You're not Jake, Ethan's not Kevin. Ethan's not going to run away like Kevin did. Where would he go? He's not stupid. He knows what he's got with you."

"Why would you want to sign on for this? He's difficult with you and unpleasant to be around. He resents you."

"You mean, what's wrong with me?'" He laughs. "I like you. A lot. You're beautiful, I think you're funny, I think you're complicated and we have great sex. Oh, and based on the one time we played, you're a terrible golfer, but you know it, and you're willing to learn."

I picture the clumps of dirt and grass flying through the air the only time we played. My club missed the ball, but not the fairway.

"I know how quickly things change, Maddy. My wife's illness taught me that. Ethan is going to leave, and I don't mean running away. He's going to grow up, one way or another, and it's going to be sooner not later. We have a shot at making a life together." His voice softens. "Ethan can learn to incorporate me into his life and you can learn to lean on someone."

"I found a therapist today."

"Good. He? She?"

"She. She's direct, like you."

"As long as she gives sterling advice."

I can hear him smiling. "Are you playing golf tomorrow?" I ask.

"No, I have a partners' meeting in the morning. You want to meet me for lunch?"

"Yes."

"At a restaurant or my house?"

I take a deep breath. "Your house."

"Good. I'll call you when the meeting is over."

And that's it. Simple, straightforward, easy.

Later that night, I lie on my back in bed, alone. I think about Phil's deep, seductive voice beckoning, imploring me to trust him. My right leg slides toward the empty side of my queen-sized bed and back again, making half of a snow angel. I want Phil next to me, to reach out and touch him, to feel his body near mine. I run my hands over my rib cage, then down to my belly. I imagine Phil's hands, first tracing, then kissing each rib as he moves down to bury his face in the softness between my hips. I crave his understanding and his passion. And I fear it at the same time.

The next morning, Ethan goes to work and I have the house to myself. I usually love to stay in bed and read or watch a movie, my fantasy come true. But so is Phil. And I want everything, namely me, to be perfect.

I'm not a bath person, but I want one this morning. I fill the tub with the hottest water I can tolerate and add some scented bath oil. I look in the mirror and am not thrilled with my naked middle-age body, the dimpling thighs, sagging breasts and extra poundage. But Phil has seen me before and knows what he's getting. He likes the love handles, the soft feel of skin that isn't taut, the laugh lines around my eyes. Still, it isn't fair that Jake got the young, toned body and Phil gets this one.

I decide to wear the same purple outfit and sneakers I wore on our first date. Phil liked it and I want to start over. I drive into Phil's circular driveway in Beverly Hills. His car isn't there. He told me he might be late and I should let myself in with the key I never returned and he never asked for. I had put it away for safekeeping in a small alabaster container on the nightstand next to my bed.

I ring the doorbell just in case his car is parked in the garage. Letting myself into the house feels strange. Phil's wife has been dead for three years, but her ghost is present everywhere. Her needlework hangs in the hallway, and family photos adorn the credenza, two walls in the den, and the top of Phil's dresser in the bedroom. I know it shouldn't bother me. I don't want it to. I don't want their love to have been any other way. But I prefer her warm, smiling face not to be watching me.

I go outside to the patio and sit near the pool. The wind chimes jingle in the cool breeze. I push the lounge chair back and read my book. My foot taps the ground, distracting me from the words on the page. I hear his car on the gravel driveway and run to meet him.

I open the door before he gets his key in the lock. He smiles and puts a large plastic bag from Canter's on the floor of the foyer along with the leather folder I gave him. He takes my face in his hands and looks into my eyes. He tilts my head back gently and kisses my neck.

"Mmm, you smell good."

I close my eyes. His lips travel up the side of my neck to my cheek.

"I had a hard time concentrating on my meeting knowing you were here." He presses his body against me.

"Your partners must have been thrilled with your lack of attention."

He kisses me in the soft hollow at the base of my neck. My knees buckle. He catches me in his arms.

"Are you hungry?" He points to the Canter's bag on the floor. "We can have lunch by the pool."

He picks up the bag and leads me outside. We sit on the lounge chair. His leg touches mine and sends an electrical charge through my body.

"Do I have to choose? Food or you?"

"No." He kisses my forehead, then my nose. He puts his right arm around my back and holds me firmly. He kisses my lips, light and playful. Then with months of stored passion, our tongues thrust and tease each other. He unzips my dress with his left hand. I reach up and run my fingers through his thick hair.

"Oh God, wait," I groan. "Do we need a condom?"

"No. Why?" He looks surprised, wounded. "I haven't been with anyone since you. Have you?"

"No, and I don't want to be."

Suddenly our clothes are in the way and the lounge chair is in the wrong position. We laugh as we tend to those details so we can tend to each other. I stand in front of him as he sits on the lounge. His eyes linger and roam over every part of my naked body. My need to run and hide disappears as he grasps my hips and gently pulls me toward him. He kisses my belly, his tongue gently poking at my belly button. I feel a pulsing throughout my body. I press his head down so he can kiss me where I most want him to be.

We lie next to each other. The heat from our bodies matches the heat from the sun's rays on our skin. I put one leg over him so I can feel him between my legs. He rubs against me as he becomes harder. I ache to receive him. Our passion is unhurried, a beautiful ballet, intimate and graceful. As it increases, Phil enters me. Our pace quickens, slows, quickens. We come together and rest in each other's arms.

Later, we sit in chairs, side-by-side, grinning. Phil brings us some shirts from his closet. Famished, we dig into our sandwiches happily gazing at each other. His eyes crinkle from the sun as he looks my way.

"This is a wonderful moment." I lift my arms toward the sky. "The day is perfect, you're perfect." I turn to look at him. "I'm glad you didn't give up on me." I take his hand. He glances at me and then out at the pool. He doesn't respond.

My body recoils immediately and folds in on itself. I withdraw my hand to get away from him. He won't let go.

"I'm not saying anything," he begins, "because I want to make sure I say it right. Sometimes you're harder to convince than a jury," he says softly, but it saws through me.

"Sex and passion," he continues, "having a good time, has never been the problem between us. I didn't want to have this discussion today, like this, after we made love."

Then why are we? I close my eyes and push my half-eaten pastrami sandwich away.

"I haven't stopped thinking about you since we met in that garage waiting room. But I'm also not sure why, since you frustrate the hell out of me." He turns to face me. "I want a real relationship with you, Maddy. I want to know who you are, how you feel about everything, the good, the bad, all the dirty laundry. I'm glad you went into therapy. It's not just for Ethan. It's for us."

I watch his face. I want my hand back. I want my soul back. I can't explain the panic I feel.

"Don't you want to say something? Help me out here?"

I shiver on the inside. "I can't. I don't know. I'm scared."

He comes around behind my chair and wraps his arms around me.

"It's okay," he whispers. "I know you're scared. I don't know what it's about, but it's okay. You're safe."

I grab his arms tightly and begin to cry.

11

SANTA MONICA
1996

*A*fter four sessions with Carol, I still feel like Wendy Darling being dragged along Captain Hook's plank toward a dark, choppy ocean. I want to go to therapy because I feel better, but I hate how painful it is. Two hundred therapy minutes covers a lot of territory but only superficially. We've just begun to delve into my childhood, my parents, Jake, Ethan, Phil, and now Anthony. I thought he was wrapped in that imaginary box stored deep in my brain, but when I open up to Carol about that difficult trip to New York, my father's operation and telling Jake that I was pregnant, there is Anthony in all his sick glory. It doesn't surprise Carol.

This week, I settle into my chair, grab a tissue and check out Carol's outfit. She always wears an expensive, dark tailored suit with a touch of red or white. My closet is mostly devoid of style, so there is no way I can compete. I pick up the oblong, brown tweed throw pillow and put it on my lap. If a session is going well, it stays there, resting. If I'm challenged to go where I don't want to go, look at things I don't want to look at, I turn the pillow from side to side and twirl one of the many nubby fabric particles. Which one will unravel first?

"Things feel good," I announce. "Ethan's home on time, mostly doing his chores without being reminded and he challenges my authority less." I smile. "And Phil and I are getting closer."

"I'm glad."

I look at the two vases filled with purple mums and crimson gladiolas this week. The clock ticks.

"Who was the authority in your house when you were young?"

"My father." I answer without hesitation.

"How did he use it?"

"It's complicated." I slump in my chair and stare at the ceiling. "I was the proverbial good girl. And when I wasn't, it was nothing like Ethan. I wasn't disrespectful, I didn't challenge."

"What did you do?"

"Just growing up, trying to find out about myself." I groan. "When I was twelve, I wanted to cut my hair. I wanted to be 'in.' I had long, beautiful thick hair, but it wasn't the style. My mother took me to get it cut. My father, who loved my long hair, was furious. It was like we'd done something personally to him."

"How did he show his fury?"

"He stopped talking to us. My mother and I got the deep freeze. It lasted weeks."

"What did your mother do?"

"Nothing, at first. But ultimately she begged me to apologize to him. And I always did."

"What happened then?" Carol's eyebrows crunch across her forehead.

"Nothing. I apologized. But he stayed angry, until he wasn't."

"How did you feel?"

"I hated it. I got a haircut, for crying out loud. I didn't deserve to be punished, and then apologize and be ignored. I was angry at my mother too, because she put me in that position. She never stuck up for me. Or for herself."

"So you took the responsibility for making it right between them, even when you hadn't done anything wrong."

I don't answer.

"Do you see the pattern, Maddy? You did it with your parents, and you did it with Jake."

"With Jake? What does he have to do with this?"

"Haven't you taken all the responsibility for the two of you? Raising Ethan?"

"Wanting to get pregnant was my idea. I told him he didn't have to do anything."

"It was your idea, but you didn't get pregnant by yourself? Jake was a willing participant."

"But he didn't need or want to have another baby."

"You're responsible, not only for the decisions you make and your behavior, but also for the decisions he makes and his behavior?" She leans forward in her chair. Her huge diamond ring sparkles as a ray of sunlight hits it. Her bracelets jangle. "Couldn't he have stopped you from getting pregnant? Wouldn't you have slept with him even if he used birth control?" She tips her head and softens her voice. "And should Ethan pay the price of not knowing his father because of his parents' decisions?"

I twist the tassel on the pillow. "You play rough."

"I want you to look at what you do. Why is it always your fault? Why are you the bad one?"

"I don't know. I end up feeling sorry for the other person. Like I can handle it and he can't."

"You had your mother as a role model. Wasn't she the one who said, 'Thank God I have broad shoulders?'" She let that sink in before continuing. "Did anyone stand up to your father?"

I sit quietly, then smile. "Ethan. He's the only one. He once defended me when my father complained about something, maybe the eggs being overcooked or the asparagus being undercooked. I don't know. But Ethan looked at him and said, 'Grandpa, why are you yelling at my mom? She's doing the best she can.' I remember my mind froze. My mother and I stopped what we were doing. And my father apologized. He said, 'You're right, Ethan. Your mother is doing the best she can. And it's pretty good at that.'" I inhale. "I taught him how to stand up for himself, so why can't I do it?"

"Interesting question. Why do you think?"

I fold one leg underneath me. "I've never told anyone, never said it out loud before." I reach for a tissue. "If I don't do what everyone wants me to do, they'll be angry at me, they won't love me." A pain grips my chest. I inhale twice. "I've thought about Anthony lately, not only what he did to me, but my father's reaction. I think he felt so guilty and ashamed he couldn't protect me that he withdrew. He stopped playing with me, reading to me, loving me." I gasp and start crying. "I thought what Anthony did was my fault, and my father blamed me. Losing his love was far worse than Anthony's grotesque game." I blow my nose. "And that's why I stayed in the windowsill. Lonely, but safe." I reach for another tissue. "The windowsill is still with me."

"Where?"

"It's a big hole, inside, that I hide in."

"That's how you protect yourself."

I twirl the nub on the pillow. "That's why I stopped seeing Phil last year."

"Lonely, but safe?"

I nod. "He wants something that I'm not sure I can give him."

"What's that?"

"He says I shut him out, won't let him be part of what goes on with me."

"Give me an example."

"He says I let him know what's going on after the fact. That I don't discuss things with him, or let him help me, until I've decided everything. Ethan was so impossible with Phil after he came back from New York that I kept them separate. Phil wanted to work it out. I wouldn't let him."

"Who were you protecting?"

"Everyone." I laugh.

"It's scary to give up your power or to share it. You're afraid to get stomped on again."

"What do you mean?"

"You were powerless with Anthony, you were powerless with your father, and with your mother. Then she modeled that powerless behavior with your father. You don't want to be put in that position ever again."

I stare at her.

"But that was when you were a child, Maddy. You're grown-up now. It's time to do things differently."

"What do you suggest?"

"You've started seeing Phil again, so you can try out new behaviors. Have you told him about Anthony?"

A chill runs through me. No way am I ready to deal with that. I sit back in my chair and run my hands through my hair, making a ponytail. I can't look at Carol, so I check my watch.

"Yes," Carol says, "the session is over. And there's always next week. You might try to trust Phil. Think about the fact that you get what you expect and if you expect nothing," she raises her eyebrows, "guess what you get?"

————

By July, I need a haircut and my hair dyed. Phil and I are going to a dinner dance at the Riviera Country Club. I want to look smashing. I buy a halter dress, with a sequined red floral print on top, and a full chiffon skirt. If we're going to do the twist I want a dress that will twirl, sparkle and shimmer.

I pull into a parking spot in front of the beauty salon. When I enter, my hairdresser Lena is working on another client. She and I have shared appointments many times before. It's amazing how personal and intimate one can be with strangers. I don't know the woman's name, but I know she's been married, has one son, and has gone through an ugly divorce. I sit at a vacant stylist station and observe the two women in the mirror.

"I'll be finished with Elizabeth soon," Lena says "How are you?"

"Good. It's summer." I look at Elizabeth. "You're off too, aren't you? The major benefit of teaching."

Elizabeth nods, then grimaces as some curly brown hairs are pulled and painted with bleach for highlights. "I'm getting my son ready for Berkeley."

I laugh. "For you to get ready or for you to get him ready?"

She looks back at me. "I suppose both."

"It was an adjustment for me," Lena says in her animated Latin way. "They don't call it 'leaving the nest' for nothing. All those years, focused on the kid, making a good life for us, and then suddenly, it's only you."

I know Lena grew up in Bogota, Columbia, married, had a child at nineteen and was widowed by twenty-one. She came to the United States with no money and no connections. She pushed a broom in someone's salon until she finished school and eventually bought her own beauty shop. We are three women who ended up single parents through a variety of ways.

"How was graduation?" I ask Elizabeth. "Did his father come?" I realize I'm on fragile ground with that question. The father was a hit-and-miss type.

"Not only didn't he come," she answers, "but he didn't acknowledge that Steven graduated."

The phone rings and Lena goes to answer it. Elizabeth turns toward me in her chair. The dye forms a widow's peak on her forehead. Some of it drips down her face aiming for the bridge of her nose. She wipes it away. "As soon as Steve turned eighteen, on June 5th, my ex-husband's court-ordered financial obligations were over and he was done. Hasn't paid a dime since."

Lena hangs up the receiver. There is only the sound of a clock ticking in the room. My gut burns. "Infuriating," I say. "New wife and kid?"

"Two little girls," she says.

I shake my head. "Why don't the new wives get it? If a man walks away from one child, he'll walk away from any child? The new wife should insist her husband be a dad to all his children."

"I wasn't surprised." She shrugs. "That's why I didn't tell Steven I sent his dad graduation pictures. I didn't want to set him up to be hurt again."

"I'm sorry."

"Me too. My son's a great kid, in spite of his father or because he wasn't around."

Lena taps Elizabeth on the shoulder and signals for her to sit under the dryer. It's my turn. I absorb Elizabeth's story as Lena's fingers massage my shoulders. I close my eyes and finally relax.

The summer flies by and the school year begins. I come home in the afternoon exhausted, rush to get the mail and walk Phanny. As I leaf through my letters I see Beth's handwriting. We talk once or twice a week, so getting a letter from her is unusual. Maybe she's sending me the essay she wrote for *The New York Times*. I sit on my bed and open it. A piece of newspaper flutters out and falls on the floor. I pick it up and read the enclosed note.

> *Madd,*
> *Thought a lot about NOT sending this, but figured you'd want to see it. Call.*
> *Love you,*
> *Beth*

I look at the tiny piece of paper. It's Jake's mother's obituary. There is a hollowness in my chest. Sixteen years and only word-of-mouth information about Jake, and now something concrete I can hold in my hand.

MILLER, Frances Barbara
1912 – 1996
Frances Miller, beloved wife of Jeffrey, loving mother of Jacob
and Daniel, adoring grandmother of Rebecca and Kevin,
great-grandmother to Lisa and Donald, died peacefully on
September 4, 1996. She was a warm, caring woman who
will be genuinely missed. A memorial service will be held at
Temple Emanu-El, 1 East 65th Street, at 10 a.m. on Friday,
September 6. Graveside services will be private.

I read it a second time. Ethan's name isn't there. Not a surprise. Frances died never knowing about him. I want to roar. I can't find a place for myself. I walk into the bathroom. I walk back to my bed. Like some sleeping giant, old raw feelings boil from behind the calm screen I show to the world. I pick up the phone not giving a damn about the long distance cost. As it rings I hope Beth will pick up and not the machine. I know her message by heart. I begin mimicking it. "Hello, you have reached Beth's answering machine. I can't . . . " But Beth picks up on the fourth ring.

"It's me. You busy?" I ask.

"You got my note?"

"Yes."

"I didn't know what to do. I kept it for a couple of days before mailing it. Are you upset with me?"

"With you? No." I bellow. "How could he do this?"

"Do I hear anger? Don't answer, I need to get a cigarette."

I wait and adjust the pillows on my bed. I picture Beth searching for the cigarettes on her cluttered desk, or mixed up somewhere in her down comforter. She just can't quit.

"I'm back," Beth says, exhaling into the receiver. "You wonder how Jake could do this? Are you kidding? He's done it for fifteen, sixteen years. Why are you surprised?"

"I'm not. It's finally smacking me in the face. How can he live with himself knowing that he has a child on this earth and then forget about him? Pretending he never happened?"

"Some men have the ability to do that."

I sit up straighter. "I never believed Jake could be so heartless and just disappear. I thought he'd come to trust that he could be part of Ethan's life, and enjoy him, without the day-to-day parenting." I stare at the blank television screen across from my bed.

"Don't beat yourself up, Madd, though I never understood how you let him get away with it."

"Sixteen years later I'm still waiting. Dumb, huh?"

"No comment. What are you going to do?"

"Not sure. Maybe I'll write him a condolence note, with a long postscript."

"Not funny, but I guess that's one option. You know you'll be opening up a Pandora's box. Jake Miller has been in denial for a long time. He's buried you and Ethan."

"Maybe it's time we rise from the dead." I hear Carol's words in my head, "If you don't expect anything, guess what you get?"

"What about Ethan?" Beth asks. "What will this do to him?"

"He doesn't talk about him, won't look at pictures of him. But I really think he needs to know his father Beth, even if it's just to check his fantasy against reality."

"I'm speechless."

"First I'll write the letter, but I won't tell Ethan." I hide the obituary in my nightstand. "No point in setting him up to be rejected again. Whatever happens, it's not your doing. This is in my face for a reason. I'll keep you posted."

The next afternoon, I sit at the computer and watch the cursor on the mostly blank screen. I write the date and salutation, "Dear Jake," the easy part. I lean forward, then hide my face in my hands. The last time I tried to write to Jake was when Ethan sent him the Father's Day card. Piles of balled up papers covered the kitchen table because I couldn't find the right words to explain Ethan's curiosity. Remembering those sleepless nights, I feel the rage that I couldn't let myself feel then. It percolated in my stomach, churned against my insides. I won't shut myself up this time, Jake.

Phanny stirs at my feet and perks up her long silky ears. Her tail thumps against the dark blue carpet. I hear the front door open. "Mom, I'm home." I look at my watch and give myself a thumb's up. Things are so much better and it's a huge relief.

"Hi honey, I'm in the den." After his backpack hits the dining room table with a thud, I figure he went into the kitchen to check out the food supply. People talk about the food teenagers consume, but seeing is believing. Ethan can empty out a newly filled refrigerator and the cupboards in one sitting.

Phanny bounds to the den door to greet him. I focus on the door also, as her tail thwacks against the frame. She jumps on Ethan as soon as he bends down to pet her. He walks over to me, gives me a banana-smelling kiss on my cheek, and then lies on the day bed and lets out a deep sigh. Phanny jumps up and scooches her long Basset body alongside his.

"Sounds like you both had a rough day."

"Just a lot to do. The rehearsals for the choral concert go on and on. I don't know what she wants from us."

"Your best. She's a taskmaster but she gets you to make beautiful music. This is your normal litany, then after a performance you're always happy."

"I guess you're right." He smiles and gets up. "I have a history paper due tomorrow. When's dinner?"

"Around seven."

He looks at his watch. "I'm hungry, but I can wait. What are you writing?"

"A letter."

"Anybody I know?"

"Not really, sweetie."

After dinner, back at the computer, I'm surprised how easily the words come to me. I know this letter isn't an exercise where you get it all out on paper, then burn it. I don't trust my energy to travel across the country on a metaphysical journey and land in Jake Miller's psyche. I plan to send it registered mail with a return receipt request. I keep writing. I will finish this letter tonight. After an hour, I stare at the finished product. It conveys most of my feelings in a somewhat civilized way. I study it looking for typos.

> *Dear Jake,*
>
> *It's been a long time. A friend sent me your mother's obituary and it raised issues that I sadly never faced. My son, your biological son, lost a grandmother he never knew, who never knew him. In fact he has a whole family who doesn't know him, beginning with his father who's never acknowledged him.*
>
> *Is there a secret compartment that you hide him in, Jake? Do you ever lie in bed wondering . . . just a little? How do you love your grandchildren without an iota of curiosity in Whatever Happened to Baby Ethan?*
>
> *I want to introduce you to your progeny. His name is Ethan Robert Gold and he's wonderful. He's cute and funny, bright and talented, goofy and struggling, like most sixteen-year-olds. He's five foot six inches and weighs about one hundred thirty pounds. He works out pumping iron, running, doing Tae Kwon Do and using the Nordic Track. He's outgoing, friendly, smart and clever, and while he does fine in school (he's an 11th grader) it's not his favorite activity. He wants to be a rapper and an actor and he's part of every theatrical performance at his high school.*

There are few people who aren't touched by him.

So where do we go from here? Ethan doesn't know I'm writing this, and before I tell him, I want to hear from you. It's time. Ethan deserves your acknowledgment. I want you to write to me so we can start moving forward. And while you do it, imagine a young boy standing in front of a Father's Day card display trying to choose the right card for a man he was reaching out to. Feel how devastated he was to be rejected and ignored by you. That won't happen again.

I'm sorry about your mother. I hope she didn't suffer.

Sincerely,

The cursor blinks. Will Jake respond? Am I doing the right thing? I press print and leave the den to the clicking sound. I walk into Ethan's room, put my hands on his shoulders and kiss the top of his head. He looks up from his desk and smiles. I see trust in his eyes. I need that trust in myself. I'll protect you one step at a time.

"I'm going to sleep, sweetie. Love you." I kiss his head again. "Don't stay up late."

I go into the den and gather the pages from the printer. I hide the letter in a personal file so Ethan won't see it and shut off the computer. I'll read it over several times before sending it, but I will send it — one to Jake and a copy to Beth.

———

I sit at the edge of Phil's pool. We eat the vegetable frittata I brought from home and I wait for him to finish reading Jake's letter. Even though I mailed it two days ago, I'm anxious to get his feedback. It's a mild fall day and I dangle my feet in the cool water. His granddaughter's yellow beach ball bobs up and down. I stretch back and let the wind blow across my body.

When Phil is done, he comes and sits beside me putting his feet in the water. His legs are tanned with sock lines above his ankles.

"Well?" I ask.

"I hope I never do anything that makes you that angry."

"What do you mean?"

"You're pissed and you let him know it. The sarcasm in that note is striking."

"I have the right to be angry. You've said that you never understood how he could walk away."

"And I don't. But what are you trying to accomplish by raging at him? And threatening him?"

I squint as I look at him. "I didn't expect this reaction. I thought you'd support me."

"I do. But what are you trying to accomplish?"

"I want Ethan to know his father and the rest of his family. I don't want one side of his family tree to be a question mark."

"Why now? Because of the obituary?"

"Because of therapy. I'm seeing things I didn't understand before. I believed I would be a good parent and could do it on my own. But I didn't understand that as much as I love Ethan, I can't make up for that mystery person in his life. It's time Jake introduced himself." My words bolster my determination. My queasy stomach is fear. "I'm not the only one who created Ethan, and although I set it all in motion, Jake was not an innocent bystander. The only innocent person is Ethan."

"Then maybe Ethan should write the letter."

"He tried that once, remember? And I let Jake ignore him. He was so crushed. And I did nothing. I chose my promise to Jake over Ethan."

"So you're angry at yourself."

"Of course I'm angry at myself." I kick the beach ball. It soars across the pool.

He moves back slightly and raises his eyebrows. "Maybe you need to deal with your anger first."

"You know what? I'm tired of being understanding, protecting people from my feelings and keeping bad promises." I jump up and look around for my shoes. "If that letter is too scary for you, then I am too. Keep the leftover frittata. I'll find my way out."

I gather my jacket and purse and head for the front door. As I grab the doorknob, Phil puts his hand on my shoulder to stop me.

"Maddy, this is ridiculous. You don't like what I say, so you're out the door?"

I turn to him, my arms across my chest.

"I'm not saying this guy doesn't deserve this letter. But if you wanted to start a dialogue so Ethan can meet his father, this might not have been the way to do it."

"I don't think being easy on him is the way either. If it were, Jake would have responded to his son long ago because it was the right thing to do." I look at Phil, begging him to understand. He puts his arms around me. My body relaxes and I collapse against him. He rubs my back.

"What I understand is that I love you. You're hurt and angry for both you and Ethan. There are a lot of issues here. All the emotions you've bottled up are exploding out of you. Sending the letter can't be any worse than it already is for you or Ethan."

I take a deep breath. "Being in therapy is like being on one of those people movers at the airport. You step on, it glides you along, and you can't get off until you're at the end." I give him a small smile. "I've stepped on, Phil, and we'll have to see where it ends."

12

SANTA MONICA

1996 – 1997

*I*n mid-November, I stand at the mailbox, envelope in hand, staring at the return address. I dare myself to open it.

> *Maddy,*
> *I will respond, but in December.*
> *Sincerely,*
> *Jake*

I've been patient, but after two months all I get is a single sentence. One fucking sentence! I stomp like a petulant child down the walkway to my apartment. You have until December. Then I better hear from you Jake Miller.

The second letter arrives after the New Year. I pick it up on my way to an appointment with Carol. Perfect timing. I read it, rooted to the pavement.

> *Dear Maddy,*
>
> *I've always thought of you in the fondest way and respected you for carrying out what appears to be a most successful job of raising Ethan.*
>
> *My intentions were to answer your questions in detail, but after rereading it, I decided not to. You don't understand*

the way I live my life and therefore, there seems to be no reason to write further.

If you wish, I will meet with you in the future to discuss this. Write and we can make arrangements.

Sincerely,

J.

When I walk the plank to Carol's office, I hold up Jake's letter and shake it.

"What's that?"

"My New Year's present. It's an offer from Jake to meet him."

I hand it to her to read and sit down. I pick up the pillow and rub the nubby fabric.

"What are your thoughts?" Carol asks.

"He thinks it's all about him. But it isn't." I twist in my seat. "And he brushes off answering my questions. He thinks I'd want to meet him? God, I don't want to."

"Are you going to respond?"

"I guess so, I started this whole thing. What am I going to say? You come here? I'll meet you halfway?" I laugh. "I don't want to meet him any way." I pause. "I wonder whether he'll bring his wife. That would be cute. The three of us sitting down for a cozy chat. Too dramatic." I go quiet.

"What?"

"Having to tell his wife, his children. I'm sure they don't know about Ethan." I close my eyes and frown. "I can't imagine having to tell them."

"It's his mess. He created it."

"But I'm forcing him to deal with it."

"It's your fault again? And now, because of you, he has to say, oops, I left out one detail about the last seventeen years of my lying, cheating, dishonorable life. I have a kid living in California, I didn't tell you about."

"When you put it that way, I guess it's not all my fault. But I told him he didn't have to be involved."

"So does that give him a free pass to just walk away? You were being sincere when you made that promise, but you didn't know then what Ethan's needs would be."

I'm stuck on Carol's words, "your fault". This seems to be a theme that's apparent to her and becoming so to me.

"I guess it's like someone leaving their house one morning and ends up causing a car accident. He didn't mean to, he didn't set out to, and yet he did. By law, he'd be held accountable. Jake should be accountable for his part in Ethan's life."

"What would you do if Ethan came home and told you he was the father of a child, and because the girl said he didn't have to be responsible for the baby, he wasn't going to be?"

"I'd kill him," I blurt out.

"Then why is it okay for Jake?"

"I don't know. It feels different. I knew Jake didn't — " I run my fingers through my hair, then bury my face in my hands. "I'm tired of going round and round. I'm so fucking ambivalent. My friends fall on either side of this conundrum. Some think I'm awful for going back on my word. Others say, 'It's about time.' You know what Julia said the other day? Regarding my promise?"

Carol shakes her head.

"She reminded me that every day people get married and promise to love, honor, and cherish, that is until they divorce. She said I was allowed to grow and change and see things differently."

"What do you think?"

"It's a great argument."

"I know it's not easy to be in conflict, battling yourself, but it's important for you to explore these issues." She looks at her watch. "It's a good place to end." She smiles. "Keep in mind that when you made that promise years ago, you didn't know what you were promising — what it means to be a parent, what Ethan would need from his father. I think you do now. You kept your promise, Maddy, for more than sixteen years. Unless you've done it yourself, no one appreciates how hard it is to raise a child with two parents, never mind alone."

Carol's understanding of my doing it alone opens a floodgate of tears and emotions. Years of questions and decisions, fears and self-doubt bubble up. I'm not used to anyone acknowledging the difficulty of what I've accepted as my way of life as a single parent. I reach for the box of tissues and take a few. Carol lets me cry. I take one more tissue and stand up to leave.

"We'll talk about this next week," she says.

I raise an imaginary glass. "I can hardly wait!"

————

Phil kisses each breast, then continues down my belly. He stops abruptly and looks up at me from the foot of his bed.

"Why'd you stop?" I sit up, leaning on my elbows. "It feels good."

"Does it?" He slides up next to me. "You seem distracted. Like there's a ghost in bed with us."

I'm embarrassed at getting caught. "I guess there is. Sorry. I was going to tell you after."

He shifts against the headboard. "What?"

I look around the room at our clothes scattered on the floor. The reflection of the water in the pool shimmers on the carpet through the patio doors. I check his dresser. The wedding picture he put away three weeks ago, without me asking, is still gone.

"Jake called this morning after Ethan left to meet you at the golf course."

"At six-thirty?"

"It was nine-thirty his time. He forgot the time difference."

"That must have started things off well."

"Maybe it was good. I wasn't nervous." I sit next to him and cover myself with the quilt. "It was strange. I hadn't heard his voice for a long time. He and his wife are going to China in February, and they will do a stopover in Los Angeles if I want to see him. He suggested drinks. Dinner. The two of us. The three of us. Like, right, I want to have dinner with him and his wife." I look at Phil. "Maybe you could come too? Ooh, a party. And it's four weeks from now."

"How did you leave it?"

"Between gasps for air?" I sigh. "I told him okay, but I wanted him to meet Ethan too. Then he began stuttering. Ultimately he thought it would be all right, but he had to get back to me. Then we hung up."

"Why didn't you tell me earlier?"

"I don't know. This feels weird." I look away. "How was golf this morning? Ethan getting better?"

"Ethan is getting better, better than you, but you both need to practice. Why are you changing the subject?"

"I don't want to see this man. And Ethan's happier than he's been in a long time. I want to protect him." I brush some hair out of my eye. "I'm opening a Pandora's box and we all know what happens then."

"Even if Jake turns out to be a jerk, Ethan can find that out and deal with it. It's better than spending his life wondering."

"After I spoke to Jake, I called Beth and Linda — the only ones I could talk to at that hour. They said the same thing."

He leans over, kisses me lightly, then more deeply. "Do you feel better now?"

"Are you wanting to get back to what we were doing?"

He smiles. "I could be up for that."

I turn on my side toward him. "One more thing, and don't read this the wrong way."

"Uh, oh. What?"

"Did you ever meet an old girlfriend after a really long time?"

"At a high school reunion. Rachel and I met in our freshman year of college and we were together ever since. Why? You're worried what he'll think about your looks with everything else that's going on?"

"I don't want to. I don't want to care what he thinks. But I do." I frown sheepishly.

"What he'll see is a beautiful woman and what you'll see is an old fart." He chuckles. "You did say he was considerably older than I am."

"And shorter." I kiss his nose. " I love you." I slide down the mattress and throw off the covers. "And you were where, doing what?"

The following Monday afternoon I run into the house late. I put my packages on the table.

"I'm home, E."

Ethan walks into the living room. "Where were you?"

"Sorry. I couldn't find a phone booth with a working phone. I went shopping after school. I needed some new clothes." I appreciate our role reversal. "How are you? Did you have a good day? Did you get your history test back?"

"Fine, yes, no. Mom, there was a weird message on the answering machine. The guy sounded confused."

"I'll listen in a minute."

I pick up my bags and walk to my bedroom. Dropping everything on my bed, I go into the bathroom. As soon as I sit down, the phone rings. Let it be for Ethan.

Ethan knocks. "It's for you. Sounds like the same guy. What should I tell him?"

"Tell him to hold on."

When I come out of the bathroom, Ethan is still in my room.

"Are you protecting me?" I laugh.

"I want to know who this guy is."

I pick up the phone.

"Hello."

"Maddy, it's Jake. I got — ."

"Hold on." I put my hand over the receiver. "It's okay, E. I'll explain later."

He gives me a quizzical look and leaves.

"I'm back."

"That message I left must have sounded strange. I called after five my time, forgetting the time change again."

In our previous conversation I told him I usually come home by five. It is now five forty-five. Jake's prompt — perhaps anxious.

"I just walked in, so I haven't listened to the machine."

"I'm sitting in my office. I can see the Empire State building all lit up. We had a glorious day today."

I cut him off, ignoring the charm. "Did you decide whether you'd see Ethan? Is that why you're calling?"

"I'll meet with him Sunday."

"Good. Why don't you plan around brunch or lunchtime?"

"Do we have to decide now?"

"No." I need to reel myself in and soften my tone. "Sorry. He'll be in Orange County. I was trying to figure out the logistics." Now who's anxious?

"I'll let you know where we're staying when I know."

"Fine. One more thing, when we meet on Saturday, does five or five-thirty work for you?"

"That's okay. You know me. We won't have slept the night before. An early evening will be good."

"Perfect. Tell me your plans when you have them."

I hang up the phone and stay glued to my bed. So it's really happening. Ethan is going to meet his father. I take my new silk pantsuits out of their bags. One is royal blue and dressy, the other, turquoise and more casual. Bright and bold, they made me feel good when I tried them on. I put them in the closet and go to face my son.

He is doing his homework at the dining room table. I pat his shoulder and go into the kitchen.

"So?" He looks at me expectantly. "Who was that and what's the big secret?"

My heart races. "I've been in touch with Jake." I rinse some carrots in the sink.

"Why'd you do that?" His voice is low, edgy.

"I thought it was time. I should have done it years ago when he ignored you. He didn't have the right to do that."

Ethan stares at his book and flicks at something on the page. He looks back at me. His mood and energy level seem to oscillate like a bungee jumper caught in a tornado.

"That wasn't the only time he ignored me." His voice is soft. He looks at me shyly, like he's embarrassed.

"What do you mean?" I march out of the kitchen, holding a dripping wet carrot.

"I called him, that summer in New York. He ignored me."

I grip the back of my chair, caught in the turmoil of the same tornado. Images swirl around me — two lovers, a bed, a nine year old, a mailbox — even the gold key from long ago. Dreams twisting in the wind.

"E. I'm so sorry. Why didn't you tell me?"

"I didn't tell anyone. I hated him. I hated — " He looks down without finishing.

"Me?"

"Yeah."

I sit in my chair. "What happened?"

"Nothing. I called his office and gave his secretary cousin Arlene's telephone number, but he never contacted me. I thought maybe, because I was older, he'd feel different. I planned it all. The L.A. Dodgers were playing the N.Y. Mets. It was perfect. I thought we could go." He looks down, then at me. "Does he want to know me now?"

His undying fantasy shocks me. All these years with so much pain, sadness and anger buried inside. I failed him. I want to cry.

"I wrote to him and told him all about you in my letter."

"What did you say?" His innocent smile reinforces the strength of his hope.

"I said you were handsome, and funny, and smart, and wonderful."

"Did he answer you?"

"He's coming to L.A. in February."

"Can I see him? Does he want to see me?" The questions tumble out.

"I'm going to meet him first on Saturday and you'll have your chance on Sunday."

"What else did you say in your letter? Were you angry?"

"You could say that. I didn't like his ignoring you and making believe you didn't exist. I told him to picture a nine-year-old child choosing just the right Father's Day card. I wanted him to understand how devastated you were when he ignored you."

"I wasn't devastated, then. So why are you doing this now?" he asks. "You always told him he didn't have to be my father."

I swallow hard and gnaw at my upper lip.

"Is that what it sounded like to you? I guess it must have. I wanted you so much."

Ethan sits quietly, tapping a pencil against his teeth.

"You know," he says, shaking the pencil at me, "he's going to have a hard time getting through God's pearly gates."

"What? Are you going religious on me?"

"No, but I see him standing there, begging to get in, and I keep saying, 'Gooooo awaayyyy!'"

"That's a pretty omnipotent fantasy." I laugh.

"What does that mean?"

"Look it up in the dictionary." I smile. "I'm going to broil some burgers." I kiss the top of his head. "By the way, I love you."

"Me, too." He gathers his books. "I'll finish this in my room." He kisses me on the cheek and takes the carrot from my hand. He walks away humming one of the songs we've been singing together since he was two. "We'll be the same as we started. Just travellin' along — singin' a song — side by side."

The day of our meeting flies by. I planned it that way. Julia insists on treating me to a manicure and pedicure, then I have my hair washed and blown dry. For fun, we window-shop on Rodeo Drive. We have lunch near her house in West L.A. so I can dress at her condo. I don't want to be alone. I check in with Phil, but this is a girl thing.

I've spoken to Jake twice. Once, after he and his wife arrived at their hotel in the Marina, and again in the afternoon to reconfirm time and place. Both conversations were strained.

In the early evening, I walk into The Warehouse Restaurant in Marina del Rey to meet Jake for drinks. I'm a few minutes early and the place is empty. The Maître d' isn't there to greet me, the bartender isn't washing and drying glasses, but Tony Bennett is singing, "Smile". Decorated like a dock with buoys, ropes, wooden crates and barrels, I scan the room. I choose a table in the bar far enough toward the back for privacy, but close enough to the entrance so I can see Jake walk in.

Sitting at the table, I remind myself why I'm here. I want Ethan to meet his father and be acknowledged by him, but I have no idea what to expect from Jake. What does he want? What is he feeling? Anger, denial, guilt, embarrassment? He suggested this meeting and he'd been pleasant when we spoke. But my letter had set things in motion, things he'd rather have kept at bay. I close my eyes and take a deep breath. Whatever happens, I'll keep my composure and do nothing to get in the way of Ethan and Jake meeting tomorrow.

At exactly five-thirty, Jake walks through the heavy driftwood doors. I'm surprised he looks like Jake, just a little balder and grayer, but otherwise the same. He's dressed in Bermuda shorts and a short-sleeve shirt. I feel silly in my more formal blue pantsuit with a gold and crystal necklace and matching earrings. My eyes follow him as he walks through the restaurant. The bounce is still in his stride, but he looks grim.

He enters the bar and I wave. He nods in my direction and comes over to the table. Will he kiss my cheek?

"Maddy," he says, nodding again as he sits down.

"Jake," I say, returning the gesture.

"How are you?" He shakes his head. "No, no, don't say anything. I want to tell you I thought I saw you a few months ago."

"Where?"

"In the Virgin Islands."

"Never been there."

"I realized it wasn't you after I followed the woman."

"When was this?"

"After my mother died. We had to get away. It was a rough time."

"I'm sorry about your mother."

"That's only part of it. My mother was sick for a long time. She died disappointed in me. Never felt I spent enough time with her. She cut me out of her will, yet made me executor." He pauses. "She left everything to my brother. Well, she left something for my kids, too." Sweat beads on his upper lip. "My brother has cancer," he continues, "and now I have to oversee his life, manage his money, and check on him. I have no money and no time."

"That must be hard." I sound like Carol.

When the waiter appears, Jake orders a vodka martini. I ask for an iced tea.

"My mother was so angry at me even though I tried to do everything for her. At the end of her life I made her as comfortable as I could. It was never enough." He blinks and wipes his lip with a paper napkin. "My business takes all my time. I don't get home until ten or eleven at night. Advertising is treacherous these days. The younger kids keep coming after my blood. It's hard." He crumples the napkin. "My mother wanted more of my time, more attention. I couldn't give it to her."

The words spill out so fast, I wonder if he's even inhaled. I'm mute. He's like an old LP recording stuck in a groove. I could easily switch the problems with his mom for the ones he's had raising his kids.

"Sounds awful, Jake."

He shifts in his chair. "What's going on in your life? And Ethan's?"

"Ethan's almost seventeen, Jake. He wants to know who you are."

He leans closer to me. "I thought you'd get married, and he'd have a father."

"I didn't know fathers were interchangeable." I snicker.

His face scrunches up. His right hand forms a fist on the table.

"I don't have time or money for this," he shouts. "It happened a long time ago. I don't remember anything, and I won't let you make me feel guilty. I can't have this in my life."

Gloves are off. The waiter sets the drinks on the table. Jake glances at his watch and turns toward the door. I look too. Is he expecting someone? The waiter leaves and Jake continues his litany.

"I don't have money. All I do is work. It takes every minute of the day." He grabs the toothpick from his martini glass and slides the two green olives into his mouth. "We're one of the top agencies, but it's fucking hard. I don't have anything saved — a small IRA, the apartment and the house on Fire Island — but that's it." He takes a gulp of his drink. "A man in my jazz group has prostate cancer. It's painful to see him. But the group is my only pleasure. I play all night and go to the office the next day, wiped. I never should have gone into this business."

I let him ramble. This perverse time warp is his message of the past that now echoes in the present: no time, no money, no responsibility.

I check my watch. He's been repeating himself for half an hour. Focus on Ethan.

I look up from playing with my straw. Satchmo is singing, "As Time Goes By". Why am I not in Casablanca having a worthwhile but tragic, love affair?

I'm about to say something when I notice a woman standing in the bar area scanning the room. She looks like Jake's second wife, who

Linda described to me a few years ago. Pleasant looking, with dark hair pulled back in a bun and no make-up, she is wearing a simple, striped sleeveless dress, fitted at the waist and flared at the hem. Not a glimmer of flamboyance.

You son of a bitch, you didn't tell me. "Jake, I think your wife's here."

He turns around and waves. She walks over as he gets up to bring a chair to the table.

"Maddy, this is my wife, Marian Clark. Marian, this is Maddy."

His reinforcement is here and I've entered the Twilight Zone.

"Welcome to California." I'm pissed, but I do my best to be convivial. Jake and I have not yet discussed what matters to me. "You arrived just in time for a heat wave. I'm sure it beats the winter weather you're having in New York."

"It's beautiful here."

The waiter returns and takes our orders — two more vodka martinis and another iced tea.

Marian scrutinizes me. "After we rested, we got a chance to walk around."

"We're in a great little hotel," Jake adds. "People from all over. Not a high class place, but that's what makes it interesting."

I turn in my chair and face Marian.

"You're an artist in Jake's office? Is that how you met?"

"Yes," Marian answers. "I — "

"Marian's a wonderful artist," Jake adds.

She smiles at him. "I wasn't making enough money. I was in a long-term relationship that was ending. I needed to do other things with my life, so I got a job in advertising."

"Do you like it?"

"It's challenging and exciting. We work long, hard hours. There's so much to do."

I almost laugh out loud. They have their routine down pat, but I'm fed up with the nonsense.

"Marian," I say, peering straight at her, "what do you think about this?"

She stares back. "I want to know your bottom line."

"What do you mean?"

"I was living with someone for a long time," she says softly. "He didn't want children. I did. It was awful. That's the reason we broke up."

"Got it. I have your baby and you're jealous."

"Well, I know someone else," she continues, "who didn't tell the man what she was doing. Now she expects him to pay for her child."

Ah, the bottom line.

"That's never been our situation — "

"What you think or what Marian thinks won't change anything," Jake interrupts. "I want to table this. We both need to eat something and get to bed. What time do you want to meet tomorrow?"

Jake's anger meter is at eight. I've had enough, too.

I turn to Marian. "Are you joining us again?"

"I wasn't planning to." Marian looks at Jake. "There's an exhibit at the L.A. County Museum. I could go there while you're at your meeting." Her tone is a question and a statement.

"I don't want you doing that, I want you nearby."

"You need your security blanket?" I ooze sarcasm.

"I don't need a security blanket." He snaps. He's at a ten.

"You guys work it out. I'll pick you up at your hotel at eleven-thirty. That way Marian can have your car."

"That'll work," Marion says.

The gavel bangs. Meeting adjourned.

We walk out into the night air. Jake and Marion cross the street to their hotel holding hands. At first I want to hear their conversation, to know what they thought about the evening, but now I'm glad to be on my own. I need to understand things from my point of view, not theirs.

I drive to Julia's house dazed, angry and disappointed. Sixteen years later and Jake is the same self-involved person, minus the charm. Poor Ethan. How will I protect him tomorrow? I want to go straight home and by-pass Julia's house, but I can't. She's invited Phil and a few of my family and friends for dinner so they can hear what happened. I park the car and before I get out, I look in the mirror, fix my hair and put on some lipstick.

For the next two hours, I hold court like a queen. I trust and love everyone present. They all have a special investment and connection with me and with Ethan. Julia has set a buffet table with several dishes of Indian food and after everyone's plates are filled, they sit around me waiting for the details.

When I describe my disbelief and frustration, they remind me he is here in the Marina, willing to see Ethan, and that I will accomplish my goal to introduce father and son.

By the time we rehash everything, I'm emotionally and physically exhausted and I still have to get through Sunday. Phil, who has remained quiet most of the evening, walks me to my car. It's a warm winter night for L.A. and a full moon lights our way down a dark side street.

"I told you you'd look terrific tonight," he says, "and that everything would go smoothly. I know it was difficult, but you did it."

We lean against my car, holding hands.

"It really bothers me that he seems to have reduced this to money. Why would he think I want his money? If that were the case, I would have written to him years ago."

"He has nothing else to give, Maddy. Money is easier than time and attention. And what he has is what he thinks you want." He puts his arm around me and kisses my forehead. Then he puts his hand on the small of my back and guides me. "I know you're tired. We can leave your car here and I'll drive you home. We'll pick it up in the morning."

I feel trapped. I resist his pressure and pull away. "I need to go home, Phil. Alone."

His face crumbles. He shakes his head back and forth. A strand of his beautiful white hair falls across his forehead. I want to brush it back, but I don't.

"I'm sorry. I thought you'd understand."

"Understand that you don't want me around? This happens every time you have an issue to deal with. You show me the letter to Jake only after you send it. You tell your friends about everything that happens to you, and then maybe, you include me. Even today, you chose to spend it with Julia. One of these days, Maddy, you're going to stop pushing me away, and allow me to enter your very exclusive world."

"I don't mean to keep you out. I'm not trying to reject you. I just can't be there for you now."

"Why would you think I want something for me?" He stares at me in disbelief. "I want to be there for you."

I look at him feeling bewildered. "I can't do this right now. Please don't ask me to. I need to figure things out by myself. We can talk later."

He shakes his head again. "There is no later. This is life now. It's not something you talk about after an event happens, and before the next one begins. There's always going to be something — Ethan, Jake, some drama's going to make you shut me out so you can handle it by yourself."

"Please don't do this."

"This isn't working." He turns and leaves. I want to go to him. I know he's right. But I can't. I watch him until he disappears around the block.

When I get home, the house is empty, quiet and dark. Phanny has already buried herself in my bed. I walk into the den and rock in the computer chair to sort out what happened. In the blackness of the room I hear Phanny jump off my bed. She comes and sits at my feet and puts her head on my leg. I bend over and kiss her wet nose, then lean back as far as I can in the chair. I cross my arms on top of my head and close my eyes. I see a little three-year-old girl with red ringlets. She sits alone in a Brooklyn windowsill, bunched up in a ball, sucking her thumb.

I open my eyes and shudder the image away. I pick up Ethan's old teddy bear sitting on top of my desk. I've never been able to throw it away. I hug it to my heart and think about what I told Carol during one of our sessions. It feels like I'm in a hole or a box and even if people are around, reaching out to me, I can't or won't reach back. And then I picture Phil.

Following a fitful night's sleep and an angry dream that had me pleading my case against Jake in front of a judge, I drive an hour south on the 405 freeway to pick Ethan up at his hotel. Ethan is a member of the BBYO, a Jewish youth group that supports cultural, social and religious events for teens. I like how BBYO reinforces the concepts of justice, kindness, generosity and the importance of being a good human being — not the religious stuff. They're having their annual meeting this weekend and Ethan has to miss the last day of the conference to meet his father.

After calling his room, I rest in the car while he gets out of bed and packs. He climbs into the passenger seat and grunts at me. This is not going to be fun. As he buckles his seat belt, I notice a nickel-size hickey on the left side of his neck. I reach over and touch it.

"Could it be any bigger?"

"It's none of your business." He wrenches his head away.

"You made it so, to me and the world. Your conquests are not to be broadcast. Sex is private and personal."

"We didn't have sex."

"You had something."

He ignores my statement and looks out the window. I start the car and wend my way back to the freeway. He turns in his seat and pulls the strap of his seatbelt away from his neck so it doesn't cut into him.

"So what happened last night?" he asks.

I shrug. "Not really sure. Jake complained about not having time and money and then his wife joined us. You might meet her today."

"Did he say anything about me?"

"He asked how you were." I look at him and then in the rearview mirror to change lanes. "He's here, E. That's the important thing. You can meet him and make your own judgments. I don't want to color things with mine."

"I'm tired. I want to go to sleep."

He closes his eyes for the rest of the trip leaving me to think about the three angry men in my life — Phil, Jake, and Ethan. When we get home, I tell him to be ready by eleven. We go into our bedrooms to get dressed. At eleven, on the dot, he appears at my door.

I smile at him, then stare in the mirror. I turn to the side and run my hand down the front of my jacket. I feel the bulge of my belly but don't see it reflected back to me. I hook one of my long turquoise and silver earrings through my left ear lobe. I'm perspiring. It's much hotter than I thought it would be, but I don't have time to change.

"You look fine, Mom."

"Thank you, honey. You look good, too." He's wearing a pair of blue jeans and a Michael Jordan T-shirt. I point at the hickey on his neck. "Do you want some make-up to cover that thing?"

"Do you think I should? Do you want me to?"

"It's up to you," I reply, hoping he'll say, 'Yes'.

"Then I don't want to."

I bite my tongue and finish putting on my lipstick. Is this a man-to-man statement to Jake? I stand back and check myself in the mirror one more time. "Let's go."

The drive to the Marina takes longer than I anticipate. I tap my thumbs against the wheel and chew the inside of my cheek. I don't want to be late. As I make the left turn off Washington Boulevard to the street that takes us to Jake's hotel, Ethan stares out the passenger window.

"What does he look like?" he asks.

"About the same as his pictures. On the short side, gray hair, balding, a little pot belly."

He points. "Is that my father?"

Men are walking in the vicinity, but no one that fits Jake's description. I look at Ethan to see if he's serious, but even if he isn't — he is. I put my hand on his arm.

"E, remember, no matter what happens, this is an opportunity to meet the real person versus your fantasy."

Ethan takes a deep breath. "I know."

I park the car and we get out.

"Do you want me to introduce you?" I ask as we walk to the entrance.

"No, I can do it myself."

I put my arm around him and kiss his cheek. "I'm sorry if this feels like an ordeal, but it's almost over."

He gives me the first genuine smile of the morning. I step away, and we walk into the lobby.

Since it's Sunday morning a lot of people mill about the desk waiting to check out. Others stand on the back patio overlooking the water. The lobby is decorated with wicker furniture, brass lanterns, and strategically placed greenery. I spot Jake between two palm fronds and call out as he walks away from the desk. He turns and comes over. Father and son look at each other. Ethan holds out his hand first.

"Hello, I'm Ethan and I'm nervous."

Jake shifts his weight from one foot to the other and takes Ethan's hand.

"Hello, I'm Jacob Miller and so am I."

Jake lets go of Ethan's hand and nods in my direction. No greeting? What does that portend?

"Are you ready to go?" I ask.

"Marian's joining us. I'm waiting for her to come down."

"That's a surprise."

He pats his pant's pocket and pulls out his room key. He fiddles with the sailboat fob, flipping it back and forth. I search for something to say.

"I hope you're open to having Mexican food. That's Ethan's first choice."

"I guess that's all right."

He turns toward the elevator scrutinizing the exiting crowd. His shoulders relax when he sees Marian. She walks up to us and stands beside Jake. Either I'm seeing her better in the daylight or she hasn't slept well. Her eyes are puffy and her bun askew. She is wearing a light pink and white striped A-line skirt and a matching pink sleeveless shell. The pale color adds to her washed-out complexion.

"Ethan, this is my wife, Marian Clark."

They shake hands.

She and Jake discuss some checkout procedures. I step closer to Ethan. He watches in silence, absorbing it all. When we walk outside, Ethan is next to Jake and I'm next to Marian.

"How come you changed your mind and joined us?" I ask.

"Jake wanted his security blanket."

I smile.

The Mexican restaurant is on the bay, next to the hotel and ironically provides a natural backdrop for our awkward and unnatural meeting. We're seated on the patio overlooking the calm water and the blue and white sailboats. Green, red, and yellow animal piñatas sway from the rafters. A mariachi quartet serenades the noisy diners.

I worry the cacophony of sounds throughout the restaurant will make it hard to have a conversation. Ethan stands up first to get his food from the buffet line. As he walks out of earshot, Jake leans toward me. "You didn't tell me he had an earring. And a hickey. Interesting." He has a smug look on his face. Is he proud? Is Ethan a chip off the old block? I cringe. My rage from the night before resurfaces. You creep. I challenge myself to maintain control.

We make civilized small talk as we rotate to get our food. Everyone settles in their seats with plates full of tacos, enchiladas, beans and rice, and guacamole. Jake and Marian don't bother to dig in. They monopolize the conversation with their similar scripted chitchat from last night about how busy they are and how hard it is to make a living. This time it's for Ethan's benefit. The two headliners perform their routine knowing when to say something and when to be silent. I watch Ethan. He takes a bite of a taco. I'm glad I prepared him for the 'how hard we work and how little time and money we have' speech. He listens politely and chews. I wait for a lull in their commentary and jump in.

"How are your other kids, Jake? I guess they're not kids anymore."

Jake takes a sip of his margarita. "They're fine. Kevin is doing better. He seems happy. He's finally making a living."

"Do they know about me?" Ethan asks.

"No."

"Not even Kevin?" I interject, remembering the morning, so many years ago, when I blurted out I was pregnant.

"No."

"Oh," Ethan says, leaning forward. "That's too bad."

"You know, Ethan, I've tried explaining to your mother that she has no understanding of the type of life I — we live." He reaches for Marian's hand. "We're busy. We go to work very early, get home very late. That's why I rarely see my kids. If Marian and I didn't work together, we'd hardly see each other."

Mariachi players approach our table singing, "Vaya con dios, my darling, vaya con dios, my love." No one acknowledges them so they leave.

Ethan looks into his father's blue eyes. "I'm going to ask you a question, Jake, but you don't have to answer it."

Like watching a tennis match, my eyes goes back and forth between Ethan and Jake. It's strange to see them together. I compare the powerful square cut of Ethan's jaw to Jake's deeply creased jowls and slack, drooping chin. He still doesn't have a child who looks like him.

"Go ahead," Jake offers.

"Why did you leave me?"

A shock courses through my body. The energy around the table shifts. No one talks and silence spreads throughout the room. It's as though everyone in the restaurant waits for the answer.

"I didn't," Jake says.

"He didn't," Marian says.

"Yes, you did," Ethan retorts. "What you did was irresponsible and amoral."

I lean back in my chair, and slowly pull down my sunglasses from on top of my head. I'd brought them with me for protection. I'm afraid I'll cry. I'm witnessing my son stand up for his rightful place in Jake's family.

"Your mother was responsible for this," Marian says. "She was the one who was amoral when she didn't tell Jake what she was doing. What do you think of someone who stops taking birth control pills and doesn't tell her partner? Is the man responsible for her baby?"

Ethan focuses his attention on Marian.

"Excuse me," he says. "You weren't there. You may not speak."

Marian stiffens. "I beg your pardon."

Ethan leans into her. "This happened way before you. My mother's told me one story, and Jake's told you another. They're obviously different stories. For all we know my mother is lying, or he is lying, or they're both lying. But you weren't there, and you don't know."

"This all happened a very long time ago." Jake puts a hand on Marian's arm. "I lived in a big house in the suburbs along the Hudson River with my wife, my children, and a dog. I wasn't happy and so I began therapy, and then started to date, and eventually left everything. I still miss my dog. It was the sixties, the sexual revolution. Everything was very free and open. I wouldn't recommend it now, with AIDS and all, but that was the way it was back then. That's when I met your mother."

Marian's upper body hovers over her plate of food. "Your mother was part of the group that Jake knew on Fire Island. She had many different relationships, too. She was involved with a man named Alex and a New York Yankee, before Jake."

"I what?" I exclaim and start to get out of my seat. "How dare you!"

Ethan cuts me off. "No, no, no, no!" He wags his finger from side to side in front of Marion's face. "You don't understand. You weren't there. You may not speak."

She looks at him with a twisted expression, then leans back and surrenders.

Ethan reaches under the table and squeezes my hand. He turns his attention to Jake. "I have an older friend," Ethan says slowly and respectfully, "whose girlfriend stopped taking her pills without telling him. She got pregnant. He was going to a junior college part-time, working full-time to save money to go away to a university. When she told him she was pregnant, she said that he didn't have to take care of the baby — she'd do it by herself. But you know what he said?"

He waits for Jake to respond.

Jake shakes his head.

"He said, 'No way. That's my baby, and I will be part of its life.' And he is. You didn't do that."

"You call me amoral and irresponsible, Ethan, but your mother set this up. She's the one who wanted you. She's the one who's responsible for you. I was duped."

"You're my father — no matter how that happened."

Jake slumps in his chair. "I can see how you believe this," he says softly. "But to be honest, I wasn't the first person your mother slept with."

My lungs feel devoid of air. I gasp.

"All these years later and you contact me with all this rage. Like it was my fault!"

I lift my glasses so he can see my eyes. "The part that was your fault was to walk away so easily, so completely. Never wondering, never asking. The part that was your fault was never to respond to Ethan when he tried to contact you. Twice. I can't believe I ever thought you were a caring and honorable person."

"People still think I am."

Ethan and I look at each other. The waiter interrupts with the bill.

"This conversation isn't going anywhere," Jake says. "I suggest we end it." He takes his credit card out. His hand trembles as he puts it on the tray. He looks at Marian and pats her arm. "We're going on a vacation and when we come back, I'll call." He looks at Ethan. "You're obviously a bright young man, very thoughtful. Maybe we can get to know each other — slowly build a relationship." He pushes back his chair. "I'll be right back." He dismisses us like his subordinates at one of his meetings.

I turn and face Marian. "You know, unlike Jake, I have a big investment in remembering everything that went on between us. And in order for him to have done what he's done these many years, he's had to be in denial about it."

"Jake is not a liar."

"I didn't say he was a liar. I said he was in denial. I told him I was thinking about having a child, and when I discussed contraceptives with him, he told me it was up to the woman." I pause and then soften my voice. "I know I could have been more direct, more protective of Jake, but I wanted a child. And if he had once said 'no' to me, this wonderful human being would not be here right now."

"And he is wonderful," Marian says, looking over at Ethan who sits quietly, watching. Marian's unexpected change in tone and attitude throws me. But she's been living with Jake for several years now. She must have some clue about him.

"Thank you. You know what a hard time Jake has setting limits for himself, how out of control his life can be."

Marion doesn't get a chance to respond because Jake returns to the table. He remains standing.

"What's going on?"

"They're fighting," Ethan says.

"We're not fighting," Marian and I both answer.

"Good," Jake says. "We've had enough of that. More than enough."

He turns and we get up to leave the restaurant. Outside, Jake motions to Ethan that he wants to talk to him privately. I stand with Marian, but I watch. Jake puts his arm around Ethan's shoulder. I feel the adrenaline course through my bloodstream again.

"Mom," Ethan calls, "when are we going to be in New York?"

"The last weekend in March," I answer.

"We'll be home by then," Jake says to Ethan as they walk over to us, "so we'll be able to see each other."

We say our good-byes and everyone shakes hands. Ethan and I walk back to our car. It's over.

"He's lying," Ethan says, getting into the front seat.

"What makes you say that?"

"He had a hard time looking at you. He looked at me, he looked at her, but he wouldn't look at you." He buckles his seat belt. "He knows he deserted me and he knows you didn't dupe him."

"It sure didn't sound that way." I smile at my son. "I'm proud of you, E. You took on two well-rehearsed and well-prepared adversaries."

"You think so?"

"I know so. And you did it calmly. You never lost your temper. Even the way you silenced Marian, 'no, no, no, no, you may not speak!' That was awesome." I relax into my seat. "What made you tell him about New York?"

"I figure we were going there, why not? He'll have to make the effort, though. I won't call him."

"Sounds good."

Ethan shrugs. "He's a very sad man, Mom. I get the feeling there's not much in his life that makes him happy."

I lean over and kiss him. "You're right. I think one of the best things he could have in his life is you. It's sad he's missing out."

"Mom, I know you want to talk more, but I'm really tired. Can we go home?"

"No more postmortems?" I buckle up and start the car. "Oh, one more thing. The under the table thing, squeezing my hand? Thank you."

Ethan nods.

"I really needed that. Knowing you were on my side meant a lot."

"Of course, I'm on your side. I know who this man is."

I smile. "You do now."

13

SANTA MONICA

1997

*B*y midweek when I don't hear from Phil, I know he's serious about me making the first move. I miss everything about him, his love, his warmth, his integrity, his counsel and his willingness to work with me and help me get beyond my trust issues — something I have to face head on.

I stand in the doorway of his office watching him from behind as he talks on the phone. He rotates left and right in his brown leather chair and every so often he leans all the way back making it screech. Occasionally he runs his long fingers through his hair. He faces a view of downtown Los Angeles to the east, and the Fox Plaza building to the south. I think of Bruce Willis in *Die Hard* and how he had gone to that building to win back his wife.

With a backdrop of the evening sky, the bright lights of the city twinkle in the distance. The clamor of the busy office is silenced for the day and the upcoming weekend. I checked Phil's schedule earlier with his secretary and we conspired so I would show up promptly at seven.

I wait at the door until he's finished. His spacious office is masculine with brown and black leather and a large teak conference table. A chrome and glass coffee table is positioned in front of a two-person sofa. Phil sits quietly for a few minutes before he turns around and sees me.

"Maddy. What are you doing here?"

"I came to see you. I want to whisk you away for the evening." I smile and hold up the tennis shoes and leather jacket that he always keeps in the office.

"I don't know what to say."

"Hello? I'm glad to see you? Come sit down?"

He stands up and points to one of the two beige upholstered chairs in front of his desk. I hesitate and then sit in one. He comes around his desk and kisses me on the cheek. His blue shirt is open at the neck and the knot of his tie falls midway down his chest.

I finger my hoop earring. "I think I'm intruding. Do you have plans?"

"It's Friday. I haven't heard from you since last Saturday."

He walks behind the desk and buttons his collar.

"I didn't want to call until I got some things straightened out."

"Isn't that our problem? You always need to work things out by yourself before you tell me anything? Am I supposed to sit around while you work things out?" He pauses. "The truth is I know I want someone in my life again — a partner. I thought it would be you."

I look down at the sneakers in my lap, and put them on the floor. I wonder how people summon the courage to ask questions they don't want to know the answers to. "Do you have a date tonight?" I ask.

"I'm supposed to go to my associate's house for dinner. It's a small get together. There's someone he wants me to meet."

"Oh." I take a deep breath.

"You didn't call, Maddy. What was I supposed to think?"

I close my eyes. "I don't know, nothing? That I'm worth more than six days of your time and worth fighting over." I stand up and drape his jacket on the chair and start toward the door.

He comes from behind the desk, beats me to the door and closes it. He puts his hands on my shoulders and gently forces me to look at him. "I don't want anyone else Maddy. I want you. I don't know how to get you." He pulls me back to the chairs and turns them around so they face each other. "What did you straighten out this week?" We sit with his legs on either side of mine, touching.

"I was going to take us to the pier, our first date. I was going to suggest we start over — again. Last time."

"And if we start over, what will change?"

I close my eyes. "Me. Maybe. At least I want to try." I look at him, my eyes brimming with tears. "It's not just you I treat this way. I don't trust anyone. I let people get close, at least I appear to, but only so far. I always keep a safe distance. From you, from Ethan, from everybody. The only thing I trust is that you will all hurt me and I can't, won't let that happen. And when I tell you this, when I show you how scared I am, how rubbery and blubbery I am, you'll run away." I cover my mouth with my hand. Tears begin to fall.

He takes my hand away from my mouth and holds my face in his hands. He gently wipes away my tears. "Hey, I deal with criminals everyday — I don't run away from them."

"Very funny."

"I'm not being funny. You're not a criminal, you're not a bad person Maddy. Your intentions are good. You're kind, generous and you're not perfect. So, what else is new?"

"I've been like this since I was three and that's like forty-eight years."

"Then we'll work on it together for the next forty-eight. But I want you to understand something, and I don't mean to threaten you, this can't happen again. I won't let you cast me aside. Twice is enough."

"Is this the three strikes law?"

He smiles and squeezes my hands. "We can work through this, but only if you're willing to risk it."

I take a deep breath, reach up and stroke his cheek. "Are you too good to be true? I've wanted 'a you' my whole life." I lean over and lightly kiss him. "I feel like I'm on the rim of the Grand Canyon ready to drop into an unknown abyss. No," I say, shaking my head. "I feel like I'm stepping outside of my box, my windowsill, and you're holding my hand."

He looks at me, questioning me with his eyes.

"I'll explain later."

I stand and pull him up. I put my arms around his neck and this time as I kiss him I surrender into his arms letting as much of my body touch as much of him as I can. I feel him get hard against my belly. His fingers weave through my hair as his mouth opens against mine and our tongues touch. He pulls back my head and kisses my neck and the hollow in my throat. That sweet moan, from somewhere deep down in my body, comes out of my mouth. Every part of me quivers. "Are you going to call your associate and cancel dinner?"

———

Julia and I walk by the ocean twice a week. We like breathing fresh sea air. Our jobs are taxing. Julia's a party planner for large corporations arranging formal dinners, fundraisers, and some red carpet events for the Hollywood crowd. We usually saunter along the path from Santa Monica to Venice watching volleyball players, street musicians and the numerous homeless people struggling through life. Tonight we drive to the Marina for a change of scenery.

"The last time I was in Burton Chace Park, I told Beth I was pregnant. God was I naive."

"Young, too."

"I thought I knew everything."

Julia's pixie haircut frames her face. Her eyes look huge. She wears red furry earmuffs and red woolen gloves. "How's school going?"

"I broke up a fight today." I roll my eyes.

"What?"

"I was at the board writing down the difference between criminal court and civil court when there was a crashing sound followed by objects whizzing past my head. I whirled around to see Sal, with his hands around Troy's throat, shaking him like a rag doll. And Troy, who's about four inches shorter than Sal, was flailing about trying desperately to connect with Sal's anatomy. Within seconds, the other kids jumped in and pulled them apart. Then I rushed in."

"Are you nuts?"

I shrug. "I threw aside a desk and stepped between the boys. Wonder Woman to the rescue."

Julia stops walking. "And?"

"Sal kept twisting, trying to get loose. I clamped my hands on his shoulders and yelled. 'Sal, stop!' I fixed my eyes onto his and kept repeating, 'Look at me. Calm down. You're okay.'" I pause. "It was wild. The other kids did a great job holding on to Troy, so I could keep my attention on Sal."

"Scary!"

"No time to think. Finally Sal's breathing evened out and his muscles relaxed."

We start walking again.

"Then?"

I laugh. "I sat down to talk with them. All's well that ends well. But it's so frustrating. They're so sensitive. They fly off the handle with little provocation."

She slips her arm through mine. "Talking about frustrating, what's with the Jake thing?"

"Nothing."

We walk in silence.

"I don't know why," Julia says, "but this reminds me of someone I worked with. She had great ideas for the clients, and she was beautiful. But she was self-centered and narcissistic. She gave everyone a hard time, including me. One day, when I was in San Francisco, I saw this white, muslin doll, with outstretched arms, like a scarecrow. It had stamps on various body parts, with curses like the Passover Plagues — boils, pimples, gas, hemorrhoids. I bought it. Every time she did something hurtful I'd take out the doll and stick her with a pin."

I laugh. "Did your voodoo work?"

"It made me feel better."

We stop by the fence overlooking the water.

"Why are you telling me this?"

"To help you feel better. You can't change Jake, Maddy. Ethan got to meet him, maybe that's all you can accomplish."

"I don't think so."

"What do you mean?"

"He can't disappear again. I promised Ethan when he was a year old that I wouldn't let Jake hurt him. I broke that promise at nine, fifteen and now."

"But you promised Jake, too."

I bend my neck back to stretch out some kinks. "I know. But the promise to Jake," I shrug, "I thought I'd be enough." A large nimbus cloud floats across the sky. I feel cold. "Do you want to get a bite to eat?"

"In a minute. What did you mean about being enough?"

"I thought if I tried my hardest, gave Ethan my love and support, he wouldn't be hurt by not having a father."

"We do the best we can, Maddy." She gives me a hug. "What are you thinking of doing?"

"Your cousin Joanne called me. She wanted the names of private schools for one of her clients. Since I had her on the phone I asked her some legal questions about paternity. Guess what she told me?"

Julia shrugs.

"Until Ethan turns eighteen, I can sue Jake to establish paternity. At eighteen, Ethan can sue Jake for child support from birth to adulthood."

Julia's eyes get enormous. "You wouldn't."

"Don't plan to, but it's interesting. It's not a voodoo doll but at least I have options."

———

A week later, I write Jake another letter. The words flow. I'm so into it I jump when the phone rings. It rings several times before I pick up, allowing my heartbeat to return to normal.

"How're you doing?" Beth asks. "We haven't talked in ages."

"I'm fine. Thanks for Ethan's birthday present. I hope he thanked you."

"He did. Did he hear from Jake?"

"Funny you should ask." I twirl the cord around my finger. "Ethan heard from you, Linda, his cousins. But not his father. I just finished writing to dear old dad."

"Uh oh, Madd, another missive? Was Ethan upset?"

"He didn't discuss it with me. I'm upset." I scroll to the beginning of the letter. "Want to hear it? It's hot off my finger tips."

"Every time I talk to you it's an episode from a soap opera: *On the Edge with Maddy Gold*, or *Over the Edge with Maddy Gold*. Which one?"

I laugh. "Probably both. Here goes."

> *Dear Jake,*
>
> *Three months have gone since we met in February. You were too busy to meet Ethan in New York in March and in April you ignored his birthday. How many times can you disappoint your son?*
>
> *I know how important meeting you was to Ethan. While I sensed the depth of his unspoken feelings of abandonment, I had no idea that he'd have the courage to confront you with them.*
>
> *I have no regrets about having Ethan, but I was naive and wrong on many levels.*
>
> *Ethan just turned seventeen and he's going into his last year of high school. He's looking into colleges and wants to go out of town. I want your help. I want you to pay for it. I've done it by myself — I've done a good job. It's your turn to contribute to his success. This is crucial emotionally as well as practically.*
>
> *I look forward to hearing from you.*
> *Sincerely,*

I wait. "Beth, you still there?"

She sighs. "It's very direct. What do you think he'll say?"

"After he picks himself up off the floor? He'll be furious. I see his response. 'Bitch.'" I turn in my chair. "This was never about money but it is now. I was going to ask for half the college costs, but I figure he'll bargain so I'm going for the jackpot. What do you think?"

"Is this what Ethan wants?"

"I haven't told him. It's between Jake and me. I don't have the right to give Jake an easy out and Jake doesn't have the right to walk and use me as the excuse. After February, it would've been easy for Jake to start a relationship with Ethan. But he didn't."

Beth sighs again. "Who would've thought all this would happen because of an obituary?"

"It would've happened regardless." I can't read Beth's reaction so I change the subject. "How are you?"

"On my way to meet a friend. We'll take a walk, rent a movie and order in Thai. I put another ad in the paper. My yearly attempt at bringing a man into my life. If nothing else," she laughs, "I get lots of responses. The process sucks, but I'd like to meet someone. How are you and Phil? I'm envious, Maddy."

I pick up a pen and doodle a happy face. "I wish he had a twin or I could clone him for you. I'll keep my fingers crossed."

"Gotta go. We'll talk next week."

I hang up. How wonderful and unique it is for me to have a loving man in my life. I pick up Jake's letter and sign it.

———

Whether or not Jake responds, my life and Ethan's will go on. By mid-July, with college looming, we'll get a head start on seeing some state colleges around California. I plan a trip to two Northern

California universities. I'm excited but Ethan is sullen. I hope the first stop at Sonoma State will change his attitude.

We fly to Oakland, rent a car and drive directly to the university. It's two hours through rolling hills and farms. Ethan sleeps while I wonder how to snap him out of his mood. I can't. When he's ready, he'll talk. In the meantime, I'll try to have a good time in spite of him.

"Where are we?" he asks, an hour into the trip.

"Halfway there." I force exuberance. "Are you hungry? We could eat on campus. Food's an important concern when you're choosing a college."

"I don't care." He looks out the window. "Is this place in the boonies? It's cows and horses everywhere."

"What did you expect? You already saw Humboldt State. The countryside is different, but it's still rural."

"I don't want rural."

"There's not much else to choose from, Ethan. You've ruled out L.A. Too close to home. You aren't interested in San Diego. So what do you want?"

"For starters, I don't want you yelling at me."

"You haven't been helping me. Can't we look at this place? Can you keep an open mind?"

"Fine."

We continue in silence. I turn left onto the campus.

"This is nice," I say, parking the car. "Let's look at the campus map so we know where to go. We can find a dorm, maybe get a tour."

I open my door and fling it shut without waiting for him. He's damn infuriating — adult one minute and a tantrum throwing two-year old the next. I locate the administration building on the map and walk in that direction. Ethan follows. Dark wooden buildings nestle amongst mature oak, pine, and cedar trees. "It's a beautiful campus," I say, into the cool breeze.

"Where are all the people?"

"It's summer. It's Friday. People go home, or out of town for the weekend."

I see kids talking, laughing, throwing footballs and tossing Frisbees. It's a carefree college environment. I want to join them and escape my petulant child.

"The housing office is over there." I point to my left. "Maybe we can look at a dorm?"

Ethan nods. We walk into the office and find a young college woman dressed in shorts and a Sonoma State T-shirt. She's happy to take us on a tour of a dormitory suite.

"This is nice," Ethan says, as he sees the two bedrooms with an adjoining den area.

"Is it hard to get one of these?" He likes something. "How far ahead do you have to apply?"

I hope asking questions and taking care of logistics will keep Ethan happy.

"Relax, Mom. I'm not interested."

"How can you say that?"

"Easy. I—am—not—interested. This place isn't for me."

Flushed and flustered, I turn to the guide. "I guess that's that. Thanks for your time." The young woman smiles and leaves.

"I don't understand you, Ethan. I thought you liked it?"

"The dorm's nice, but I'd go nuts in this place."

"Then that's the end of our trip. Chico State is more in the boonies than this is." My heart pounds. I want to have a temper tantrum. "Do you want to go home?"

"Can we eat first? And not here."

"We'll find a restaurant on the way to the airport," I say exasperated. We get into the car. "Will you tell me what's going on? Your attitude sucks. You're not pleasant and this is costing a lot of money."

"That's the whole point."

"What is?"

I back out of the space.

"Money. How are you going to pay for college?"

I stop the car. "That's what this is about? You're worried about money? I've always told you that you'll go to college. I have money saved. Grandpa and Grandma saved money for you, and if I need to I'll get loans. You'll go to school. I promise."

I start driving. This is a good time to tell Ethan about my letter.

"I wrote to Jake. I told him I want him to pay for college."

"You what?" He glares at me. "How could you?"

I stare back. "I did it after he was too busy to see you in New York, and then when he didn't acknowledge your birthday."

"That's my call. Why are you butting in? Why didn't you ask me?"

"It wasn't a decision you needed to make. This is between Jake and me."

I pull into the crowded parking lot of a roadside restaurant. Its flashing neon sign says, OPEN. Ethan exits the car and slams the door. He walks ahead.

Seated in a booth, he immediately confronts me.

"You had no right to do that. Did you get an answer? Was he angry?"

"I didn't get an answer. He probably was angry. So what?"

"When he was too busy in N.Y. weren't you the one who said I shouldn't burn my bridges? And now if he gets angry, then what?"

I press myself against the back of the booth. "First of all, I'm the one who's asking, not you. He can be angry at me. Secondly, it's not like he's paying any attention to you. He could have called or sent you a card, or even a birthday present." I pause. "I don't think there's anything to lose."

"You should have asked me. It affects me." He leans across the table. "I don't understand you. You're making him out to be the bad guy. You're the one who told him that he didn't have to have anything to do with me. You're changing the rules on him."

My heart races. "Is that what you think? I'm the bad guy?

"You picked a loser and set this up."

215

"It's not that simple. But I did. I wanted you."

"And now we're both stuck."

The waitress appears and takes our order.

"What happens if you don't hear from him?"

I take a deep breath. "I might call an attorney to establish paternity. I don't think that will happen. Jake's too smart. I asked him to pay your college expenses figuring we'd settle on half."

"You'd really take him to court? What if I don't want you to?"

I shake my head. "I know you believe this is a decision you should be included in, but if I'd asked you about sending this letter, you would have told me, no. I believe it was the right thing to do. Let's see if I get a response." I take a sip of water. "For now, what are we doing about college? This trip?"

He scratches his head. "I don't know."

"We could go to Berkeley," I suggest. "See friends. We could even go across the bridge and visit San Francisco State."

"Will you tell me if you get an answer?"

"No more secrets. And I'll listen to what you have to say. But I'll make the final decision."

Ethan laughs. "We'll see about that."

When we arrive home, I get the mail. It's about to overflow from collecting five days of mostly junk. I find Jake's letter stuck in the middle of a bill from Macy's and a flyer advertising home mortgages. I check the envelope as I walk to the apartment. His chicken scrawl is spread across the front in black ink. I wonder how a handwriting expert would interpret it.

I rip open the envelope. I read it several times. My body tenses, yet I find him funny.

Dear Maddy,

I was shocked by the content of your letter. I'll answer you at some future time.

Sincerely,

J.

A two-sentence letter! Dismissed and put on his back burner, I go into the house and find Ethan. He's in his room, unpacking. I hold up the letter.

"It's from your father." I can't hide my contempt.

"What'd he say?"

"Read it. It's not long."

I hand the letter to Ethan and watch him.

He looks at me and gives it back. "Now what? We wait? Do you think he was angry?"

"I do. Maybe he went running to his lawyer to check out what this means, and he's stalling for time. I'm willing to wait. If I do something it has to be before you're eighteen. We still have plenty of time."

Ethan pushes aside his suitcase and sits on his bed. His dirty laundry is strewn around the carpet.

"What exactly would it mean if we took him to court?"

"What I want to happen is that he'd have to admit, legally, that he's your father, and that he has some legal responsibility to you."

I lean against the dresser.

"I don't want him made out to be the bad guy. Would they do that?"

"I don't know, Ethan. I've never done anything like this before." I toy with a Michael Jordan action figure that is part of his ten-year collection. "Why are you asking? Have you changed your mind?"

"I've been thinking. He's used to getting his way, and he thinks he can play you along somehow. I don't like that. Maybe we do need to take him to court. If he has more money than we do, he should have to pay for some things for me. But I don't want to see him crucified."

I'm surprised. "You've been doing a lot of thinking. Look, we don't have to make any decisions now. We can take things one-step at a time. Let's see if he writes again, and if he doesn't, we can meet with the lawyer and ask her all sorts of questions."

"All right," he says. He seems solemn and thoughtful. Then he perks up. "When can we go to the kennel and rescue the pup?"

I smile. Phanny is definitely Ethan's security blanket. "Give me thirty minutes."

The next Saturday, Ethan, Phil and I go to the Encino driving range. Even though it's crowded it's the only time we could all get together. Ethan stands on one side of me while Phil is on the other. Each of us has our own bucket of golf balls. Mine is half full and theirs are completely full because they're having so much fun teasing me with old jokes they find hilarious.

"Maddy relax. Keep your left shoulder higher than your right. And you're standing too close to the ball — after you hit it."

"Don't try to kill the ball, Mom. I've seen a better swing on a gate."

"Okay, you guys," I say, placing my hands on my hips. "You seem way too focused on me and enjoying it way too much. I'm going to get my book, a cup of coffee, and sign up for lessons with a pro. Then, some day soon, I will come back and whip your butts but good."

Phil and Ethan look chastised.

"Are you sure? You're not angry are you?" Ethan asks.

"Nope." I smile. "Challenged. You, gentlemen, are going to be very sorry."

I walk away swinging my club and whistling. I'm actually very happy. The two men in my life like each other. Ethan has even begun to call Phil on his own, asking for advice, or just wanting to say hello. When they find me, an hour later, I'm almost finished with *Turtle Moon*, by Alice Hoffman, and the three of us are ready to go for lunch.

We drive from the valley to Malibu by way of the Santa Monica Mountains and land at Geoffrey's. It reminds me of a Mediterranean restaurant, or at least what I imagine one would look like. It's a clean white building with a large outside dining patio perched high upon a cliff overlooking the Pacific Ocean. Magenta bougainvillea hangs everywhere contrasting dramatically against the white of the building and the blue of the ocean and sky.

Ethan's mouth drops open as we sit at our table. He looks around. "This is great."

"This was one of the first places I took your mother to after we met." Phil smiles at me. "I was trying to win her over very early on."

"This place could do it. It would be great to come here for dinner on prom night, but it's probably too far from the hotel."

I look at Ethan. "You're already thinking about the prom? It's, what, eight, nine months away? Do you have a date in mind, too?"

"No, but I'm looking." He smiles broadly. "There are some really beautiful girls at Samo."

The waitress interrupts Ethan's fantasy. She hands out the menus, announces the lunch specials and takes our orders. I want to update Phil about my legal plans. We haven't talked about it since I got Jake's note a few months ago. There hasn't been a reason to. But yesterday I reached my limit and made a decision.

"Ethan and I have an appointment with two attorneys on Monday."

Phil takes a sip of his beer.

"Family law attorneys," I continue. "We're going to find out what it means to sue Jake for paternity."

Phil looks from me to Ethan. Ethan appears oblivious to our discussion. He stares out over the water.

"When did you decide?"

"Yesterday. I hadn't heard from Jake since his last note, and some future time, as he put it, has long come and gone. If this is something I want to do, then I need to know what it entails. Ethan will be eighteen in April and that's not so far away."

"Who's the attorney?" His voice sounds strained.

"Julia's cousin and her partner."

"Why didn't you ask if I knew anyone?"

I'm unprepared for his reaction. I did it again — I shut him out.

"I don't know. I didn't think about it. I told you that Julia's cousin, Joanne, had called me a while ago to ask about special education programs, and that I had asked her a few questions about paternity. Her field is family law, so I called her." My voice rises an octave. "Are you upset about that?"

Ethan turns around and looks at us.

"I'm a lawyer. I would think you'd have asked me."

"But you're a criminal lawyer. It's not your area. Every time I've ever had a legal question out of someone's field of expertise, I've been told, 'I can't answer that.' I didn't think to ask you."

"You two aren't fighting are you?"

Phil and I look at each other and then at Ethan.

"No." We answer in unison.

"Do you want to know their names and check them out in whatever book you check lawyers in?"

"No," he says. "I trust you to do what's best for you."

I want to say, "Well, thank you," but I know that won't be helpful.

"Ethan has some questions and so do I. I thought we'd meet with Joanne and her partner and get some answers. We're not committing to anything."

Ethan looks at Phil. "I want him to stop lying about my mother and lying about me. I exist, because of him. No matter what my mother told him."

The waiter interrupts again, this time with the food. When the dishes are served, napkins placed on everyone's lap, and the forks and knives raised, Phil stops the action. He takes my hand and Ethan's, holds them up high and makes a toast. "May all your questions be answered and all your issues and concerns be resolved. Successfully."

Ethan smiles. "Hear, hear."

14

SANTA MONICA

1997 – 1998

*O*n **October 17, I pick Ethan up at school** and drive to Hamburger Hamlet in Brentwood. We have a three-thirty meeting with the lawyers. A waitress is taking Ethan's order, when I see two women scan the restaurant. I wave. They walk over smiling and introduce themselves.

"Hi, Maddy. Hello, Ethan. I'm Julia's cousin, Joanne Lippman. This is my partner, Alexis Strauss."

They sit down and adjust their briefcases and note pads. I study these two women who might represent me. Joanne is tall and blond and looks more like Julia's younger sister than her cousin. Alexis is a petite brunette with her sunglasses resting on top of her head to keep her long curls from falling in her face. They're more than partners, they're friends who genuinely like each other.

"Alexis will be handling your case," Joanne says. "I'll be there to help her and reassure you. We know these situations aren't easy." Joanne's sparkling blue eyes radiate warmth as she smiles and looks at us. "Why don't you fill her in on what's happening — what you're thinking of doing."

"Where to begin?" I say. "Ethan is seventeen. I'm a single parent, and his father has had nothing to do with him for all these years. I told him he didn't have to and he didn't. His name isn't on Ethan's birth certificate."

I relate the facts in a monotone. Alexis takes notes on her yellow legal pad.

Well," Alexis says, "it doesn't really matter what you told him." She adjusts her eyeglasses. "If he is Ethan's father, he is responsible for him and always has been. The courts recognize this now, and don't permit deadbeat dads to walk away from their children."

The waitress interrupts bringing Ethan's hamburger. No one else orders anything. Alexis continues. "First we'd have to establish paternity, and custody. That's — "

"Custody?" I interrupt. "I have custody. He's mine. I raised him," I sputter. "Are you joking?"

Alexis shakes her head. "No, I'm very serious."

"You mean Jake could have taken Ethan away from me? All this time? I don't believe it. I mean he never would have, but to think he could have, and I didn't know."

Alexis nods and goes on. "We'd file a Complaint to Establish Parental Relationship, and an Order to Show Cause for Custody and Child Support. I'm warning you, his attorney will demand you all have a DNA test."

Alexis looks at Ethan and at me.

"You mean like O.J.?" Ethan says.

"Not quite as involved," she laughs, "and in family court, unlike criminal court, the results are accepted as proof of paternity."

"I understand that his lawyer would insist," I agree. "It's a waste of money. I don't have a problem with it." I shake my head. "Oh, God, Jake's going to die. All this coming out in the open, needing to get a lawyer, going to court."

"If he's smart," Alexis interrupts, "it will never get to court."

"Have you had any contact with him recently?" Joanne asks.

I give Alexis and Joanne all the information about my contact with Jake, our meeting with Ethan and my letter requesting financial support for Ethan's college education.

"Can he pay for it? Does he have money?" Alexis asks.

"I imagine so. He won't be happy. I'm sure he's thinking of retiring."

"What does he do?" Joanne asks.

"He owns an advertising agency."

"Well," Alexis explains, "we'll ask for a lump sum for Ethan for college plus child support payments for you. He won't want to deal with Ethan in court when he becomes an adult. Right now, because you waited so long to do this, Maddy, you can only collect child support until Ethan is eighteen. And that's when?"

"April of next year," Ethan says.

"Okay, from the day we file in court until then. But Ethan can sue him when he turns eighteen. And that's from day one through eighteen. This man will definitely not want to have that happen. You're in a very good position."

I feel my chest tighten and a pain in my stomach. "Can't we just ask the court to legally recognize Jake as Ethan's father? This was never about money, until I got angry by the way he treated Ethan."

"It's not that simple, Maddy," Joanne says. "The courts are protecting the rights of children, and not many judges are going to look kindly on a man who walked away from his child and refused to take care of him financially."

Ethan speaks up. "I don't want him to be the villain. He's not a mean person."

I sit quietly.

"I understand." Alexis focuses right in on Ethan. "We can file the court papers for paternity and custody and at the same time let him know that we would like to handle the financial settlement out of court. That would be the more gentle way of doing it."

I watch his reaction.

"Okay," he says finally, "I think he should have to pay something, but I don't want him dragged through the mud."

I take a deep breath and plunge forward with my questions. "What is this going to cost? A small fortune or a big one?"

"We can't give you a definitive answer," Joanne says. "We charge by the hour, but we're lowering our fee for you because you're Julia's friend, and we think this is an interesting case. Beyond that, we can only hope that he doesn't decide to drag this on with continuances and other delaying tactics. That will make it very costly."

I purse my lips and turn to Ethan. "Do you need to discuss this with me privately?"

He's quiet for a moment.

"No," he says, "but if it's going to cost you a lot of money — "

"Let me worry about that, E. I have money saved and if Joanne and Alexis think we can win, then it's worth the investment. This is important to me and to you. I think your father should have honored you after he met you. But it didn't work out that way." I turn back to the two women who are now my attorneys. "What do I do next? Do we sign a contract?"

"No." Alexis says. "We'll need a retainer and some information, like Ethan's father's name, his address, things like that. Then I'll get started."

I open my folder, pat Ethan's hand and turn my attention to Alexis.

———

The days, weeks and months fly by. October turns into mid-December. I'm settled into my new teaching assignment while Ethan bounces back and forth between the joys of being a big man on campus and the doldrums of senioritis. He loves his success but hates the sameness and being treated like a child. I'm happy he shows these signs of being normal and typical.

As for Jake, although I haven't heard from him, he's on my mind and most days in my face. Lawsuits do that — so much time, energy and money. Alexis and I trade phone calls four or five times a week, and each call costs a minimum of a quarter of an hour's fee. My mind turns into a cash register and a stopwatch every time I hear the lawyer's voice. As the bills come in, my panic escalates. How can I afford this?

Finally, unable to stand it any longer, I discuss it with Alexis. She calms and reassures me. She explains she doesn't charge for phone messages left on answering machines so that's the way we communicate. I call Alexis at night and speak to her machine. She calls me during the day when I'm teaching and leaves messages on mine.

On the last day of December, I receive a letter from Alexis. I read the Post-it on the outside. "As soon as you authorize it, he will be served." My hands shake. I sit down before unfolding the letter. While it's written in legalese, the message to Jake is simple. Let's settle this or appear in Los Angeles Superior Court and answer to paternity charges. I read it three times. I ask Ethan if he wants to see it. He declines. I hold it in my hand and walk around the apartment not knowing what to do. Finally, I go into my bedroom and call Phil.

"This is really happening," I say. "I have the letter to Jake and as soon as I give the go ahead, they'll send out the little subpoena man to serve him."

The call waiting beeper beeps.

"Oops, can you hold?"

I press the button.

"Hello, Maddy, it's Jake."

I freeze except for my thudding heart. "Uh, hello. How are you?"

"Fine. I'm calling because I haven't written. Are you coming to New York soon?"

His voice sounds casual, friendly.

"No, Jake. I have no reason to. Why?"

"I thought we could sit down, face to face, and talk. I find it hard to respond to you when you write such angry letters."

"Can you hold?" I want to get back to Phil and I need some breathing time.

I click back to Phil. "It's him," I wail.

"Who?"

"Jake. How could he call the day I get the letter. Do you think he knows?

"He's not the psychic type, Maddy. Take some deep breaths. You'll be fine."

"Okay. I'll call you after."

I click back to Jake.

"Hi, I'm back."

"How's Ethan?"

"He's fine. Up and down. Teenage stuff. And you?"

I swing my legs off the bed and plant them on the ground. I need more time.

"I'm good. No, actually I'm depressed. Things have been very difficult. The pressure and stress. People are getting sick and dying. You know about my mother. And now a friend died. My partner had triple by-pass surgery. Someone else has prostate cancer. I'm working hard. My house is a mess. It wasn't ready for our annual Christmas party, so we canceled it. I don't get out of here until late at night. We're still at the office. I'm well respected. But it's hard."

I pick up a silver bracelet on my night table and toy with the clasp. Jake keeps talking. "Ask me if I'd run this kind of business again?"

I don't say anything.

"Go ahead, ask me."

"You mean now? You want me to ask you now?"

"Yes."

"All right. Would you do it again?"

He begins his second soliloquy, when I realize I don't have to listen to him anymore.

"Jake." I yell into the phone. "Stop! This has nothing to do with what we need to discuss."

"What do you mean? It has everything to do with it. It's, it's about me, my life, and — "

"Jake," I interrupt again, speaking more softly, "this isn't about you. It's about Ethan."

"No, it's about me. My life is not like yours. I don't remember the last time I saw my daughter and she lives in New York. I'm living my life this way, and I choose to. I have fun things in my life, but I work very hard. You can't make me feel guilty."

"This isn't about guilt, Jake."

"You can rewrite history and change the way it happened," he says, "but this is what you wanted. Having a baby was your agenda."

"Absolutely," I reply. "I definitely wanted a baby."

"I've no room in my life for another child. I liked you, Maddy." His tone softens.

"I cared about you. Really respected and trusted you. This wasn't our agreement."

"You were a part of this, Jake, and I was wrong. I had no idea how what I set in motion was going to affect Ethan."

"I believed you, Maddy. I'm not prepared for this. What do you want? There are state schools. And if you live in the state they don't cost anything. California has good state schools and they're free."

"They are not free."

"That's what I was told."

"You were misinformed."

"I'm willing, even though people disagree with me, to go for DNA testing."

I gasp. I never expected Jake to request that. An attorney would require it, but Jake?

"That's fine," I say.

"It'll take several months. I'll pay for it."

"That's fine," I repeat. "Look, Jake, I've been to a lawyer."

"What?" he bellows.

"I wrote to you in July. It's now December."

"Well, well, that might change things. If you go into litigation, I might have to change my offer."

"That's fine."

"You know that I talked to Ethan. If he's part of this then there's no way for us to continue a relationship."

"What kind of relationship have you had since February?"

"I'm not getting into this with you. Since you're pursuing litigation, I withdraw my DNA offer. This conversation is over."

"That's fine." I put the receiver into its cradle.

I stare at the ceiling, my feet glued to my spot. Oh, my, God. I pick up the phone and dial Phil's private line. He answers on the first ring.

"Are you all right?" he asks.

"Yes, I am." My heart rate slows. I feel oddly proud of myself.

"What happened?"

"Same old litany."

"How did it end?"

"After he suggested getting a DNA test, I told him about the lawsuit. He was less than happy."

There's a long silence.

"Phil?"

"I'm here."

"What's wrong?"

"I know you're hurt and angry, and while I could never do what Jake is doing — "

"Yes?"

"Men are different than women, Maddy. An ejaculation doesn't necessarily make a man a father, emotionally. Jake didn't carry Ethan, he didn't even see you pregnant. None of it was real to him."

I smooth out the wrinkles in my quilt.

"Just because a man can jerk off into a cup," I say, "or jerk off into a vagina, doesn't mean he's not responsible for what he produces."

"I'm just pointing out another side to you."

"You don't think I know that side already? I argue with myself all the time."

"Only when you tell me."

"Are we going there again? Aren't I better? I've been trying to tell you what's going on with me."

I hear him sigh. "Listen to me. Don't get scared or run away. But I want you to think about what I'm saying. It's not that you have to do anything about it."

"Uh, I don't think I'm going to like this. Hold on." I turn around on my bed so I can support my back against some pillows. "What?"

"You know that dream you told me about. The one with the gold key and how you're digging through the dirt and you can't find it. I think you found it in Jake — only it wasn't gold."

"What do you mean?" I sit up straighter.

"You chose someone you couldn't trust, who not only wouldn't be there for you, but wouldn't want you there for him. You've spent most of your life depending on yourself, and you were not about to do it differently. It's the same reason we've had so much trouble, only I'm not Jake."

I stare at a watercolor of tribesmen dancing in grass skirts with huts in the background. I bought it in Kenya when I was in the Peace Corps. I don't know what to say.

"I'm confused. Is this about you and me, or me and Jake?"

"You and Jake. Although I suppose I was pointing out some similarities."

My stomach tightens. I feel threatened and defensive. When Carol confronts me, tells me things about myself that are hard to look at, and painful to deal with, I'm never afraid she'll leave me. Phil is another thing.

"So this is all my fault? I deserve what I'm getting? And Ethan deserves it too?"

"If anyone deserves it Maddy, it's Anthony for scaring you and taking away your innocence, and for your father because he didn't know how to handle it. And consequently your feeling like you did something wrong. But that's not the point. For this to truly be about Ethan and for it to end positively, you have to look at what you contributed — and not only that you gave Jake permission to walk away, but that you could have banked on it."

I close my eyes, purse my lips and feel the heat of stinging tears roll down my face. I picture Phil's kind and gentle face, his laugh lines, and his inviting smile. He's not leaving me. He's not leaving me.

"Are you okay?" Phil asks.

"Not happy."

"I know. But that's temporary."

"I know."

I place my hand over my heart, my voice just above a whisper. "I can't believe you've spent so much time thinking about this."

"That's because this is the first healthy relationship you've had. I care about you and that's what people do in healthy relationships. They care."

"Thank you." I pause. "I'll think about what you said."

"Good. What time do you want me to pick you up?"

I think for a second. "As soon as possible. Ethan's meeting here with his rapper friends and I don't want to be anywhere around. You know how Phanny howls? You should hear her when they get together. It's very funny. They have to lock her out on the back patio." I smile. "Honk, and I'll meet you outside."

———

By early January the attorneys for both sides are busy faxing and phoning and filing papers with each other and the court. Jake has hired a California family law specialist to represent him and each side is sizing up their opponent to get a fix on what real or imagined threat there is.

A court date is set for March 9 and I wait for the final confirmation that a lab had been chosen for the DNA testing. The message comes on January 16.

"Maddy, it's Alexis. Arrangements have been made for Jake to have his blood drawn in New York and mailed to the lab in Palos Verdes. You and Ethan can make your appointment and have your blood drawn. Test results take about two weeks."

I listen twice and check my calendar. Between my schedule and Ethan's, I settle on January 30. I call the lab to confirm.

I couldn't have chosen a better day. When I pick Ethan up at school, he is so happy, he can hardly contain himself.

"We won. We came in first at the rap contest today. The finals are next week and we'll be even better."

"Whoa, slow down," I laugh. "Congratulations, but I want to hear everything from the beginning. Don't leave anything out."

He settles in his seat and puts on his seat belt.

"First of all the amphitheater was packed. There were security guards and teachers all over. We came on last, which was great for us, and not good for the other groups. Josh and I blew them away. The audience went wild. They were standing, waving theirs hands in the air, and dancing with the beat. It felt great. There must have been a thousand people there — all eyes on us!"

More than Ethan's words, I listen to his energy and passion. Nothing, not even going to establish who his father is, could put a damper on his joy.

"You know, sweetie, you've always had that charisma."

"And you've always been prejudiced."

We drive down the 405 freeway in silence. When he finally speaks, the magical spell is broken.

"Mom, what happens today? When we get to the lab?"

I laugh, trying to be light and get the joy back. "I don't know. We'll have to find out together. It's kind of weird, isn't it?"

Ethan shrugs. "I can't believe he's making us do this."

"His lawyer is. She wouldn't be doing her job if she didn't demand it." I realize I'm protecting Jake again, so I add, "On the other hand, he wanted us to do it, too. I guess he has the right, but it is crummy."

"Can we stop and get something to eat? I'm starving."

"I bought you a tuna sandwich at school. It's in the bag on the floor."

He reaches down, unwraps the sandwich and takes a bite. He waves it at me. "This is what I want to do, be a rapper."

"And you tell me all the time."

He turns on the radio. We're ten minutes away from our destination. It's strange to be going through this. I joke about immaculate conception with my friends, but nothing about this is funny.

I turn off the freeway and find my way to the lab. We sit in the waiting room.

"Ms. Gold," says a man in a white lab coat, "please come with me." We follow him into a tiny room. There are two chairs, a cabinet, and one picture of a Mexican village on the wall. A small table holds syringes and empty vials.

"I'm Stan Robbins, your lab technician. Before we get started, I need your photo I.D.s and to take your picture. Then I'll draw your blood and you'll be done."

Ethan and I look at each other. We each take out our driver's license and hand it to Stan. He writes down our numbers and then we stand together for a Polaroid. Ethan puts his arm around my shoulder and crouches beside me. We watch the picture develop before our eyes. I note that we smile happily and broadly. No one would imagine it's being taken for anything but a joyous occasion.

"Who wants to go first?" Stan asks.

"I will," Ethan says. He rolls up his shirtsleeve. But before he sticks out his arm, he looks at Stan, "Do you know why they bury lawyers eight feet under instead of six?"

Stan smiles. "No."

"Because deep down they're not so bad at all."

The three of us laugh.

"Don't say anything like that while I'm working," Stan says, holding the needle in the air, "I've been known to miss."

He wraps the rubber tubing around Ethan's arm, feels for his vein, and sticks in the needle. I watch as Ethan's blood fills the vials. Within ten minutes the whole thing is over and we're on our way home.

I smile, pulling out of the driveway. "You can't say that your mother doesn't offer you unique and unusual experiences. I'm really sorry you had to go through this."

"It wasn't your fault." He wrinkles his nose looking impish. "What if he's not my father?"

My eyes widen and I roar with laughter. Ethan joins me.

"We would definitely have to rethink things. Not to worry, honey," I wrinkle my nose at him, "he is your father."

———

"What a life," I tell Carol sitting down. "Not a dull moment."

"What's going on?"

"We got the DNA report back. The probability that Jake is Ethan's father is ninety-nine point nine percent.

"Is that a problem?"

My face twists and feels lopsided. "Not high enough for them," I scoff. "They demanded more tests. They can use the same blood samples, though." I pick up the pillow and play with it. When that doesn't calm me I begin pushing back my cuticles.

"Alexis called yesterday," I continue. "Jake and his attorney want a settlement hearing next Monday. That's less than a week away — the day before we go to court." I close my eyes and lean back in the chair. Then I sit up straight. "I want to ask you something." I hug the pillow to my chest. "Do you think Jake is getting more than his fair share of my wrath?"

"Why do you ask?" Carol tips her head to the side. I love the way her hair fans out on her shoulder, like the shampoo commercials on television.

"Phil thinks that because of Anthony and my father, I chose Jake. That I couldn't have handled a real relationship with a man. That inside I knew Jake wouldn't be there for me — or Ethan."

"What do you think?"

"It's possible. Putting everything together, and knowing what I know now."

"Is that why Jake is getting his unfair share of your wrath?"

"Yes. No. I don't know."

"I think Jake is getting Jake's share." Carol leans forward in her chair. "You know, Maddy, you must remember who you were when I first met you. Your feelings were so shut off and disconnected that you wouldn't and couldn't entertain that you were angry when someone hurt you. You swallowed everything, made nice, and came back for more."

I frown. "I don't want Jake, or anyone, to be angry at me."

"I know," Carol says, "and that's how you get abused and trampled on."

I sigh. "I won't see you before the hearing. I'm going to be a mess." I take a deeper breath. "Both my lawyers, Alexis and Joanne, will be there. And I'll have Ethan. At least, I won't be alone." I'm babbling. "I'll be quiet now."

We continue the rest of the session talking about Ethan and Phil until Carol checks the clock. There is a minute left.

"Anything you want to say about Jake before we end this session?" I ask.

Carol smiles. "You seem to be handling things very nicely." She stands up and embraces me. "Call if you want to see me earlier than our usual time. Good luck. And you'll be fine."

15

SANTA MONICA

Winter 1998

*I*t's the Sunday before the Monday of the settlement hearing, and for the first time in a week I almost believe I'm relaxed. I touch the necklace I bought myself yesterday — a delicate chain with a solid gold key. I'm not usually extravagant but this charm is a symbol to remind me I am a survivor and a woman who stands up for herself and anyone she loves. I realize the dream isn't only about having a man and being married. I curl up on the brown leather couch in Phil's den with a burgundy chenille blanket wrapped around me. My head is in his lap. On the coffee table a bottle of Merlot breathes and a fire glows in the stone fireplace. We're solving *The New York Times* crossword puzzle together. He does most of the solving, but he swears with a cute smile, that he values my input. I turn on my side and look at my watch. When I sit up, I feel his hand on my shoulder stopping me.

"What time is it?" Phil asks, reaching over me to retrieve his wine glass.

"Four-thirty."

"You've made it in one position for exactly twenty minutes. That's a record for you today." I look up at him, his head is cocked to one side and his lips are pursed. "Just an observation."

"Are you timing me?" I smile.

"Attempting to change the activities, so I keep you from focusing on tomorrow."

"I'm sorry. I know this hasn't been easy for you. I've been a 'Johnny One Note' for a long time now."

"It will be over soon. The fact that Jake's attorney is asking for a settlement hearing means they want to resolve this, so hopefully, tomorrow, it will be done."

I take Phil's hand from my shoulder, and still holding on to it, I sit up.

"I don't know what being done means. I sue Jake, Ethan gets money for college, and a piece of paper identifying his parentage. Does he get a father out of this? That seems to be what he really wants. And of course, if I were Jake, I would be so angry that I wouldn't want — " I stand up, walk over to the fireplace and struggle with the wrought iron tongs to put another log on the glowing embers. I turn back around as the sparks fly behind the black mesh curtain. "It doesn't make sense to finish that thought because I'm not Jake, and if I were, all of this would have been handled differently. Actually if I were Jake, Ethan wouldn't even be here. Weird, huh?"

Phil leans forward and puts down the magazine section and the pen. "What time do you expect Ethan home?"

"*Man of La Mancha* opens Friday night. He's been rehearsing everyday. Sometimes with the whole cast and sometimes," I raise my eyebrow, "just with Amy. He really likes her. I've never seen him so happy. After he was chosen as Don Quixote, he hoped Amy would get the female lead. He's going to ask her to the prom after opening night. I tease him all the time by singing, 'Once in love with Amy, Always in love with Amy.'"

"I have it in my calendar."

"And you do know I'm going to all eight performances?"

"I'm going to four."

I nod. "Right." I begin pacing back and forth across the hardwood floor. My loafers make a clicking sound.

"Do you want to go home?"

I stop in mid-step and turn to face him.

"What?"

"I know you, Maddy. You've held it together most of the day, and now you're starting to flutter about, acting like a trapped butterfly." He stands up and walks over to me. He puts his hands on my shoulders. My heart is racing. "You've been very good today." He takes my face in his hands and strokes the length of my nose with his thumb. "And I appreciate it."

I look into his face — open, trusting, welcoming. "I — "

"Don't say anything. I know how hard it's been." He smiles. "And it's okay. We're making progress."

Tears form along my lower lids like a dam barely able to hold back a flash flood. "I don't know why it's so difficult. You're the best thing that's happened to me, in forever, and I love you." I shake my head and tears plummet down my cheeks. "I don't want to shut you out. I just don't want you to see this part of me."

I shiver as he pulls me to him. "And what part is that? That you get antsy, that you might get short-tempered?" He holds me at arms length. "What is it that I'm going to see?"

I reach for his hand. "Before Anthony did what ever he did to me, and before my father withdrew from me, do you know what my nickname was? Did I ever tell you?"

Phil shakes his head.

"I was called, 'Giggly Gertie.' And I see that little girl too, in old snapshots — a redheaded Shirley Temple with ringlets and a smile just like hers. But I think after Anthony, I went into the windowsill to feel safe and be rescued by my parents, and when I wasn't, I never came out. If I can't be perfect, I'm afraid people will be disappointed and abandon me."

"So how, in this situation, are you going to disappoint me?"

I reach over to stroke his face. "I want to be there for you, and take care of you. But I can't do that now. I just want to be alone."

He takes my hand and guides me back to the couch. We sit down facing each other.

"Look, I'm not Carol, and I'm not a therapist, but it sounds like you made an unconscious decision as a three-year-old that has outlived its relevancy." His face breaks into a big grin. "I told you this before, and I'll repeat it for however long it takes you to believe it. You're not perfect, and you don't have to be for me to love you. And I know you're going to think I'm nuts, but after tomorrow or Tuesday or whatever day this nightmare with Jake is over, we are going to attack this head on."

I look at him like he's crazy. My face feels scrunched and wrinkled like a Sharpei's.

"I don't understand."

"The only way you're going to trust me, and yourself, and learn how to be real in a relationship, is to do it."

"What do you mean?"

"We can live together at my house, your house, or rotate."

"You want to move in together? Are you serious?"

"Very."

I'm speechless. I stare at him and then at the fire. "You are totally nuts, you know that? A glutton for punishment." After a few seconds, I scratch my head. I get up and face him. "It makes perfect sense, doesn't it? I can't run away from you if I'm home and that's where you are. Could it possibly be that simple?"

"We'll be fine."

He stands and we kiss. I look into his eyes.

"I don't really understand any of this, but I know I love you."

Phil slides his arms around my waist and pulls me close.

———

Monday arrives and with the first drops of rain the streets clog up and overflow. Driving is always a nightmare in L.A., but now on my way to pick up Ethan, I'm sandwiched between cars on all sides. I inch my way through a water-filled intersection on Venice Boulevard. The windshield wipers, in high gear, can't out swipe the raindrops fast enough. I settle back in my seat and bemoan the cold, gray, rainy weather and the time. I'm late and I'm stuck. I tap my newly manicured, red fingernails on the steering wheel. With all I have on my mind, I don't need this.

I think about Ethan and the meeting at our lawyers' office. Am I right to put him through this? And what about Jake? What's he feeling? At least teaching today kept me focused.

I check my watch again. Seven minutes late so far. The radio reports the traffic and weather conditions every few minutes, in between the gloomy forecast on talk radio about welfare, taxes, and health care. I fiddle with the tuning dial searching for something to distract me. I listen to the lyrics from *California Dreamin'*. Years ago, as the Mamas & the Papas blasted forth from my lemon-yellow Mustang convertible, I drove the FDR Drive in Manhattan singing my heart out, planning my own California dream. And I'd made it happen. A perfect thing to keep in mind today.

I pull into the Santa Monica High School parking lot and look around for Ethan. Fifteen minutes late, I hope he isn't drenched waiting for me. I reach over and unlock the door. My hands grip the steering wheel and my thumbs tap against it imagining what this upcoming confrontation will be like. God, I need to be strong. Jake must never think I question my decision. And that decision — was it two years in the making or seventeen? I shiver and inhale. No Ethan. I sit tight and wait. I raise the volume to drown out my thoughts.

Raindrops continue to fall between the white beams of my headlights and the red hue of rear brake lights. The downpour, hypnotic and intense, hits puddles and creates miniature fountains. Ethan opens the car door and I jump.

"Hi." He throws a dripping wet black umbrella onto the back seat.

"Hi honey. Are you drenched?"

"No. Just got out of my drama class. Sorry I'm late."

"Was Mr. Marx, Groucho or Harpo today?"

"He went ballistic when I told him I was leaving rehearsal early. And he's got a point." His voice is strained. He runs his hand through his wet hair and wipes it on his damp jeans. "We open this weekend. I better be able to go to school tomorrow or he'll throw me out of the play."

"Doubt he can do that. You're the star."

We drive onto Lincoln Boulevard. I see him look at me.

"All dressed up, Mom. Nice."

I nod. I had gone hunting in my friend Deborah's closet, the next best thing to shopping at Nordstrom's. I'm wearing her new red wool dress and gold hoop earrings. She says she feels honored to lend them to me.

"You nervous?" he asks.

"You could say that." Even now I can argue the pros and cons of what I have set into motion. I smile though. "But my kids made me feel good. When I took my break today I went into the ladies room to put on make-up. You should have heard them when I got back to class. 'You look so pretty, Ms. G. Where're you going? Why don't you do that every day?'"

"I'm starving." Ethan says, a long, loud growl coming from his stomach. "Can we get something to eat?"

"Damn. I totally forgot. Look at the weather. We're going to be late and I don't know where we can get you something fast."

"Mom, relax. So what if we're a little late? Stop worrying."

I nod. He's right, to a degree. My need to be on time and not keep people waiting borders on the extreme. And in reality, they can't start without us.

"I'll stop at the Subway on Pico." I glance at him. He's looking straight ahead. He has such a strong profile even with his button nose. "How about you? You nervous?"

"Not at all. In fact," he pauses, "I look forward to seeing him." His voice is emphatic. "I can't wait for him to say one wrong thing."

"E, you're not supposed to say anything. The lawyers do the talking, not us. We're supposed to sit, perhaps glare at him, but not speak."

"I'll glare," he says, "and stare him down. But if he speaks, I speak. You can be sure of that."

I laugh. "Not a doubt in my mind."

I pull into the strip mall and wait in the car while Ethan gets his sub. I don't doubt that he will tell Jake everything that is on his mind. If I taught him anything, it is to be assertive and not be intimidated by anyone. It's a lesson I'm learning myself.

———

The traffic on the freeway barely creeps along. But when we enter the reception area of the attorneys' office, a large brass clock announces we're only twenty minutes late. After a short wait, we follow a receptionist into a room decorated in pale Southwestern colors. I sit down on the beige love seat against the wall with Ethan next to me. This can't be easy for him. The door opens and Joanne, a tall blond, take-charge woman bounds in. She reminds me of Julia. Her energy fills the room.

"We're almost ready for you. Alexis is finishing a call and she'll be with us in a minute. They're not here yet, so you can relax." She pauses. "We're going to get this settled today. I know it."

"How does this work?" Ethan asks. "I mean, what do we do?"

"Each case is different, but we'll all meet in the conference room downstairs, and Alexis and his attorney, Bertha, will do the talking. My strength is as a mediator and that's what I'll add to the meeting." She gives a sly smile. "We'll outnumber them. This man does not want to go to court tomorrow. He's already been complaining about all the time he's spent on the lawsuit, and he wasn't happy having to fly out here."

"I really feel for him," I say.

"He doesn't want this to go public. And going into a courtroom is very public."

I perk up. "How do you know? Did he say that?"

"His attorney hinted at it."

"They're on their way," Alexis announces entering the room.

"Has he admitted paternity?" I ask.

"No," Alexis answers. "I didn't expect him to."

Ethan and I begin to talk at the same time but I defer to him.

"How could he not admit it? The paternity tests prove it. He is my father. I am his son!"

No one speaks. My heart goes out to Ethan. What can I do or say?

"You are his son," Joanne says. "And Jake will acknowledge that. It will be written in the final settlement and court records will show it. But right now it's part of the legal dance where neither side shows all their cards. This has nothing to do with what's decent, or even what's right. It has do with money, and winning, and the law, and not necessarily in that order. We have the law on our side, and we're going to get you as much money as we possibly can. Sadly, we can't make him into a sensitive, caring guy."

There's a knock on the door and the secretary comes in. " They're here."

I cover my face with my hands. "Do I really have to see him? Can't you guys just handle it?"

"We can," Alexis says. "You can stay in here and we'll come back and forth with their offers."

"No way," Ethan retorts. "I want him to look me in the eyes."

"I know, honey. Just kidding."

"Ethan, I'm sure you have a lot of things you want to say to him," Alexis cautions, "and we'll try to get that to happen. But we just need to make sure this doesn't turn into an emotional brouhaha. Okay?"

"As long as I have my say."

"Do I have time to go to the bathroom?" I interrupt. I need a space to calm myself and breathe.

As I wash my hands, I look in the mirror at the face staring back at me. Fifty plus years show. There are small bags under my eyes, a few crow's feet, and some sagging under my chin. But all in all, when I put on make-up and do my hair, I still look younger than my age. I stand up straight and remind myself to stay centered.

My side waits for me in front of the conference room. Joanne opens the door and Alexis and Ethan go in first. As I enter, it reminds me of an upscale dungeon with no windows. The room is barren with cement gray walls, fluorescent lighting, and a cherry wood conference table and chairs. No art, no warmth, no amenities. Jake is standing to the left of the door with his attorney, Bertha Shapiro. He's still wearing his raincoat and a brown beret, while Bertha, well into her sixties and overweight, is dressed in a tailored black suit. She's probably someone's mother and grandmother and a perfectly nice person, but at this moment, I'm not that generous. Alexis does the introductions and Ethan sticks out his hand to both Jake and Bertha. I simply nod, look at them briefly, and turn away. This man, who I once cared about and respected, is a stranger — a nondescript stranger who I would pass on the street without a second glance or thought. He has become not only a man small in size, but also in moral stature.

The opponents face each other around the oval table. Ethan and I sit between Alexis and Joanne. Jake sits next to Bertha on the opposite side. Alexis, seated at the head of the table, begins.

"The first thing we need to establish, before anything else gets discussed, is paternity."

I glance at Jake quickly, still hoping to find even a speck of the humanity I once believed he had, but his head is down.

"We won't acknowledge paternity until we're sure of other stipulations," Bertha counters. "If you try to sue my client for support payments beyond eighteen, we will sue Ms. Gold for fraud. We have letters that prove she told Mr. Miller that he would not need to be responsible for her child."

"You can threaten future lawsuits if you wish, Bertha, but I don't think that's very productive," Alexis says. "We need to deal with the lawsuit that's on the table now. I know that my client is a very reasonable person, and she only wants what is beneficial for her and Mr. Miller's child."

Two points for Alexis.

"Mr. Miller is willing to pay child support payments until Ethan graduates from high school, but we seem to disagree on the amount," Bertha says.

"Until today we haven't had all of Mr. Miller's income tax information. You and I can run the numbers through the computer later and see what comes up."

"Good," Bertha says. She pauses and looks at me, and Ethan. "Now, it's important for everyone here to understand that none of my client's children ever had it easy. Neither one of them had a car; in fact they both had jobs."

"I have a job," Ethan says.

"Oh, you do? That's nice."

I don't like Bertha's patronizing tone.

"And we feel," Bertha continues, "that Ethan should start college at Santa Monica Community College and then transfer — "

"Oh, no he won't," I cry out.

"Oh, no I won't," Ethan shouts at the same time.

He rises out of his seat and then sinks back down. He leans forward on the table and stares straight at Jake's attorney.

"Look, his other children had their father all the time."

His eyes bore into Jake. "Where were you in my life? Where were you when our house was broken into, and all our things were ripped up and destroyed? All my baseball cards, everything I had was stolen. We had to borrow money to move because we weren't safe in our old place. Where were you then?"

I gasp. The room sizzles. Jake bolts out of his seat. What seemed like barely controlled rage before pours from his eyes and his tongue.

"Your mother lied and deceived me," he yells. "I didn't want any more children. I — ."

"You mean you were a helpless victim, and you couldn't do anything 'not' to have a child?" Ethan tilts his head. "Are you saying that my mother took advantage of you?"

Pow. I watch Jake and know the question made impact. He paces and stutters, his hands in his pockets, and then at his sides. His navy blue suit hangs loosely on his body.

"Yes, she did. She lied and told me she was on the pill when she wasn't."

I leap out of my seat. "You liar." Joanne pulls me back into my chair.

"Ethan," Jake says, as he sits down, his voice softer, "before we go any further with these proceedings, I want you to read this." He holds up a manila folder and waves it in the air. "It tells my side of the story. I know there are a lot of strong feelings on both our parts, but I want you to read the letters your mother wrote to me. We cannot proceed until you do. Your mother has been telling you stories all these years, and until you know my side, I will not go on with this. I want you to go into a room with me and read what I wrote. Your mother lied to me, and I want you to see that. I won't say a word while you're reading, but I want to be in the same room with you, alone, while you do it."

I turn to Joanne to protest, but before I can say anything Ethan responds.

"Okay," he says. "No problem."

Joanne stands. "I'll take you downstairs and give you some privacy."

I look around the room. Only Alexis and Bertha are left.

"Maddy," Alexis says, "I'd like to talk to you outside. Will you excuse us, Bertha?"

"What just happened in there?" I begin talking as soon as the door is shut. "How could you let Ethan go off with him alone?"

"Jake won't be alone with him. Joanne will be there. I know that you're very upset, but you'll have to trust us. I have to go back in there and talk to Bertha. That's the way these things work, Maddy."

"But Jake lied!"

"Joanne's with them. We read what he wrote. It's outrageous fiction coming from a desperate man. Ethan knows the truth. He's not going to be manipulated."

"But he lied. Doesn't that mean anything?"

"No. People lie all the time. That's why there are lawsuits. It doesn't matter right now, anyway. I know that it matters to you, but not to the litigation. I have to get back in there. Why don't you go back to my office? As soon as Bertha makes an offer, I'll come and discuss it with you." Alexis smiles. "It might be hard to believe, but this is normal. I still feel we'll get this settled today. I'll see you in a little while."

I meander down one hallway, then another. I find the office we had all been in a mere hour before. Where is Ethan? I'm dissolving. A muscle in my thigh twitches and something weird is happening to my eyes. Everywhere I look are colorful squiggly lines surrounding the objects in my peripheral vision. I stand up and circle the room, then sit down. I pick up a magazine and try to read. I look at my watch. It's only been twenty minutes. Alexis walks into her office. I jump up and almost pounce on her.

"I want to see Ethan."

"He's doing fine, Maddy. Joanne's bringing him in right now. She told me that you have one terrific son."

"Oh." I need to get control of myself.

"He did a great job," Joanne announces as she and Ethan enter the room. She closes the door behind them.

I walk over to Ethan and give him a hug.

"You all right, sweetie?"

"I'm fine, Mom. He's a mess, but I'm fine."

"What do you mean? Would someone please tell me what's going on?"

"Your son is incredible," Joanne says. "He was calm, cool and direct. He never lost his temper. And he made Jake take responsibility for what he did."

"I thought they weren't supposed to talk. I thought Jake would be quiet while Ethan read."

"Yeah, well I needed to say some things to him," Ethan replies, "and that got us talking. He tried to blame this all on you, and I told him he was nuts if he thought I would believe that."

I sit down. My eyes return to normal and the twitch in my thigh calms down.

"And," Joanne adds, smiling at Ethan, "you got him to admit he could have made other choices."

"He was crying, Mom."

Alexis smiles at me. "I would say he's finally getting it."

I look from one person to the other. I'm confused.

"I know I haven't seen his performance today, but I saw it last February. He was shaking and sweating then. Why are you all falling for this act?"

"We're not falling for anything," Alexis says. "We're working out a settlement, Maddy, and getting Ethan the best deal we can. If Jake is feeling sorry for what he did or did not do, that's good for us. Bertha's worried. She wants to keep Jake away from Ethan. She knows Jake is caving. That's why she stopped their meeting. So let me tell you what they're offering." She pauses to look at her folder. "He's willing to — "

"Wait," Ethan calls out. He looks at Alexis and then at me. "I don't care what he's offering. I don't even want to know."

"What?" Joanne, Alexis and I respond in unison.

He walks over to me and sits down. "We won, Mom. He had to admit he's my father and he did. I want to stop the lawsuit."

I struggle to get a handle on what Ethan is saying.

"Ethan, this doesn't make sense," Joanne says. "If you do this, Jake doesn't have to give you or your mother anything. He can walk out of this office, go back to New York and ignore you again."

"Maybe he can," Ethan says. "And maybe I'm doing what my mother did a long time ago by letting him off the hook. But she got what she wanted — me — and so have I. I don't care about his money. That's all he has and he can keep it."

"But your life will be harder for this decision," Alexis says.

"You don't understand. It doesn't matter. I'll get a job. I'll get loans. He's a very sad and lonely man and we're a lot better off than he is."

I'm numb. I put my arm around him.

"We are a lot better off," I agree. "I don't know what went on in that room, but I trust your decision. All I wanted was for you to know both sides of your family, get some questions answered and feel some closure. I'm proud of you."

I continue, facing Joanne and Alexis. "Can we just do that? Withdraw?"

The two women look stupefied. "This case has been unusual from the beginning mainly because Ethan is almost an adult." Joanne says, pausing to process. "But if Ethan's guardian ad litem agrees to his decision, I would think the judge won't have a problem with it. We can draw up the papers tonight and finalize everything tomorrow morning. All parties will have to be present in case there are questions." Joanne's voice trails off.

"Good," I say, "then I suppose we're done here. Do you want to tell Jake, Ethan?"

He shakes his head. "No. I want to go home. I got what I needed and if he wants anything from me in the future, he knows where I am."

I smile at him. "Okay." I turn to my attorneys. "I guess we'll see you in court to get things finalized."

We thank Joanne and Alexis and walk outside. The rainy gray day has turned to a clear dark night. I look up at the stars, inhale the air, and put my arm through Ethan's. We're ready to go home.

Epilogue

*T*he **subway lurches to a stop at Church Avenue.** The middle of summer isn't the best season to go for a ride to Brooklyn, but here we are. I look over at Phil to see if he's as sweaty as I am. His short sleeve shirt is open one button lower than usual and the gray hairs on his chest glisten. I take his hand as we exit the station. Memories of this walk, of skipping alongside my father — my two skips to his one step — come back. I stop. The signs on the front of the stores are in Spanish, the faces of the people crowding around us are different shades of brown, and the colorful textiles the women wear make me feel like we're on vacation in South America.

"Are you okay?" Phil asks.

"Just surprised. My childhood friend Esther, warned me it would be different, that I wouldn't recognize it. I didn't believe her."

"I'll remind you again."

"I know, '*You Can't Go Home Again.*'"

We walk toward Ocean Avenue, the heat rising from the pavement. Sweat drips down my left leg.

"I know you think I have a lot invested in this," I say, "but I don't. If the people who live in my old apartment are home, and let us in — fine. And if, for whatever reason, we don't get to see the apartment and my windowsill, that's okay too."

We pass what should have been a delicatessen where I ate potato knishes, a candy store where I spent my allowance, and the corner drugstore that served malts and ice cream sodas made from scratch at a black counter with red stools. They're all gone. A bodega, a bank, and a zapateria have replaced them. We walk by Esther's apartment building and then come to mine.

"Things have vanished or they're smaller," I say. "My six story building is tiny. And Ocean Avenue is narrower than Santa Monica Boulevard."

Phil doesn't answer. He squeezes my hand. We stand on the sidewalk in front of my childhood home. The courtyard feels familiar but the bushes and flowers are different. The big tree I hid my eyes against to play hide and seek with my friends has been cut down leaving only a stump. I point to the windows on the first floor.

"There they are," I say, leaning against a car. "All three of them. I would sit all scrunched up in the corner one. It was a cozy box. I could see my father with his hat. His body would tilt under the weight of his big leather briefcase. Sometimes my mother would stand behind me, and I'd smell whatever we were having for dinner on her hands and apron. It was all so normal, except for the reason I was in that box in the first place." I turn to look into the eyes of the man I love, the first man I totally trust.

Phil leans down and kisses me. "Say the word and we'll see if anyone's home."

I smile. I try to move but I'm stuck to a hot car, in a foreign world. Suddenly the absurdity of where we are and what I've convinced him to do takes hold and I burst into laughter. When we talked about it weeks ago in L.A., we were on the couch in our den and I was so excited, I bounced on the cushions.

"We'll go to Brooklyn, ring the bell of my old apartment and I'll tell the tenants living there that I want to come into their home to revisit my childhood. Then I can sit in their windowsill for a minute. It makes perfect sense Phil, symbolically and realistically — you'll be there to give me your hand, to help me out, and then I can put all of it behind me — behind us."

"Fine, great in fact. We'll stop in New York on our way to Italy. Ethan can stay with Phanny and take care of the house. And don't worry, you'll be back in plenty of time to get him ready for college."

And now, here we are in Brooklyn, in a place I realize I no longer belong.

"What's wrong, Madd? You okay?"

I hug him tightly.

"Even better. Seeing it is enough," I whisper in his ear, still laughing. "I have you. Let's go back to the city."

I put my arm through his and look at the window one last time. I silently say good-bye.

———

ACKNOWLEDGMENTS

It took forever and a village of friends and family to write this novel. Without the unwavering support and encouragement of so many people, it would never have happened. Thank you so much to Adam, Al Moore and Sherrill Johnson, Barbara Bozman, Barbara and Bob Brown, Barbara Corlin, Barbara Temkin, Barbara Thompson, Beth Swartz, Christina Kahn and John Mayer, Debbie Curling, Devera Harris, Diana Escudero, Diana Lafayette, Dotty and Al Schmalholz, Duncan Smith, Greg Doll, Greg Elliot, Hinda Handschu, Jane Golbert, Jane Seskin, Jodai Saremi, Judi Helfant, Judi Weiss, Judy and Jay Messinger, June Whittaker, Kate Gale, Kate Holt, Maggie Shelton, Marilyn Culbertson, Mary Chunko Kay, Nita Nash, Sharon Marshak, Sylvia Levin, Tamar Levin, Toby Salter, Wendell Liljedahl. And to my Editor and friend — Martha Fuller.

———

CPSIA information can be obtained
at www.ICGtesting.com
Printed in the USA
FSHW01n1853040618
48799FS